# Soothing Music for Stray Cats

# Soothing Music
# for Stray Cats

Jayne
Joso

ALCEMI

First impression: 2009
© Jayne Joso 2009
*This book is subject to copyright*
*and may not be reproduced by any means*
*except for review purposes*
*without the prior written consent of the publishers*
Published with the financial support of the Welsh Books Council
Alcemi is represented in the UK excluding Wales by Inpress Ltd —
www.inpressbooks.co.uk. In Wales it is represented by www.gwales.com

Editor: Gwen Davies


ISBN: 9780955527258
Printed on acid-free and partly-recycled paper.
Published by Alcemi and printed and bound in Wales by
Y Lolfa Cyf., Talybont, Ceredigion SY24 5AP
*e-mail* ylolfa@ylolfa.com
*website* www.alcemi.eu
*tel* 01970 832 304
*fax* 832 782

*For Mum*

'The mass of men lead lives of quiet desperation.'
Henry David Thoreau as quoted in Kurt Vonnegut - *Timequake*

'Human life lasts but an instant. One should spend it doing what one pleases. In this world fleeting as a dream, to lie in misery doing only what one dislikes is foolishness.'
Samurai, Tsunetomo Yamamoto - Hagakure

# CHAPTER ONE

## *february 2005*

## KEEP PASSING
## THE OPEN WINDOW

My name's Mark Kerr, I'm 35, and one of what my dad calls '*Thatcher's youth*, and the generation who thought they could have it all'. I don't even know what that means anymore, I'm not sure I ever did. And now that my friend, Jim Jakes, has jumped from a window on the twentieth floor, all I do know is, I've been living the wrong life. I guess Jim was too.

When we were kids, me and Jim, we dreamt of writing songs together. We should have tried, should have given it a go, and written the songs, and lived the lives we wanted to.

The thing is, you're supposed to keep *passing* the open window. But once you need to keep passing it, in some ways it's already too late – because you start to notice it in that particular way, and then you notice it more, and the pull gets greater, and then you're stuck with finding *ways* of passing it, dodging it, putting it off, until finally it pretty much *sucks* you out. That's what happened, I guess, what must have happened, to my mate Jim. 'My mate Jim'. That statement feels so awkward, because it isn't entirely true. We *were* mates, when we were kids, teenagers. I'd never really given it much thought, but we must have been friends for quite some time, in fact right from being little kids until we were about eighteen. That's why his sister, Julie – *Jules,* had tracked me down. In the end she got hold of me through my dad. He was the only one who'd never moved.

Jim's family had moved to the other side of town when his dad got a promotion, it had meant they could afford a semi, and later they planned to go detached. I guess me and Jim would have been about seventeen then, so it must have been just before I moved away to university. I think Jim stayed more local for that, truth was, neither of us ever dreamt of going to university, it was just that time when suddenly every Tom, Mark and Jim got the chance. Anyway, like I said, Dad was the only one who'd stayed in our old terraced street. I think he'd got stuck, specially after Mum left, and more so once she'd passed away. The big 'C' as people call it. And it hit Dad hardest because it meant finally facing the fact that she really would never come back. While she was alive he'd managed to fool himself that she *just might* come back, one day. She would never have come back, but people have to tell themselves lies, stories, that make life easier to deal with. And the possibility of *Mum's return* was his. In the end the house was all he had to hang on to. That and his mates. — He'd been there so long he'd taken root, and the only memories he thought to be of any value at all, belonged to that house. He couldn't ever contemplate the idea of new dreams, stuff that might make more good memories, he was too loyal to the past. Sad in some ways, but that's how it was, that was Dad. And that house contained the only sense of life he'd known or ever wanted to know. He loved it. I think 'I'd' loved it, well, sort of, but it was always too quiet after Mum had upped and left. Quiet, that uneasy, queasy sort of quiet that gnaws away and messes with your nerves — Dad said he liked it like that. But I think he just didn't have any way of filling in that empty sound without her around. It was as though it would have been an act of adultery, a betrayal somehow, to tune the friggin' radio in, or get a sodding disc player.

That was another thing, he lived in a different time. He even called the radio a sodding 'wireless'; it felt like he did it to annoy me, even me granddad never called it that, that word was well gone even before me dad's time, in fact that word's so well gone it's looped right round and come back in again — anyways, me dad, he was stuck, and not even in a time warp that was his, more a sort of *pre*-warp. And he lived it for real too, no 'half measures' with Dad (those old phrases crack me up, they sound totally lame now). But me dad, he did genuinely, and I suppose, legitimately, still inhabit a time when you bought stuff and kept it forever and fixed it when it got broke. I kept telling him, no one, Dad, no one lives like that anymore. He never listened. And in some ways he was right, I could see that, and really, what was the point in finding more ways to *make a bleedin' racket,* when you didn't make use of what you'd already got? And he always added 'son' in that tone of his. I didn't mind. He was stuck, that was all. And what's so wrong with that? Thick with dust, his radio was. — Anyway, the reason I'd gone back up there, was 'cos Jules wanted me at her brother's funeral, 'Best mate he ever had,' she said. I must have looked as uncomfortable as I felt because she said it again, I suppose to reassure, *'His best mate, you really were, Mark.'* Yeah, right. Like I said, she meant it nice, but I'm telling you, when the guy's just chucked himself out of the glass of a twenty storey building, and the last time you saw him was… *was?* I don't even fucking know when it was. How long ago? Years. Years and fucking years. So 'nice' just doesn't come into it. Wasn't his fuckin' mate when all that happened, was I? Wasn't around when he jumped – to stop him jump. — *So where was I?* — *And just what the fuck was going through Jim's stupid bastard head?* I wasn't his mate, not anymore. I'd moved on. That's how it is. We've all got opportunities now, so-called *opportunities… yeah.* So things get all separated out, people move away, and lose touch. That's what happened with us. It was my fault. When I had a moment to myself I thought it through again, trying to make sure – exactly how old was I when I left? And was that really the last time I'd seen him? I bit into my lip. Tried to calm my breathing. Yeah, I reckon we'd just turned eighteen the last time we met, thirty-bleedin-five this year, seventeen years back.

I've always been useless at keeping in touch. Even with me dad. I go up from time to time but not that often. And no one sends letters anymore, I've never done cards, and Christmas, dunno but somehow that's always been more of a bird's thing. I suppose now though, I could've emailed, sent the bastard a text, but we didn't have all that then. Tell the truth, I don't care for texting much. It's not my thing. People send messages. I read 'em and I mean to reply, but then, then I can't be arsed. I'd made my lip bleed. Should have kept in touch. Should have done something. I read the details in the paper, Dad had kept the clipping. There wasn't hardly anything to read, it was like Dad

11

said, 'Don't write nothing special about you do they, not if you're no one.' I looked up and half smiled, agreeing. 'Sad that,' he added. And then he noticed the date, 'Jim died on the Monday – *February Seventh*,' he said, with some depth of meaning as though I ought to realise the significance, 'That was Ellen MacArthur's day, *the sailor.*'

'Who?' I said, but Dad wasn't listening.

'They're making her a dame, 71 days, 14 hours, 18 minutes and 33 seconds.' He got up and went into the kitchen, I could hear him shuffle through the recycling bin (recycling was one of the few things Dad approved of in the 'modern world'), he gave a few disgruntled sighs and then a hushed and contented 'Yeees', as he found what he was looking for. He practically waltzed back in, saying, 'They described her as, "diminutive",' and he smiled approvingly, as though he was proud, like on a personal level, as though she was someone he knew. 'The fastest person to circumnavigate the globe, *ever*. Don't suppose it matters much what size she is, eh?' and he laughed awkwardly, the way people do when they aren't really sure about jokes, how to make them, how they work, the timing. I laughed along to keep him company, but he was no Dave Allen. And then I thought back to when I was a kid, and how I used to hide behind his chair; he'd forget I was there and think he'd already sent me to bed, but I'd be curled round the back of his armchair distantly taking in Dave Allen on the telly, and Dad would be laughing along, bottle of beer in hand to Dave Allen's fag and whiskey, but you can't get comic genius just from watching it, you can't time gags like Allen if it ain't already streaming through your veins. And despite smoking and drinking being the best punctuation that ever was, it don't make every fag-ash-Harry and barfly a bleedin' comic, despite all our delusions. — Dad was still on about Ellen — icebergs, oceans, whales, and he was right, *'What a bloody achievement!'*, and normally the whole *Moby Dick* thing would grab me, but I couldn't stay with it just now. Too much other stuff had just happened, and I'm not like Dad, I can't push it all away and pretend like stuff ain't happened. I don't blame him for doing that, in some ways I even envy him, but me, I don't quite know how to do it. Can't push death away. — I wanted a fag, and Dad knew I did 'cos he kept noticing my leg twitching. 'Not in here son,' he said in that disapproving, whispered tone, 'best go outside.' I felt like the bleedin' dog sometimes, as though he thought I was gonna cock my soddin' leg or something. We didn't even have a dog.

That was the last time I went up there. The funeral. — Jim had done well for himself, was how Dad put it, engineer, fully qualified and everything. 'It's not good,' he said soberly, 'not good at all', and after that he didn't say too much else about him. He looked at Mum's photo a few times, but he didn't mention her, and I didn't. Didn't know what to say.

I met up with Jules in the pub, it was the day before the funeral, she said it was going to be a burial, and Jim hadn't left instructions – *instructions?* – so they'd thought that a 'proper funeral' was best. Jim hadn't got as far as thinking about all that. Guess you wouldn't. Guess he just wanted to be 'gone'. — Jules had known his girlfriend, and at first I was curious, but the more Jules talked about her the more I didn't like her, and the more I wished I hadn't asked. *Girlfriend*, total fuckin' witch more like. And what the hell kind of a name is *Trudy* anyway? — So, there we were, sitting in the pub, I had a pint, and Jules had a rum and coke. It didn't matter, but it felt weird somehow, like we should've been drinking something else, I don't mean like tea or coffee or anything lame like that, more as though there should be something… something different that you drink when something so big and tragic happens. But there isn't anything, not that I know of. Bastard Britain. So there I was, sat in a friggin' pub with a pint and a dead guy's sister, and her rum and coke. I stared at the ashtray. — Jim had been depressed, yeah, 'depressed' was how Jules put it. Proper, full on depressed, I think the docs call it depression when it gets that bad. I ran the word round my head, swilling the last of my beer round the bottom of my glass. Better get another round in. But Jules' glass was still full — Depression. Makes sense, the word, I thought, like you have a *de-press* switch or something and somehow it suddenly gets flicked, full — on. The whole thing had been getting on Trudy's tits, Jules said. And it was weird, I couldn't tell what Jules really felt. Not about her brother, not about Trudy. She carried on talking.

My glass was empty now. I'd have to get another, but Jules still hadn't hardly touched hers. I'd have to wait it out a bit. It was fine, we both smoked, loads in fact — funny the things that cover over the cracks, the time and distance, my guilt at losing touch, not knowing what had been going down, but it was easy with Jules somehow, it was like smoking covered that stuff over. It fills up pauses. Smokes 'em up. I took another drag. I never know what non-smokers do about all that, how they deal with pauses, awkward stuff. Guess they just sit there, knowing there's a fucking great awkward pause hovering, waiting to crush you or swallow you up. But then there's drinking. People drink a bit more I guess, that would cover it well enough. So, Jules talked, and I listened, both of us smoked. Match made in heaven, 'cept it was more like a graveyard. — We were back to talking about Trudy's tits again. And Jim, getting on her tits. Bitch. Jules said this bird had *tried and tried*, tried *everything*... but Jim, he was still fucking miserable, Trudy had said as much. I stabbed my fag out, that one hadn't tasted too good. I looked into the distance. I didn't want Jules to cry. Looked like she'd cried for England already. It's awkward when girls cry. I don't mind, but I think they do, and I think they feel awkward. I'd wait a minute. She'd got a tissue and that, I could see from the corner of my eye, she was dabbing. Yeah wait a minute, don't look at her, that way she'd get herself together again, *composed* I guess you'd say – then she'd be alright, then she'd carry on.

I thought it was time for another fag at least. I was feeling pretty crap by now. I should have kept in touch. I ought to come and see Dad more often too. — Jules still hadn't finished her drink but it was no good, I couldn't wait any longer, besides, I thought the time alone would suit her, she could sort herself out while I was at the bar. 'I'll get another one in,' I said as I got up, and I didn't look at her. I feel a bit bad about saying this, but frankly I was glad to have some time-out at the bar, I just didn't like sitting there seeing her hurting, and I felt like I should cry, but I couldn't, and it all felt weird. To tell the truth, I drew the time out quite a bit chatting to the geezer behind the bar, letting him wag his tongue about local shite, all that ordinary stuff that holds a place together.

I pulled my wallet out of my back pocket to pay him, and as I opened it a piece of paper fell out; it was ripped out of my old notepad with a name and a phone number scribbled on it, only I didn't recognise either. It was my writing for sure: *Ron Pope*, I ran the name round my head, I hadn't got a clue, but then I vaguely remembered writing it, and I remembered copying it from an email, a chirpy looking mail in blue, but I couldn't remember anything else, not even who'd sent it to me. I was feeling pretty frazzled. — When I looked up again I realised the guy was still waiting for some dosh so I passed him a twenty and shoved the paper back inside my wallet, couldn't be that important and maybe it would come to me later.

Jules seemed a bit better when I got back to the table, just a bit lost looking, and now I worried that I'd been *too* long at the bar. — I sat back down and lit up again. It turns out that Trudy had encouraged Jim to take a promotion, in a city he didn't know. He found a bedsit. Jules said it was a hole, but the idea was that it'd be easier to save more money that way. Trudy didn't go with him, she couldn't leave her friends, and anyway he was good at making friends, he'd be alright, the move was what he needed, it'd be good for his CV, his career, and later he could come back, and it'd be so much easier to get a bigger first home after he'd been earning decent money for a few years, then they'd have a 'substantial deposit', get on the property ladder, get started; and it wouldn't be such a hardship them being apart, she'd come up at the weekends, when he wasn't working through, well, *some weekends*, she'd got her pilates class and the gym, oh, and her mates.

So there he was, in a hole, with an a-hole job, in some fuck-wit city. On his own. Staring at the walls. Saving up to *get started*. I was glad I'd got another beer. Then Jules said he must have got really down, *really* down, he was on Anti-Ds though he'd said they didn't suit him. He'd lost a load of weight; he'd never been big, not fat or anything, but 'cos of his height Jules said the docs might have miscalculated the dose, she said she'd looked into it since… and then she stopped talking. She looked down and fiddled with something, her fingernails I think, dead agitated. She could have done with a beer mat to tear up, that was always their best use, only there weren't any. I leaned back in my chair and let her be. This stuff wasn't easy for her to get out, and to be honest, it wasn't easy to listen to. It seemed like we had to do it in stages, steps. Slow, easy steps. I thought it best to leave it alone a while. For a few moments I tried to listen in to the conversation at the bar, really it was too far away but some of the blokes were a bit pissed and acting up so I could catch some of it. Then after a while Jules took up from where she'd left off, saying as how, yeah, it might have been too high a dose, specially with his weight loss. Who knows. She finished up her drink and stared at the second one. We both watched the ice slipping. The pause was hellish long, neither of us said anything for ages. I scanned the floor, as though a pub's stinking, piss and beer ridden planks were gonna pass up any wisdom, *jerk*, but what can you do? And then the sun streamed in, all cheerful, and right there and then even that felt annoying. I turned my back to it. Then it fell across Jules' face and she tried to force a smile, but only for that moment, only to be brave, and maybe she was thinking the same as me 'cos then she shifted round and turned her back on it too.

She said she wished she'd known how far down he was, and known more about the drugs – sorry, *medication*, at the time, but then she wasn't sure what she'd have done about it anyway, maybe nothing. But at least she could have told him that sometimes Anti-Ds make it worse. Anyhow, even if Jim *had* known, he wasn't really in a state to deal with it, any of it, and most guys just don't do that kind of thing – ask loads of details, side-effects and stuff, that's just how it is. And I guess no one realises you're not in a state to deal with things until, well, until it's too late. She wasn't sure if anyone was to blame about the anti-depressants, and maybe it wasn't them, but at the time Trudy seemed to know more about that kind of stuff, and she'd said it would probably do the trick if you took them long enough. You probably just needed a high enough dose and to 'stick with it' in order for them to work.

When it got really rough Trudy took a day off work and went up there. So, she did her best. Jules was grateful, it can't have been easy. She'd offered to go, but Trude said it was something she needed to sort out, and in any case, she knew Jules was too soft, she'd probably get him to quit his job and move back home, and then everyone would just be back at square one. Square one — yeah right, and we can't have that, *'cos fuck knows, if we have people back at square one the bleedin' sky'll fall in!* — Trudy spent three days with Jim, from Friday through Sunday. She knew he'd be hard work, and this had gone on long enough. She told him to pull himself together, and then she went back home. On Monday, Jim went into the office as usual, he worked all day, and at 5pm he opened the window, and jumped. Jim died that day, and none too quickly. I lit Jules' cigarette. She drank down the rum, and I was glad I'd made it a large one. She said she'd be seeing Trudy later in the evening and didn't know what to say to her. What I wanted her to say was, '*Next time, try being kind!*' but I kept quiet. It seemed as though Jules had built some kind of compassion for Trudy, and I guess she needed to hold on to it, it wasn't fair for me to crush it, and I, I should have kept in touch. Jim was my mate. I should have been his.

# CHAPTER TWO

## *the day after the funeral*

## TRAINS

The sun was out. I was looking out of the window, it was ten minutes or more before the train would be leaving, but I imagined it already in motion. The engine starting up, that strange rumble and hiss as it breathed into life. I like trains. I like moving. I like being out of my life a while, not being anything to anyone for a while, just sitting there, pondering, staring aimlessly out the window. And I never quite get it, I never really understand why people take stuff out of their lives and bring it with them on journeys – laptops, paperwork, and phones switched on. Don't they get it? 'Train time' is separate, time to be nothing and no one. Like pressing 'pause', and sucking back a bit of time for yourself. I love it. And I'd readily spend my life travelling, not in any backpacker kinda way, more simple than that, just moving over land, and it could be any land, anywhere, just contemplating things, watching stuff go by, letting the land shift by just like clouds and sea, towns and cities rushing past, and all the time, inside, you, keep still. — I was glad Jules had listened to me and decided not to come and see me off. I'd deliberately shied away from looking for her at the ticket office and on the platform, just in case. I figured she'd cry again, selfish I know but it was all a bit more than I could handle, and the funeral, that had been something else. And then after the funeral; back at their house, the sandwiches… the tea, the brandy, brandy *in* tea… and cake, *cake!* at a funeral… is that OK? I dunno. Does it matter? It's 'unfathomable' to me, all of it. Isn't there a rulebook somewhere? Or rather, the opposite, the bleedin' opposite, isn't there a way of making it personal, singular, of marking out *Jim Jakes'* 'particular existence'? – *Cake!* Somehow, that was the worst of it for me. – One of the older ones said what a lovely spread Sandra, that's his mum, what a lovely spread Sandra had put on.

I went outside into their backyard, it was freezing but I couldn't care less. I had a beer and a fag. His mum came out to me, said I could smoke inside, said she and his dad were about to have one. But that wasn't it, I just needed to be outside, away from the 'spread'. She said as how it must be tough for me – *how'd she work that out?* I had it easy; her kids were her whole life and now one of them hadn't just died, he'd *jumped!* — I gave Sandra a cigarette, she smiled and said did I remember when I was a 'youngster' and used to nip round to their house for a 'sneaky fag'? — They'd lived just a few doors up. — I smiled, must have smoked round their place from when I was about thirteen, Dad would've gone spare if he'd realised, but then he went spare anyways. Sandra asked if I'd settled anywhere. I told her I'd moved about a bit, here and there, bit of time in London; she interrupted me then, wanting to know how that was, I told her it had been OK for a short while, 'til all my mates moved away, but it wasn't until I mentioned how they'd mostly got opportunities elsewhere, abroad and so on, that I noticed her looking down. 'Mates'… 'opportunities', these were to become two of my least favourite words. And if Julie bleedin' Andrews was ever lookin' for a new verse, I was sure I'd be the man to put it together. — We didn't speak for a minute or two, just smoked. I could hear the traffic going past the front of the house, a siren in the distance, people arguing in the street, it seemed noisy all of a sudden. I was glad. Then bit by bit it died off and the silence made things tricky. I scratched my foot around and tried to think of what to say, but everything seemed useless. — Eventually Sandra started to talk again, and somehow there was a note of brightness in her voice, forced of course, but stoical's much easier to deal with than tears. I really appreciated that. She said as how tall I was, and how she'd forgotten, and then how could she forget what with me always being able to do all the 'tall' jobs round their 'ouse, and then almost teary-eyed she blushed. I lit a fresh cigarette. And then it occurred to me that Jim wasn't really that much shorter, just that I'd always

19

been an inch or so in front while we were growing up, so it was like being stuck with a nickname when there was no need anymore, and now I came to think of it, Jim could just as easily have done the 'tall' jobs, or his dad for that matter, and that was it, wasn't it? It suddenly hit me, of course it was; Jim or his dad could easily have done those jobs, but Sandra − she was just making me useful, making me *feel* useful. I knocked the ash off, and took a long drag, some cigarettes taste better than others, depends on all kinds of stuff, the mood, the company, the place, that sort of stuff. − It struck me as funny, what you don't realise at the time. And now I knew that whilst me and Sandra were both mourning Jim, she must always have mourned for me − for me not having a mum. We smiled at one another, and for a moment I thought she looked dead young, like a teenager almost − it's nice, how old women, I mean, *older* women, can still be filled with so much youth, I guess it's always there, on the inside. She started to talk about how their lives had panned out since they'd left our street. And then her husband, Ray, came out to join us, he was half cut, mug full of brandy, long trail of fag ash falling away. He was a gentle sort of bloke, soft spoken. I hadn't heard him mention Jim all day, in fact I think he'd barely spoken a word to anyone. He looked completely crushed. And Sandra, she'd kept herself busy talking to everyone about anything and everything, except Jim, anyone and everyone, except Jim, and I guess for a lot of people, it's still an unspoken British rule, never to talk about what's actually going on. Ray knocked the ash off his cardigan sleeve, and as he did, the cigarette fell from his fingers, he moved towards it, following its arc as though he might catch it, but then he seemed to give up halfway. He crushed the last of it with his shoe, and then warmly, he asked what we were up to. Sandra smiled and said she was just 'filling me in'; she explained how she'd had to take on two extra part-time jobs to make ends meet; they'd had trouble keeping up the mortgage repayments once Ray had got laid off. 'We never made it to a detached,' she said and not unkindly, but the thin laughter running through her voice was sort of fake now, and awkward. 'Should never have moved,' Ray piped up. And like a complete arse, I said, 'Or at least not to a street called, *Burn-hope*, eh!' Ray looked away, catching me briefly from the corner of his eye with a look that hovered somewhere between hurt and spite. I didn't mean any harm. — He hadn't worked in ten years, he'd be retiring soon, 'cept he already was. I wondered if he missed me dad. I wondered if they felt at home, round Burnhope.

I used to worry about me dad, but he always kept up with his mates, and enough of 'em had never moved away, maybe a street or two, but not out of reach, and not like these had done, and not like me. — Now Sandra, she was what my dad called 'a real good sort', it's funny, he idolised me mum, but I never remember him saying that about her. I suppose it was as though Mum was, what would he call it? — 'A cut above', as though she had nothing to prove, not to him anyway, she didn't have to live up to anything, she was beyond all that, above all that, whereas other people, other people's wives, husbands, sons, there was some sort of measure for them. Mum scored 110% just for ever having looked his way – even after she'd left him, the rest of the world didn't have it that easy, the rest of us still had to prove ourselves. At a rough estimate, I reckon Dad would've scored Sandra a meagre 60%, nothing too high, could do better. — I realised Sandra was still talking, but my head was derailed somewhere, useless.

Jules came out, her pretty eyes all swollen to bursting, like a boxer. I knew it was natural that she'd cried that much, of course it was, but still, it didn't seem right her being in so much pain. Sandra was doing all that old-fashioned brave stuff, she'd do her weeping in private, but that ain't right neither somehow. There she was, trying to take care of everyone, me included. I wasn't any good at this. Ray went back inside. Then Sandra said that she'd 'leave me and Jules to it'. Jules was coughing a bit so I stubbed my fag out, she said it wasn't bothering her, said she probably just needed another drink. And then she swayed, I think she was a bit pissed. I didn't know what to say. She leant against the wall, her head slightly heavy, still too many tears onboard. I started to wonder why she looked so different from when we were kids, because if she hadn't been the only girl sitting on her own in the pub the day before, I might not have recognised her at all. I tried hard now to picture her from before. And then it dawned on me, *ten*, she must only have been about ten when they moved to Burnhope, and me and Jim were seventeen, eighteen, and quite rightly never really had anything to do with her, she was just a kid. She must be twenty-seven or eight now. The grown-up Jules. I felt myself blush a bit. Tosser. But she wasn't looking so it was alright. I noticed her hair, I'd noticed it, sort of guiltily, in the pub the day before. Long, dark, silky brown hair. Gorgeous. I wouldn't know how to judge, but I don't reckon it was dyed, too shiny and soft lookin'. It was dead long, but some shorter bits curled round her face. She was looking down at her shoes or something, maybe at nothing at all, but it meant I could keep watching, I shouldn't really have done that though 'cos they reckon, scientists that is, they reckon that people can actually feel you lookin' at them, specially if it's 'prolonged'. Fuck it. I carried on, anyways, I was concerned about her. — Her eyelashes, they were super long, and they curled up, like they were drawn on, like in comics. But then I haven't looked at any in ages – lately I keep reading novels, tons of 'em. And that's weird, 'cos I never read at all as a kid. But so it goes. And then I wondered if Jules read, and I wondered if she read novels, and I wondered whether to ask her. But I didn't. I might fuck it up, it might come out wrong, those 'random questions' and 'idle remarks' – sometimes they totally screw things up. And I think I'd been clumsy enough for one funeral. I wished I hadn't said that stupid thing about *Burnhope* to her dad. Best try and keep things steady.

It turned out that I wasn't the only one screwing things up; Jules said Trudy never showed up the night before, and that she must have had her phone switched off. I said I'd tried to pick her out at the funeral, only I hadn't a clue what she looked like. She wasn't there apparently. She didn't make it to the funeral, 'good ole Trude'. Jules said it must have been too much for her, too much to face, and then she added, 'Bless' — *Bless!!! How could Jules do that? How could she be that nice? And where did she dig out all that compassion from?* — *Bless my bleedin' arse, 'Bless!'*.

There's something so automatic about being a smoker, half the time you don't remember lighting up, or even taking the pack out of your pocket, so it wasn't until Jules coughed again that I realised, 'Sorry,' I said, about to put it out. 'No, you're alright. Got a spare one?' she asked. I lit it for her. The smell of matches lingered in the air. There's something comforting about that smell somehow, I reckon it's like that even if you're not a smoker. 'Not much of a funeral was it Mark?' and her words made me nervous, partly because it was as though she wanted me to agree with her – because she was right, it hadn't seemed like much of a send off, and then at the same time not wanting me to agree, because it hurt too much to acknowledge that as well as not being there for him when he was alive, we might have got this part wrong as well. It was cowardly I know, but I hid under my hair a bit, nodded occasionally and managed not to say the wrong thing on account of the fag in my mouth blocking the exit for my usual careless drivel. But soon enough my mind raced ahead, and before I knew it the fag was out and under my foot, and I was already halfway to suggesting 'all manner' of funeral alternatives. Jules looked up and smiled, as though she read my thoughts, 'Maybe,' she said, 'maybe the music could have been different... not so sad sounding,' and then we both fell quiet a minute lest we get the next bit wrong. 'Like what?' I asked after a bit, trying to come over gentle sounding. So far, so good. Things seemed OK, and after a moment she picked up, 'Like, something jokey,' she said, 'maybe from a cartoon or something...'

'The theme from: *Hong Kong Phooey* maybe... d'you remember that?'

'Sort of,' she said, and then she started to sing it a bit, and rather quiet and delicate considering how much she must have had to drink, '*Hong, Kong Phooey, number one super guy...*' and then I started the talking bit, and dead quiet so as no one indoors could hear, it wouldn't sound right to anyone else, and it might seem like we were taking the piss, and that couldn't have been further from the truth. So I quietly mimicked the voiceover from the start of the cartoon, like an arse of course, but Jim wouldn't have minded, he'd have laughed, and I'm no actor, '*Who is this super hero?*' I said, and luckily Jules knew the next line, I guess she must have heard it enough from us two bastards, and so she asked, '*Is it Sarge?*'

'*No,*' I answered, and now we were a double act.

'*Rosemary, the telephone operator?*'

'*No,*' I replied, and I liked having the shorter lines; like I said, I'm no actor.

'*Penry,*' and then she stopped a minute, 'is that right?' she asked,

'*Penry*, not *Henry*?'

'I think so,' I said, 'doesn't really matter too much though does it?' and happy enough she carried on, saying, 'Could it be, *Penry, the mild mannered janitor?*' and I wanted to say the next line, all cool sounding, '*Could be!*' with that sort of mischievous rising intonation at the end, only I couldn't get it out, I thought I might sound like an arse, and I felt myself blush, and now I had a knot in my chest. Everything seemed too quiet suddenly. I heard a door slam. Then nothing. And then just the wind distantly howling round the chimneys high up, cold and shrill, and a car screeching past at the front, and suddenly everything felt so lonely.

Jules started to cry. I put my arms around her. There was rain in the air and we should have gone inside, but I just couldn't face it, I couldn't face any of it anymore. My shirt was wet, right to my chest, and I tried to hug Jules like a father would, or like Jim would, and I wished that Jim was there to hug her, as though only he'd know how to hug her properly, how to handle it right, and then I realised how stupid that was. But Jim would have known how to be a big brother even if he hadn't had any practice at all, and I felt like there were some things in life I could have all the practice in the world for and I'd still fuck up. — What was I thinking, trying to pull ideas together for a *jolly* funeral? Dickhead. Now I'd got Jules crying again and she must barely have stopped these last days.

I carried on holding her. And for a few brief moments, out there in the cold, I found myself imagining – that Jules was my girl, and that Jim wasn't dead, as though he might just be inside chatting with his mum and dad, maybe having a beer, just how it might have been on a Sunday, and Jules, she was upset for some other reason, and being her bloke, I was caring for her, holding her, and maybe later we'd all go down the pub together, have a few more beers, a rum and coke, try and cheer her up. But then Jules spoke, and her voice brought me back, cutting me back to the scene we were really in, in a Burnhope backyard, light rain in the air catching your cheek.

Jules' voice was soft, she said she remembered how me and Jim had wanted to write songs, she said that since *what had happened, had happened,* she'd had a dream about it, how we'd written songs and never moved away, the way that it wasn't, but might have been, and she asked if I'd actually written any more songs or had I given up on that as well? I didn't answer, and then through her tears she whispered that she was sorry, but there wasn't any need.

I held her a bit closer as my hopeless way of avoiding saying anything, hoping she'd read it to mean all the things I should have said and would have said, if I'd had half a clue. Then, trying her best to put on a brave face, she said I shouldn't leave it so long before I came back up again and how they'd all like it if I kept in touch, if I wanted to, that was. She couldn't have been nicer, but it cut me to the quick, and all I could do was look back on our lives and dream them as better, and truer. Lives with songs. — That was one of the hardest days of my life.

The train still wasn't moving. Must be delayed. I looked out the window again, daft really, Jules wouldn't be coming to the station. It was probably for the best. I took a deep breath. And Dad, Dad never did goodbyes, it wasn't his thing, so we'd done what we always do, this casual, manly goodbye as we each crossed the living room, as though I was just popping out for a paper and might be back in a jiffy. Kinda nice in a way, 'cos I would be back, just not that soon. — *No Smoking* – can't have a fag on a train, not anywhere, not anymore, no separate carriages, not even the *one*, can't even have one in the bogs. And now my leg was shaking. I tapped the pack on the corner of the table; the bird sat opposite shot me a look, but people don't understand, it's not like issuing a challenge, I'm not about to piss her off and light up, and see if she's got the bottle to take me on, I just need to hold on to the pack to kid myself that maybe, maybe I *can* have a fag, soon-*ish*. Ah, fuck it. I got up, this train didn't seem like it was going anywhere soon, and as far as I knew, you could still get away with a smoke on the platform. — Anyhow, they taste best, forbidden ones, I felt myself grinning, *jerk*. But so it goes.

It was cold on the platform, the woman in the train was now giving me the once-over through the window, she blushed a bit when she realised I'd clocked her, and picked up a magazine. I turned away and looked about, but no, there was no one else coming down the stairs, no one on the bridge. We'd be going soon. Then I almost jumped out of my skin as they made an announcement, some sort of problem, we'd be in the station a few more minutes, they'd give us more information as it came to them, bollocks they would, but that's alright, that's our trains for you, that's Britain. — And then without another bleedin' word, and in what seemed like no time at all, the geezer blew his whistle, and the doors started slamming one after another, hard and loud and somehow 'empty' sounding. Cold. What a wind-up. I felt a kind of panic, I looked about a bit, crushed the fag out with my foot; by now the geezer had his hand on the last door and he was giving me that look which meant I should get a bleedin' move on or risk being left behind. Steady on mate. I looked up at the bridge one last time, and the stairs, down the platform, and then opposite in case she'd made a mistake, but she wasn't there. She wasn't there. Jules wasn't coming. The guy shouted was I getting on or what? I shrugged and got on.

It was probably better like that, and in any case, I did tell her, I couldn't deny that, I told her not to come, she'd probably got things to be getting on with. She asked if I was sure, because she'd like to come and see me off, but I said I wasn't one for goodbyes – *not one for goodbyes!* – what was I on? Who the frig talks like that? (my dad!). '*Not one for goodbyes.*' — Note to self, and a word of advice: *try and stop saying shite you don't mean.*

# CHAPTER THREE

## *soulmates*

## FURTHER DOWN THE LINE

I slumped down in my seat, my mouth was still full of the taste of that last 'lusty' cigarette, I had that nice tingly satisfied feeling that follows, and my head was finally growing empty, it had to, too much had happened, and I hadn't eaten or slept properly in the best part of a week. There was too much to think about: Jim, and everything that had happened, his death, his life, his family – my dad – all of that, and then there was still all the other stuff, the stuff that had been shunted to the back, the stuff that had been happening before all of this, before Jim jumped and made the rest of us press 'pause' – because all of that was still there, my life – for what it was – was still running on in the background, and I guess it needed some looking at. Coming up here had pulled me out of it for a while, but now it was time to go back, time to face the life I had, the life I *have*, go back to the place I live, the friends, job, colleagues, you know, the 'usual run of things', only *now*, things had changed, everything had changed, except I wasn't quite sure how, and for the moment I didn't have the energy for it, all I could think of doing was leaving it alone a while. And just for now, that was alright. I was on a train, just sitting on a train, starting on a journey, and the rest would just have to wait. — I felt quite sleepy. — It would all come right – *somehow*, Sandra used to say something like that when we were kids, '*It'll all come out in the wash,*' that was it. I slid down a bit further in my seat trying to hold on to that thought, only lines like that, sometimes they're just too flimsy, sometimes they simply *don't* friggin' wash, but right now they had to because that was all there was. A few familiar words, sometimes, that's really all there is.

For a time there, someone else's crisis had taken the floor, and that wasn't even Jim's, we were all too late for that one, this had been Sandra's and Ray's, and Jules' crisis. Jim mate, you've left a mess behind. And I knew, I knew that the three of them were always going to suffer, always going to wonder, just as I would: *was it me, was it my fault, something I did or didn't do, said or didn't say?* – always, that's just how it was. — But then I tried to tell myself to let go of it, at least for a bit, to just stop thinking about it, stop driving myself insane. And as the train pulled out all I could do was repeat in my head, '*It'll all come out in the wash. It'll all come out in the wash.*' What a wanker. But what are you supposed to do? Sayings like that run way back, and lame as they sound, they try and cover all kinds of human tragedy; I guess it's some dopey means of survival, and it sounds like making light of things, but it isn't that at all, more like: light words for heavy matters – and I suppose they help convince you, trick you, into taking things easier, specially when you can't do anything about them. A small way of stopping stuff hurting so bad. The train moved on. *It'll all come out in the wash. It'll all come out in the wash.* Maybe now I could get some sleep. I hummed the line in my head, just to help it empty.

When I came to, I wasn't sure if I'd slept for long, the woman opposite was still clamped to the same magazine so it might only have been minutes, but at least it had felt like deep sleep. I always think a short deep sleep outweighs the long shallow kind, but I don't know if that's true, *scientifically*. And now that I was awake, my mind started to wander, but just so long as I kept it away from the tricky stuff just for a while longer, I figured that'd be fine. I sat up and pulled out my ticket to show the train geezer, and that piece of paper fell out of my wallet again, I looked at it hard: *Ron Pope*, and *Ron Pope's* number, which was a London number, fair enough, but I still couldn't figure it. I tried to picture the email I'd copied it off, but all I could remember was it being chirpy sounding and the fact that it was blue. What's the use in that? I posted Mr Ron back in my wallet. It'd come to me eventually.

I felt conscious now of a guy at the table opposite, I hadn't even noticed him before, and for some total splice of a second I thought he had a look of Jim about him; my neck and spine ran cold. *Songwriting and suicide*, it suddenly occurred to me, though I didn't much like the idea, that if you did indeed have a real deep passion for the writing of songs, how not doing one could lead to the other. Jim, mate. — Man, I was doing a really rubbish job of keeping my head away from the dark stuff, total basket case. Things had to be kept a bit more steady. Yeah, so try a bit bleedin' harder mate.

I looked down the aisle instead. People were still moving up and down the train, hunting down that prime position, only I'd got that on account of getting on early and sticking my bag and jacket there, *yes*, it makes me a tosser, but I'm a tosser in prime position, which means: near the buffet, but not so near that the rank smell of microwaved meals can reach; a seat with a table and not one of those pull-down bastards; and a half-clean window so as I could watch stuff outside like I would have done as a kid all dead excited – *way* tall buildings, practically skyscrapers; factories, houses, and walls, *walls and walls and walls* with graffiti – some top tagging, and then finally, fields, and field stuff, what I think of as 'field furniture', because despite having legs or wheels, most of the stuff in fields looks pretty static to me: sheep, cows, tractors. Doesn't it? Doesn't that stuff stand still when you are moving? Seems that way, and I kinda like it because it increases my sense of moving, of moving away – it's good that mostly no one knows what goes on in another geezer's head and passes for entertainment, *what a nonce*, but that's how it is – and a part of me can't help feeling that there *is* some virtue in being easily pleased, finding some amusement, 'contentment' if you like, in the easy, ordinary stuff of life, I reckon even me dad would see the merit in that.

I sunk down again in my seat, cosy. And I wasn't far off from sleeping again when I spotted this kid running up the aisle, but then not so much running as skipping; he was the blackest little kid I'd ever seen, his whiter-than-white teeth inside the biggest, happiest, mother-of-all smiles, and he was chanting, cool and beautiful, bouncing the words along with his walk, eyes beaming, *'I'm black, I'm black, I'm black, I'm black, I'm black...'* total even pace. I looked at his dad and asked if the lad, who looked about six years old, had only just noticed, or was he chanting it as a declaration that it was simply the coolest thing? He laughed and said his son was, '*Just nuts!*', then just as he moved on after him he added, 'The thing is, most of the time he wants to be *blue!*'

I could still hear the boy's voice as they trailed off behind me, and it helped me feel relaxed. Nice one. Two more kindred spirits, happy with the easy stuff. Somehow, the two of them looked all the blacker for being on an unusually white train, I scanned up and down, but no, so far everyone else I could see was white. — I stared back out the window. — Some days in the summer, me and Jim, we'd just buzz off like, take a train and head off to the beach. We'd only be about nine or ten, so we had no money, couldn't buy tickets or anything, but Jim had this brilliant uncle on the railways and he'd turn a blind eye; and if he wasn't on, one of us would just take a shufty now and again for when the guard was about, and then we'd piss off into the bogs till the coast was clear. — People complain about stuff nowadays, but train bogs, I'm telling you, they used to be well worse. *Man, they were stinkers.* Can't be the case though can it, not really, I mean piss is just piss, it's just that it seemed that way back then and this one time when the pair of us were about as close as you can bleedin' get to passing out. We could hear the train geezers close by, some arse or other had snitched on us, or so we thought, and these big train geezers (unfortunately neither of 'em Jim's uncle), were muttering stuff about *knocking our little bastard heads together*, so we were rammed in the bogs there for friggin' ages. Terrified. The pair of us, damn near knocked out by piss fumes! Well nasty. I was wedged in the corner, we felt the train slow up just before the station, and we knew, we just knew, that this was it, this was where we had to make a major move, get off that train, or lose our sorry little heads to them big blokes. But when it came to it we were almost wasted from the heat and fumes and barely had the strength to even open that soddin' door, we practically had to bust the bastard open. But we ran for the exit, and afterwards, that sea air, oh man, imagine it, set against a background of train-bog claustrophobia and the scent of pure rancid piss, I'm telling you, that sea air, it was beautiful. And the seagulls, Jim said it was as if they knew, and it really was, it was like they really knew, and they screamed, man, their wings splitting up the skies; and Jim running on ahead of me, singing away after them, his wings stretched wide. Free and full of life. I was always a bit more self-conscious like, so I watched from a distance and wished, wished I could just run out the same like, my arms in the air, splitting the skies, coasting along. And what was I worried about? It wasn't as though he looked like an arse, that wasn't possible, and maybes I wouldn't have either – difference is, I would have felt like one. Shame really, we were only little lads.

My mind drifted back again and I could hear that little lad still singing away in the distance. It seemed as though he must have been running down the next carriage and then back again, entertaining the troops, so to speak. His voice, distant and sweet, lulling me back into sleep, and I found myself dreaming about Jules, about me and Jules, and I was picturing the pair of us on a beach with warm yellow sand and pale blue waves in some place where everything was smooth and quiet, with just that gentle ripple of notes as the blue lapped over the shoreline. — But then there was this sudden evil jolt as the train pulled into a station and whiplashed me back to the moment. *I friggin' hate that. What is it with some drivers?* The things some bastards do for kicks, – but maybe it gets that way at times, even for train drivers. — People shuffled about getting on and off, and when I looked across I was almost in a state of panic, worrying if the guy opposite was still there. But why? Why should I panic? I didn't even know him! And why should he still be there? This might be his stop, for Christ's sake! Man, my head was all over the place. Right now, all I really needed was just some small way of keeping my thoughts from straying too far off the map. — *Was that really too much to manage?* Stop thinking about Jim, *or* the geezer opposite, or anything else. Just for a while, just so as I could breathe a bit, keep the whole anxiety thing under control. But straight off, and I got to thinking about Jim's bird, *Trudy*, speculating just how he got himself caught up with someone quite that crap. The thing is though, it's always loads easier to see how someone else might be just about to fuck up and get themselves saddled with a wrong un. When it's yourself it only ever seems to be something you can look at with hindsight, yeah, an after-sight, after you realise you've gone too far too fast, rather like me and that bird in my flat

31

back home. — I mean, really, what's that all about? I can't even sleep in the same room as her anymore, 'cos I talk in my sleep, I talk 'loads' apparently, and it bugs her. — But I suppose the bottom line is, she makes me feel used up, second rate. Spent. I can't explain. But she ain't a Jules or a Sandra any more than I reckon that Trudy is, and right now I don't even wanna think about her. Not her, not Trudy. Best if I could stop thinking altogether 'cos for no good reason I was starting to feel angry.

As we moved off I sat back up and distantly I could make out the little geezer still singing away there, '*I'm black, I'm black, I'm black, I'm black, I'm black....*' People started to smile, and sensing this as he entered, letting the electronic doors work their stuff, he blasted out, big and bold, '*Come on everybody!*' and this was his instruction to the rest of the carriage to *join the hell in*, his big eyes smiling; he jigged his ass down the carriage, I turned and leant out, offering a look of approval and support like. He'd got himself a notebook and pen, and clutching these he ran to my table and started to drum out a beat.

The magazine woman opposite totally missed the vibe, and reading him purely as '*child*' and not as the *song writer-genius-in-the-making* that he was, started singing that rainbow song: '*Red and yellow and pink and green...*' and warmly so, to his ballsy, '*Black, I'm black... I'm black... I'm black... I'm black...*' – he stopped singing as she 'affectionately' pushed on, '*orange and purple and blue, I can sing a rainbow, sing a rainbow....*' He butt in, he had to, his tone all round and soft, 'No, no, no,' he said, and he knew she meant well, you could see that, but he wasn't speaking *kid,* he was speaking *tunes!* And he told her so. The carriage started to laugh, he shot them a look, unsure of what they took as funny, and checking that it wasn't him they were chuckling away at. And then some big old guy, a white guy, shouted loud and firm, 'I'm black!' and that was how it started, soon the little guy had the whole carriage singing, '*I'm black... I'm black... I'm black... I'm black... I'm black*', and he strutted up and down checking on the beat, tilting in and listening, correcting where it was needed, strumming his fingers on the tables or the plastic at the backs of the seats. Even I was singing, but happy that there were voices enough, and a few *real* voices too, to drown mine out. The boy spotted his dad in the doorway, and the song reached its climax as the kid smiled big, and yelled, '*I'm blue!*' His dad stood shaking his head, half proud, half embarrassed, the carriage, half laughing, half singing. 'You're nuts, boy!' his dad hollered warmly, his arms stretched wide. The boy ran and they hugged big to the approval of a sound and colourful carriage. From the doorway his dad said how he'd been 'up and down, up and down, chasing this boy, and maybe I shouldn't waste my energy, 'cos you can never lose a child who is always singing', and with that the boy took a bow, a few of us cheered, and the two were gone again, deeper into the train. A posh old lady got up, and as she did I heard her say to the bloke next to her (probably her husband), 'I rather like being black, Sidney,' Sidney smiled at her. I settled back in my seat, content, and I found myself thinking of Maya Angelou – I've got her smile on the back cover of a book of her poems. — I don't claim to know about poetry, not anything at all, I'm what you might call the *know what I like* breed of reader. And I like Maya Angelou. I like her poetry, and I like her smile. I closed my eyes and tried to see if I could remember any of the lines, maybe even a whole poem. I'd never tried to memorise them, but I guess bits get memorised anyhow, almost by themselves, some lines just sort of tiptoe in and find themselves a nice cosy home. '*Still I Rise*' – that's one, one I like a lot, and how's it go again? I don't remember all of it, but there's a verse that goes:

*Does my sexiness upset you?*
*Does it come as a surprise*
*That I dance like I've got diamonds*
*At the meeting of my thighs?*

I think Maya Angelou's genius with words. Once when I was reading that poem I felt all sort of seduced. And that verse especially, that 'particular' set of lines, I don't mean anything rude if you follow me, I just mean that the words had an effect, intense, sexy, – *argh shite*, this is gonna sound all wrong, but I know what I mean, and Christ knows, I couldn't write anything that would turn someone on – believe me, I've tried.

I must have nodded off again, we were at another station only it seemed too early. We were totally still, and this time I'd had no sense at all that we were stopping, must have been dead smooth – nice one, driver, maybe he'd chilled out a bit. Then I realised the magazine woman had gone, so I must have been well out of it. But the guy opposite was still there and that was enough. Just a little continuity. He was sleeping, yeah, and like a great big kid; and for a moment I almost thought I could hear Jules saying, *'Bless,'* like she would, all gentle and soothing. *Jules.* Maybe I'd write to her, say something, keep in touch like she'd said. I wasn't sure, like I wasn't too sure about anything anymore.

It was proving to be a strange ole journey. On the way up it was as though I had a purpose, I was going to Jim's funeral, but now, *now* where was I headed? I was meant to go back to my own home, get on with my life there, but really, that just didn't seem right anymore, it didn't feel that simple either, but I was so exhausted, brain-fried even, I could barely think. — It seemed we were already about to move off again. I glanced out the window and saw the black lad and his dad on the platform, they were looking right at me and started waving, I waved back, and just as I did I caught sight of the lad's notebook on the table in front of me. I held it up in a panic, but they'd already moved, turned to walk on, and just in that second, they were too far away. The train was moving off, gathering speed, and they were gone. I slumped back in my seat feeling a bit downhearted. I looked at the book and realised I'd panicked so much I'd nearly crushed it, I did my best to smooth it out, flatten it down again. It had a dark blue cover with thin, blue lined pages inside, and a margin in red. It reminded me of my 'rough book' at school, the kind we used to take notes in or use for what felt like dead-tough maths questions before doing them in the 'proper' book in 'neat', or we'd use them to try out essay ideas with the same thing in mind. I wondered if they still had rough books at school, maybe this was supposed to be one, only I reckoned this kid would probably have elevated it to the loftier task of songwriting. And maybe he was too little for a rough book, I wasn't sure. I had a flick through it, scribbles, sketches, words going round the page and back again, stuff written upside down, doodles, stuff written neat, stuff written messy and stuff crossed out, nothing too much like a song, but definitely the seeds for some. I looked at the cover again hoping to find his name, maybe a school name or an address so as I could get it back to him. The initials: CA were scratched into the cover, but that was all. My little soulmate, separated from his book. I put it down, turning the corner of one of the pages, and just as I did I heard this woman's voice – an older woman, soft and sweet, she must have just got on, 'Don't bend it, you'll spoil the page', she smiled at me and then looked for somewhere to put her bags (they didn't look too heavy or anything, so I didn't offer to help), and then she took her coat off and folded it, dead neat. She had these really pretty eyes, blue, very pale blue. She was about fifty I suppose, or maybe even as much as sixty, it was hard to tell 'cos she was what me ole nan would have described as 'well kept'.

Nan, now there was a woman, 'formidable' I guess is the word. She was the only one who was ever honest about me mum, and maybe it seemed a bit harsh it being her daughter and all, but I always liked Nan's honesty, it was usually pretty brutal but it was a bloody welcome change from Dad's delusions. No flies on you, Nan. — 'All hat and no knickers' she called me mum, and that never made any sense to me as a kid 'cos Mum never had a hat.

Nan passed away just before Mum left. And I'd always had my suspicions about that. Not that I thought Mum had done her in or anything, nothing sinister like. But I reckon Mum must have been aching to get away long before, only she couldn't bear to face Nan, so she must have waited, wondering what to do, measuring up whether or not she could take her mother's wrath. Nan, the only person in her life who'd tell it like it was. You see, Dad, he'd forgive me mum anything. It's fucking mental when I think about it, but Dad couldn't see it, and now, I look back on it and I think about Sandra, and I wonder how Dad could possibly have looked down on a woman like her, and I really think he did. Didn't he know, that 60% of *something* counts for so much more than 110 of nothin'. You see, she hadn't wanted me, she was bored of him, and he was the only one around who couldn't see it – 'I almost missed the train,' the woman said, breathlessly but warm, snapping me back to the present; her voice, I suppose it was the kind you'd want to hear if you were a kid and someone was about to read you a story, like Sandra maybe only posh.

I realised I'd let go of CA's book, losing the page; and I suddenly found myself sitting upright as though in response to this lady's voice, pulling myself up like, it was automatic somehow. It's weird how gentleness can be that powerful, and this woman seemed to embody something nicely old fashioned and worthy of respect, and respect in that old, true sort of sense, and not like the respect of now, which I guess is more like: *reeeeee-spec-me-man-or-I'll-smash-your-fuckin-face-in.*

I grinned to meself as I sat there 'behaving myself', and happily so – *and happily so?* – see, I only have to think of Julie bleedin' Andrews the once, and look what happens, stays with me for days – it's amazing to me that I'm not a soddin' cross-dresser. — Anyway, the lady, can't call her anything else, she took a book out of her bag, I couldn't see what it was but it had a posh bookmark in it, leather with some gold writing on it, she put it on the table as she started to read but I couldn't make out the writing on it too easily, too small, but then she caught me looking and pushed it over to me saying, 'I think you could do with one of these.'

'Yeah, maybe,' I said in my dead politest, and then I caught her glancing over at CA's rough book, and worried lest she think a six year-old's rough book was mine I pulled Calvino out of my bag. I know, I shouldn't care less, but I did, and I wanted to impress her, I wanted her to glance across again and think that what I was reading was top stuff – 'cos it was, I was reading *Invisible Cities,* by Italo Calvino. I took a proper look at her bookmark and the writing on it:

'*I have nothing to declare, except my genius.*' Oscar Wilde.

I figured that '*Wilde*' must have been a right flash git, but what do I know, maybe he *was* a genius. Really, it looked like the kind of bookmark CA deserved, but it was no good for me, I'd look like a right arse carrying that about, and the thing is, people think things like that say something about you, only it all depends on who you are to start with. In CA's case it would be accurate, he *is* a little genius, and the lady who owned it, well it just added to the fact that she came over all sort of proper and cultured, but me, I'd look like a total prick with something like that. A plain bookmark would be more my style, if I was to have one at all. Anyway, I had to get rid of this fancy one. I picked it up, 'Nice,' I said, still trying to sound polite. I laid it closer to her side of the table, 'Nice squirly writing on it,' *squirly?* yeah I know, but I'd already said it, some words just sneak out on their own. 'Actually, I've almost finished this,' I said, looking at Calvino and hoping to distract her from the poncy bookmark, stop her from insisting on me using it like. She looked at the Calvino cover and read the title. I felt dead nervous, and then I blurted out, *'You can have it if you want,'* I pushed it over to her adding, 'I've read it before, it's dead good.'

'In that case, you must have mine!' and she gave me this dead big open smile, 'unless you've already read it?' I shook my head, but to be honest I still didn't know what she was reading, I couldn't see the title too well. She carried on talking, 'I read it as a youngster, and I can't get on with it just now, but that's not to say it's not a good read, I think I probably just need a change. It's set in London.' And with that she snapped the book shut and pushed it over to me. I didn't know what to say. I hadn't actually wanted to part with Calvino, and neither did I want to rob this lady of her read, but it seemed like a done deal, the exchange already complete. Then she placed the bookmark on top of the book as though it was a *nice little added extra*, a freebie. So there I was, with a book, a lady's sort of book, and a poncy bookmark, and don't get me wrong, I was grateful, but my energy was so damn low I felt I had no sense at all of how this came about. I felt like I was coming off something, or going down with something maybe, hard to describe, but I wasn't quite with it somehow. To tell the truth, I don't think I was really with it *at all*, but I guess that sort of thing isn't too easy to figure by yourself.

The ticket guy came along again, he remembered me from earlier so he concentrated on checking the lady's ticket, but then his eye flicked across the book she'd given me. There was some posh bird on the cover and the title was actually a woman's name, and then of course it happened to be written by a bird as well. *Bollocks.* The wanker grinned all superior at me as he gave her back her ticket, and like a total tosser, I dropped my jacket over the book to hide it, trying to make it look as though I didn't realise what I was doing, all casual like. I breathed out and wished I'd woken up sooner, got off and had a smoke, a long deep smoke. *Argh, screw it*, what do I care what some arsehole thinks about what I'm reading? I can't be a dick all my life. *Read what I fucking like, matey.* I moved my jacket, got hold of the book and placed it in full view – and the bookmark? Well, everyone has their limits, 'You'll need this,' I said to the lady, 'for when you start Calvino. I can use me train ticket. Cheers though.' She gave a half nod and a smile, I think she could read me, but it seemed OK.

I took out my ticket to demonstrate that I really did mean to use it (obedient to the last), and as I did I came across that *Ron Pope* again on that bit of paper. I began to run his name around my head, and all the while with the distant murmur of the lady's voice in the background. '*It's set in London*,' she'd said, dead matter of fact, '*...in London... it's set in London*,' and suddenly I'd got it! Because ole *Ron Pope* there, he was also '*set in London*'. I knew him from London and I knew him from university. *Bingo*. And now that I'd made the connection, the rest came back easy as anything, and it made no sense at all that I couldn't remember it before, but now I could picture the whole friggin' email, clear as day. We'd gone to uni, not exactly *together*, but at the same time like; we'd shared the same halls in our first year, that was all as far as I remember. I'd never kept in touch with Ron, but from time to time I still got included on the geezer's mass emails despite my never replying. — I always reckon that if you're included on an email addressed to say 5-10 other people, it means something, it shows a little 'discernment' at least on the part of the sender, whereas being part of a list of 200 other sods just means the tosser who sent it out is a 'quantity' not 'quality' kinda guy. I pictured his email, it was blue, a cheery bloody blue. It said how 'Ron Pope' (written in a larger font *and* in italics, I kid you not) was taking time out from his job, *and what was his job?* I couldn't remember, safe to say, chief arsehole somewhere, anyway, he was going off to 'find himself', 'overseas', and to top it all, the whole friggin' mail had, *of course*, been written in the third person, I guess to suggest that his assistant: *Little Ron*, or *Ronda* had written it – I think that's partly why I hate email, it's far too easy to fuck up, and being a jerk really isn't something to advertise; but anyhow, back to business, and it seemed Ron was on the lookout for someone to house-sit for a few months.

'Do you live in London?' the lady asked. I jumped, and I could feel myself not answering, I felt as though I was somewhere else, half dreaming, and then for some stupid reason I answered, 'Yes,' only that wasn't true. I paused while I got my thoughts together, then I corrected it, 'No,' I said. 'No, I don't live in London, but I used to, a while back.' The thing was, we were in fact on a London-bound train, but I was supposed to get off at some stage and change, change and go back '*home*'. I felt myself trying to explain, but I can't have made much sense. She smiled, and I think I must have interrupted her, it was as though she'd had a follow-up question that I must have cut in on, I wasn't totally sure. To be honest, I couldn't concentrate too well, and then I realised that now she was saying something else to me. It was something about me looking tired, but somehow I couldn't connect this with the idea of actual *sleep*, 'cos when you are that tired it's no good that people hint, it's just too subtle; and looking back I think that was what she meant, only like I said, it was way too subtle, and she was way too nice, and so I pushed to stay awake, thinking I should try and chat away, only I couldn't put the words together.

After a while the lady started to busy herself, going through a diary or something. I hoped I hadn't been talking shite. Half-heartedly, I flicked through CA's little blue book some more, backwards and forwards, reading some of the stuff written upside down, well, trying to; weaving back and to on the page like, and then, on the second to last page, almost as though it was meant to be hidden, there it was, CA's song, in full. *Sorted!* I felt this sudden rush. I was well made-up. I knew he was a star. And I felt dead weird, sort of emotional, like a rush of happy and sad feelings all mixed up. Then the lady's voice came back in again, and this time she was more direct, she said I should try and get forty winks before my stop, 'a wee cat nap' she called it, and warmed by this I finally let my eyes close, this was, after all, 'train time', time-out, time for sleeping. Beautiful. CA's rhythms drumming gently in my mind.

And I didn't know how, I can't explain it, but I began to feel like things were somehow different; and I didn't know by what degree, maybe not by much at all, but it felt like something inside me had changed; and maybe I wouldn't get off, I could stay on this train, maybe even go all the way. Why not? Head off to London – *and that life of mine in some place else?* – the so-called friends, the job, the colleagues – *leave that all behind*. Who knows, I couldn't quite decide, but right now it made no odds; for the moment even the very thought was enough, and I felt like maybe something good was gonna come. Lulled to sleep by this, I felt like I'd been collecting soulmates: the lady; CA and his dad. Yeah, felt like collecting soulmates.

# CHAPTER FOUR

## *change of plan*

# SO SHOOT ME

I yawned. 'You've had a very good sleep,' the lady said, 'I expect you feel better for that don't you?' I smiled at her, and she was right, I did feel better, much better. I looked out the window. It was hard to gauge where we were, so many places now, they end up looking the same, all that shopping-centre shite all sprawled out, it looks like a place just got puked on what with all those pale yellow and flesh coloured bricks. And how did that happen? So many cities, they just look like nowhere, or anywhere, like their souls got bricked up. — But I guess there are still a few places left that aren't run by arseholes for city planners — I suppose that's the kind of thing Jim would have had something to say about. — Personally, I love all that big fuck-off architecture, all that silvery looking stuff, or that brilliant glass shite, I like that, that and the old stuff, the dead old stuff, cathedrals and stuff, or a mosque or something with the occasional gold dome; and I don't care what the building is, just as long as it's got a bit of soul.

I glanced out the window again, but no, it wasn't any good, I still couldn't figure where we were, so I checked with the lady, there was still a while to go till my stop. A bit further, then I was supposed to change trains. A part of me felt disappointed that we hadn't already passed that station, then I could feel like it was already decided, because in my present state of mind, that and ole Ron's email would have been enough to convince me that I was 'in-diddly-deed' *meant* to head off to the Big Smoke and house-sit for the bastard. Anyhow, we weren't too far off that 'changing post' now, so at least it gave me a deadline. I reckoned it gave me about twenty minutes to decide: *Stay on the train to London, give it a go, see what happens, or, change trains and go back to my old life.*

Now, taking only twenty minutes over this decision might sound pretty flimsy, I agree, but if I looked back on the last few years, it's a darn sight more thought than I'd given most things. And to be honest, mostly all I'd ever really done was let life 'happen' – without thinking hardly any of it through. I suppose that for a while that might be OK, but I began to think that if I didn't intervene at some point, and carried on *just letting it happen*, then it would probably go on like that all the way through, and I could well wind-up with an entire life that 'just happened' instead of a life I'd taken a bit of care over, a life I'd bothered to 'live', so to speak – *shit*, hark at me, what a wanker: Mark Kerr, *philosopher*, but like I said, mostly no one knows what shite passes through your head, so as long as you're not dick enough, or should I say, *Ron enough*, to splat it in an email, it's pretty much OK.

So there I was with my twenty minutes. The lady was now deeply engrossed in Calvino, it's got some dead good lines, *job done*, I thought. That whole book swap thing had totally taken me by surprise but I was pleased enough by it. It was painless enough despite my attachment to Calvino, and it was weird really, I mostly can't understand that writer, I just like the challenge, and the title: *Invisible Cities,* and I like the places too. I chuckled to myself. Nice one.

Anyway, seventeen minutes and counting. I think that half the reason I must have stopped actually making any decisions was because I no longer knew what I wanted, so I'd just made the most obvious moves. I had no reasons, and no great passions anymore, no intuition either, and I really missed that gut feeling, that sense of just plain knowing what you ought to do. Having an instinct about things. Being that way always seemed so clear to me when I was a kid, and I loved the certainty of that feeling. When me and Jim bunked off school like, I don't remember going through any great stages of decision making, well, none at all in fact, and it was never a case of: *What would I rather do today? School or fishing?* And despite all the trouble it caused, past, present and future, there was never any contest, that's just how it was, we just *knew* what we had to do, what we wanted to do, what was best like. So, we just didn't end up at assembly that morning, and we didn't wind up in the classroom, our names being ticked off the register. No matey. We just went fishing. Me and Jim. Two rods, some bait, a pack of ciggies, usually ten No 6; and a box of matches. And we'd sit for hour upon hour, smoking our little lungs out, skinny as rakes, the rods wedged, the lines just bobbing gently with the movement of the water, grey clouds moving overhead, rain threatening but never actually raining, and not much said, 'cos that's what we observed with other fishermen (the old geezers), nothing much was said; it seemed that between fishermen, things were simply understood. So we sat there for hours, watching, waiting, like two skinny-arsed Buddhas meditating on the ripples on the surface; the water, almost like steel; and there wasn't much hope of catching anything, we probably needed better bait, but it never seemed to matter. Easy. And my idea of heaven. — But now, in these last minutes, and without even the pale shadow of that childhood clarity, I was being made to think things through, and in the words of the song: *Should I stay or should I go? (The Clash – can't beat 'em)* — But what the hell was I doing? This was supposed to be 'train time', it's meant to be like going fishing, it's time-out. Only today, I'd have to make an exception, break my own rules, 'cos things were really in a big ole fucking mess, and something needed sorting. I hunkered back down in my seat and stared into the cover of *Invisible Cities* as the lady read on. — Twelve minutes. *I fucking hate watches.* I took it off and stuffed it in my back pocket. I felt like the lady seemed to notice, she sort of smiled a bit. Soulmates. — I got to thinking, that actually, it's pretty much as simple as this: I grew up and at some point, and I'm not even sure that it was a conscious thing, but there was this sort of notion, of being responsible, and it implied a whole heap of things, particular type things: getting a job, getting a 'good job', finding your own place, making your way, (and by now of course I felt like I'd got Jim's soddin' bird, *Trudy,* sat on my shoulder, droning on about, 'getting started'). Except that the '*what*' and the '*why*' of it all had got lost somewhere. And don't get me wrong, I'm not arguing for *not* doing that stuff, you just need a sense of why. A life needs a little shape, that's all. Somehow you were supposed to know what all those things meant, only no fucker ever gave you the manual. Let's face it, even learning to drive requires looking over a friggin' handbook. So, at some stage this stuff just found a life of its own, and the jobs, the friendships, relationships, where I live and how I live, and what I do on the weekends, it wasn't that it didn't happen, it was *all* happening alright, all running along like clockwork, but it was doing it by itself. A life was going on, for sure. But what the frig did it have to do with me anymore? — I wondered if that was how our Jim had felt… and I felt a knot in my throat, and a sickness in my stomach, a sort I'd never known before.

Looking back on it, I think I felt as though I'd been betrayed by Jim — *yeah, he betrayed me* — and all because it was him who moved to the other side of town, him who'd moved first. But Jim only moved because he had to, because he was still living with his mum and dad, so it wasn't as though he had much of a choice. He moved with his family, simple as that, only I remember, it really pissed me off. And then I moved, only further. I guess I was more of a full-on 'deserter'; and after that I never bothered keeping in touch. Thinking about it, we'd lost touch long before there was any real, geographic distance in the equation. There's that website isn't there? 'Friends Reunited'. *Reunited, and it feels so good…* I hate that fucking song and it'll be stuck in my head now for ages. — But it's not my thing, looking geezers up on the internet, admitting that you miss someone; anyhow, I get so sick of email I don't even want to think about it. Not about anything. I'm on a train, looking out the window, things just shifting along, and nothing, nothing going on. — And the truth is, I can't even track how things started going wrong in my life, but at some point loads of stuff just started powering itself along, and you think you made decisions about it all, but if you stop, just stop, sometimes you realise that you didn't decide any of it, it just happened. It all just happened. But I guess that's how it is when you take your eye off the ball, when you start out with ideas, then let them fly away: the dreams, the jobs, the women, life.

Fuck.

Then I remembered Jules' voice, *had I written any more songs, or had I given up on that as well?* — On that and everything else Jules, it seems I'd given up on the lot.

I needed a fag. Like I said, I don't even know when things started going downhill, but at some stage I must have caved in, and without even realising, I let things slide, little by little, I just let things start deciding themselves.

I thought back to the 'spread' put on after Jim's funeral, and how it had irritated me, how upset I'd felt – what a wanker. Didn't I realise, it wasn't the 'spread', or the 'tea', or the 'brandy *in* the tea', nor the bleedin' *cake* that was wrong, and it wasn't his mum and dad neither, it was me, it was *me!* That's what was really pissing me off. The mate who wasn't a mate. Sandra, Ray, Jules, and everyone else, *they'd* made an effort, *they'd* done the right thing. Tried their best. I'd moved on, I had, as it were, *got started.* — My chest felt tight. — I needed that smoke. — It's just that I don't remember, I don't remember thinking: shall I take this job or that job, is 'this' or 'that' a more reasonable bet, will it be 'fulfilling'? And I don't even remember *choosing* to be with this particular bird that lives in my flat back home, who, despite not being able to stand me, insists we have a relationship, I mean, for fuck's sake, *do we?* Is that what you'd call it? She's there, in my flat alright, but now that I come to think of it, she's actually only there out of some random set of events, events that seemed to start with her being too pissed to stand up in a bar one night, me helping her to a cab, him refusing to take her, her crying and puking, puking and crying; her sleeping on my sofa, then sleeping in my bed and me sleeping on the sofa, *and then*, well, there you have it. I call her Doris, though that isn't her name, it's just what I called her that first night on account of her behaving like one, a *right Doris.* And now Doris considers us to be 'an item'. So you see, where I live, what I do, even *who I'm with* – no thought at all, but supermarkets, what fucking boozer I drink in, which bookies I go to, now that stuff gets some serious consideration. I am such a fucking dick.

Jim mate, Jim. There's no going back. No undoing things. My eyes and head felt heavy again. The train composing its own sweet soddin' lyric as finally I realised, there was no going back. As lame as it might sound, all I knew was that the life that I had before Jim jumped was one I didn't want. Not any part of it. Leastways, not right now.

Ron Pope was going away, and I was going to be his house-sitter.

CA had left his song writing in my care, and the lady had swapped her novel for mine, so I had two new books, and a bag with not much in it, perfect.

Sometimes the pull really is too great, and some people do, some people jump. When it isn't quite as strong as that, I figure some people can walk out of their lives instead. Yeah, some just walk, and for the moment at least, I still had that option.

Aside from looking up Ron, I had no real idea how things were going to pan out, but right now it didn't much matter. Things had got too weighty; deep down I knew now that there was a window with my name on it, somehow I had to keep away from it, and for the time being, this was the only way I knew how.

## *london*

# STOP THE WORLD MATE,
# I WANNA GET OFF

L ondon, Euston. I'd arrived. So far, so good. I helped the lady off the train with her bags (turns out they were heavier than they looked, and I felt like an arse for not offering to help earlier), and I bid farewell to the guy who'd been sat opposite — well actually that part's a lie, he just got off the train in front of me and walked down the platform, up the ramp and out of sight, the farewell was in my head.

So, there I was, standing under the arrivals board at Euston station, a regular Dick Whittington, except that I didn't have a cat so I was probably more like Paddington Bear. I toyed with the idea of scribbling on an old luggage label, something like – *please take care of this geezer* – what a dick, but so it goes. I took a deep breath and stood a moment, adrenaline rushing, beautiful. And now I could have a fag.

I lit up and contemplated what a good move I'd made; and since my arrival in the capital, a full three minutes ago, things had been perfectly satisfactory. No ticket inspectors, which meant I'd not been compelled to make any lame explanations as to my change of plans and destination, and so, no excess ticket fare or fine. Bargain. My kind of city. I stood there as people whizzed about at top speed, arriving mostly looking either tired or overexcited, or else leaving at break-neck speed, and legging it for a train to some place else.

London, I figured this city was pretty much alright. I yawned and then had a wander about the station; it had this weird kind of brightness that practically seemed to X-rays things so that everyone walks around looking through one another; then I realised that it looked bright outside too, but the natural kind, so I stepped out.

It was close to being warm, and I know I'll sound like a plank – *of course the bleedin' South's warmer*, but it always takes me by surprise, it's like a little added extra: it's a nice change coming down here (*now I sound like me nan!*), yeah, a nice change *and* it's warmer. Sorted. But the thing was, it was still only February, so you might still expect it to be parky. Outside it was easier to see, easier to focus on people. A girl sloped past, she had big fat tears rolling down her cheeks. She was in a suit, all smart looking, I thought maybe she was an estate agent or something, well she could have been anything to be honest, a doctor, PA, who knows, suits sort of mean anything nowadays, but she was on her own, just walking along as though there was no one else around, like she expected not to be seen, just crying, silently. I watched her walk through the automatic doors and get swallowed up by the station.

There were flies in the air, loads of them, and I felt like they were taking the piss, it wasn't *that* soddin' warm, and I hate insects, flick 'em away and the bastards just zoom straight back, even smoking doesn't bother most of 'em. I moved a bit to get away from them. Then I looked up and just as I did I saw the buses. Red, London buses. *Shit!* I chuckled to myself like some big kid. I was enjoying a 'private moment'. I had a top train journey behind me, a class cigarette in hand, and now there were red London buses, double-deckers, smoothly cruising by. Nice one. But it was a shame about the cruddy buildings nearby, I don't know what they are, but coming from the train station they half block the view of the buses with their big ugly pillars, and then there were these odd sort of structures, maybe they were sculptures, I dunno, but I thought it would be much more cool if you just stepped out the station and *bam*, there they were, a fleet of beautiful red double-deckers, with a traditional red pillar box close by, and one of them dead old red phone boxes like a mini tardis – the full experience. Anyway, that's how I'd have it.

This last smoke and the whole Dick Whittington thing had gone right to my head. But fair play, I was just a bit over excited. As I stood back I noticed a statue, only what with all the other grey shite around, the pillars and that, it was sort of lost. I looked a bit closer, it was some dapper lookin' chap, I read his name: Robert Stephenson 1803-1859, cool, our major locomotive man! Real poncy lookin' get-up, and his pose! But fair dos, each to their own like. Anyhow, I figured this statue was pretty damn important, and that was another reason to get rid of them buildings and pillars and shite, so as it could stand alone, and be *seen,* if you get my drift. But I guess all that sort of malarkey is the remit of ye olde Lord Mayor of London, and not this ordinary dick. Still, maybe I'd write the mayor a postcard, make a few suggestions. Couldn't do any harm.

As I came to the end of this hugely satisfying smoke, it occurred to me that I'd made a pretty major move. I could see that it might have seemed rash, hasty even, but I bet there isn't anyone on this planet that hasn't, at some point, just wanted to stop the world a while, and step off; and no one that hasn't felt as though all they wanted to do was just leave the life they've got, set out of the house one morning, and just keep on going. Just walking, and without looking back. Go on, tell me, tell me it's never crossed your mind?

I had another fag and stood a while longer, half giggling to myself, like an arse, and I wouldn't exactly say that I was pleased, nothing arrogant or tossy like that, just sort of relieved. And maybe things would be alright... somehow – '*All come out in the wash*'. — Of course, I had no idea if Ron was actually following his idea through and going abroad, and even if he was, he may well have found a house-sitter already (friggin' should have done, number of contacts the bleeder's got), but so what? I'd find a B&B, some cheap hotel, it didn't much matter. And it was strange, I couldn't even picture my old life just now, my place, my job, Doris, so-called mates, I couldn't care much somehow, all those things were hazy, as though a bit of my head needed to shunt them even further to the back.

I decided to get a coffee before I settled down to call Ron. I went to one of those places that has a major list, more kinds of coffee than you can wave a stick at, so much friggin' choice, I can't be doing with that. I thought about Nan and smiled, she'd have had a lot to say about a coffee menu, especially one that despite all the complicated options served up in cardboard: *lattes, cappuccinos, mochas, mocha-chinos...* didn't offer: *a nice ordinary cup of coffee in an ordinary china cup*, how 'remiss'. Anyway, the geezer finally gave me a cup of some bastard with loads of froth and some sprinkly shite on it, and I joked, like a dick, about how I was just grateful he wasn't behind a bar pulling me a pint what with all that crap on it. Again, it's the Dave Allen thing, I just don't have the timing, besides which, the geezer was foreign, Czech or something, and British humour takes a serious amount of understanding, appreciating, I suppose you could say, 'initiating into' (though that sounds a bit weird) but I reckoned he'd need to watch at least 12 hours of top comedy just to stand a chance. I could sit him down and make him watch it all on a loop, *him*, arsy waiters in general, Welsh traffic cops in particular, and traffic wardens everywhere, three sets of miserable fuckers all in one 'fell swoop'. *Only doing their job.* Yeah, and like me nan would say, '*So was Hitler*'.

I lit another fag and decided to get off my soapbox, sit myself down, and stop being a bastard. Sorted. The thing is, Jules is the kind of person who gives the benefit of the doubt to a girl that pretty much helped her brother out of a window, whereas me, I'm the kind of wanker that gives a hard time to a waiter on less than minimum wage, who's doing the job, not because it's his fucking dream, but because the other options suck even more.

I started to wonder how to put it to Ron about how maybes I could be his house-sitter, I wasn't sure how much to say. I could text him. *Nah.* Best just call. I pulled my phone out and started to tap in his number. Of course it took him a bit to remember who I was, but when he'd finished being a dick, he said he'd have to have me over for dinner, and joked about 'interviewing me' to see if I was what he was looking for in a house-sitter. OK, I was over generous, he hadn't finished being a dick, *that* the guy couldn't help, it was simply his default position. And you have to credit his arrogance, '*interviewing me*', who was he kidding, he said he had less than a week to go 'til his 'adventure' started, and he still hadn't found anyone to keep an eye on his place. Of course I was supposed to believe that this was on account of him being so 'particular', but like I said, his email was a total give away. Mr 200 mates, was really a no-mates, and further evidence of this was him inviting me over 'straight away'. 'That's a bit short notice,' I quipped, but he asked for it, and needless to say it went right over his head. Then he waffled on a while about how busy he'd been, arranging stuff and packing, and how there were a lot of things to set in place before heading off for three whole months. I said I thought it might be best to keep things simple, but he assured me that it was quite the opposite and that the whole thing was like totally stressing him out. I looked down at my half-empty rucksack, different strokes for different folks I guess, but I smiled to myself all the same, I can be a right smug git.

Like I said, I'd no idea how things were going to work out; Ron was assuming that the three months bit was a given for both of us, but I wasn't sure of my plans, time didn't seem to be something I wanted to care too much about right now, and the one and only thing I was sure of was that nothing ever really turns out quite the way you think (specially when you've had your eye off the ball for as long as I had). — I'd made a rough mental note of the directions to his place, and pleased enough with my progress, bought some more ciggies by way of celebration. I figured I should take Ron some beers, but my guess was he was a wine man. I shivered, but fair play, someone's gotta drink that shite.

All smoked up, it was time to whack some shrapnel into a machine and get myself a ticket – *a ticket to ride* – the Victoria line, and then the Piccadilly, but I was running short of dosh by now. I looked down and spotted a 50p, then three 2p coins, and I bothered to bend down and pick them up – yes *Dick*, the streets of London, while they may not be paved with gold, are well and truly paved with small change. Bingo! 56p was hardly gonna make much odds, but it felt good. And so what?

I wandered around and found a bunch of cash machines. — That was something at least, I'd pretty much 'earned and not spent' since I was a kid, it was something Dad had drummed into me, one of the 'useful' things, and there was cash enough in my accounts to cover bills back home and leave ole Doris worry free for bleedin' eons, (and that was all she'd worry about, believe me: *was the room she lived in paid for?* 'A shag' she could, and would, pick up anywhere.) In fact, if

I never returned at all she'd probably do alright out of me for several years. It might be nice to think she'd worry about my whereabouts, but I doubt she'd even notice I was gone, and certainly she wouldn't miss me. Doris was about as loyal as a tomcat.

Standing in line for the cash machines I got to thinking, it totally weirds me out, the *non*-relationship we have with our own cash, sometimes I feel like my whole fucking existence is wired up by direct debit. Fuck it. For once I wanted to live with a few readies in my hand. My credit cards could go sing a while too. I got a wad of cash out, and felt like the King of Siam, only I don't know if he ever really existed or if he was a rich bleeder or not, but anyhow. Now I needed some change. I'd buy some wine for Mr Ron, and pick up a few postcards, maybe write to Jules later, fill her in.

I hadn't been on the underground for ages. Nan had first taken me as a kid, and that was brilliant, best person for the job, her being a Londoner and all, and I wondered why it was she'd left London, but it was obvious really, that was down to me granddad. *Love.* It's a powerful ole thing. Back then it can't have been any mean feat, a Londoner taking on some Northern git, though Granddad wasn't exactly a git, least I don't think he was, but I still reckon it must have been a major culture shock, moving up north back then (as would the reverse like). I suppose it would have been a shock for both of them. I tried to think back, see if I could remember what Nan had said about him in the early days. One thing I do remember was asking her about this big dark mark on the wall, it was about the size of a big ole frying pan, and it looked like an upside down smiley face with darker marks making the eyes and mouth, and it was freckled looking. I used to try and turn my head upside down to see it better, 'Try a handstand,' Nan had said, but I wasn't really strong enough in the arms for that (though I wasn't a weakling or anything). I asked her what the mark was, and how it got there. 'You ask too many questions,' she said at first, well she said it for ages, 'cos I kept on about it (persistent little bugger), and then finally she told me that it dated back to when her and Granddad were 'just married' and her trying to serve him up some shrimps as a treat. She said she'd left them intact, just as her mum had always done, with the shell and the tails all proud, and she'd thought how beautiful they looked on the plate, and how pleased her George would be (that's me granddad). She paused for a minute now and rubbed her hands on her apron, and for the moment I'd all but forgotten the mark on the wall. I'd never seen shrimps done like that, and what with my nautical interest I was keen for detail so I asked her if she'd draw me one, 'Well I'm no artist, duck,' she said, but actually she was, and I remember I'd kept that shrimp sketch in with my fishing tackle for ages. Anyway, Granddad had never had shrimp served up like that in his life (if they'd ever had any in his family, his mum had always taken the head off and the shell and the tail and all). Then Nan said, 'He took one look at the plate, then there was this great thundering silence before he yelled, '*Don't you go bringing your bloody posh London ways up 'ere girl!*' She stopped and drew a breath before she said the last bit, 'At first I thought he might be teasing,' she brushed her hand over her apron, 'but then he turned in his seat and hard as he could, he threw that plate right at the wall.'

'*Shrimps and everything?*' I asked, all wide-eyed (I was a dick from an early age). 'Shrimps and all!' she said, and then she looked at me and we laughed, we laughed so much my guts hurt.

Granddad had wanted the wall papering over, but Nan insisted the wall was left as it was (though she secretly cleaned it up as much as she could on account of the smell). She told Granddad that a marriage had to bear its scars (she said that she made that up on the spur of the moment because it sounded so dramatic and that she wanted to take full advantage of me granddad while he looked só ashamed), and then she giggled but her eyes looked a bit sad, and that was when I changed the subject to fishing. Nan smiled. And I got to thinking that maybe that's how we learn stoicism, we just cut to something else, just before it gets too much. Dad once said that stoicism was the kind of thing Americans would call a million dollar idea, only we Brits just do it as a matter of course. — '*You forming a relationship with that machine or what mate?*' Shit, I was at the front of the queue, nose to nose with an underground ticket machine, daydreaming like some mad fucker. 'Sorry, pal,' I said and I whacked a load of coins in, I would have said 'mate' rather than 'pal', only I didn't want him to think I was being sarcastic. I'd have been pissed off if I was him, and fuck knows how long I'd been standing there.

I collected the ticket from the bottom of the machine and headed off down the escalator, – all the commuters there dashing past me, professional tubers, as it were, and I started to feel that buzz of excitement again. London! – *I can be such a total kid.*

On the platform, I love those distantly visible neon signs telling you how long till the next train, and it's always so precise, you just have to learn how to translate it, *so*: a train due in one minute means one that will arrive in five; one due in three minutes will take ten; any longer and you might as well walk – leastways that's how it seems, in cities no one can wait, there's that whole manic thing going on – poor sods, *slow down mateys! Slow down!*

On the train I realised I hadn't picked up any wine for Ron, but I had bought cigarettes for myself like, two packs in fact, only I guess that's a given, but I'd also bought a stack of postcards, and I mean a *stack*, it didn't matter but what was I thinking? I don't think I'd written to any bastard in my life, and now I was planning on becoming some total *'master of communication'*. Nuts.

I wished I could write one to CA, wished I had his address like. I'd tell him I'd got his book, and I'd tell him about the cool red buses down here.

And then I started thinking about me nan again, and me granddad thinking she had *'posh London ways'*, my nan was anything but posh – she was beautiful, well dressed an' all, but she wasn't posh. She was as working class as the rest of them. Some blokes just get a bit insecure and have to give their birds a bit of a put down, 'don't let them think they're special or anything or you might lose 'em', and always keep an eye on your pals, that sort of thing, total pile of crap like.

I expect Nan didn't know what had hit her, moving up there, living away from home for the first time, and living with my granddad; and then I thought back to the 'sarni episode' she'd told me about. She'd asked me granddad what he wanted on his sandwiches, it being a Sunday afternoon, and he got dead cross and said he wasn't having any of it, that what he wanted was a buttie. I guess there's no point saying, 'same difference' when a guy's being as difficult as that. After that Nan had always offered people both as a joke like, except being a kid, and a thick one at that, it took me ages to catch on to the irony. She'd say, 'Fancy a buttie anyone?' and then add, 'Of course, I could always make sandwiches if you'd prefer,' and she'd put on some slightly actressy type of voice, fake like. I really admire me nan for doing that, making a joke out of it like, not letting him put her down. And he was good about it too, fair play, he didn't take it bad, and he'd laugh along. His eyes full of love and that. Still, that was when they were old; I expect it took a few more splattered shrimps before they got that far.

The train came in. I sat down thinking I'd start reading the book the lady had given me, only I was way too distracted; I wondered what she thought about Calvino, she'd probably understand it better than me, but I really rated that book whether I got the whole thing or not, and then I started looking about, trying to see what sort of books other people were reading. — They do that in London, folks read novels in droves – in public like. I think that's well cool. — It wasn't easy though, trying to see what other folk were reading, in fact it was really quite tricky 'cos mostly people hold books in ways that make it impossible to see the cover, but I bided my time, like a proper little sleuth, and snatched a look when they moved enough.

I spotted this one guy with *The Lord of the Flies*, which I have in fact read – I remember, it totally blew me away, that one boy so shouldn't have trusted that ponce and told him his nickname was *Piggy*, that was such a major mistake, he was *so* bound to use it on him, it practically made me wanna climb right in there and protect the little geezer, major mistake, *major*, – top book though, and it got to me just like that John Irving book and his Owen Meany character, *shit*, that little geezer damn near broke my heart.

I looked about some more, there was a Stephen King, though I couldn't quite see the title on that one; and that kids' book that everyone's reading, and then some book with a brown cover, *The Code* or something by some geezer called Brown, Dan Brown, that's it – in fact I spotted three of those. Weird.

It had felt like the start of a great big adventure when I got on the tube, and I wasn't going to, but I half felt like I wanted to bunk

55

off from meeting ole Ron chops, and just cruise around on the underground a while, take it easy, just 'people watch'. There were all these nationalities, I couldn't even guess at half of them, and I haven't ever really travelled much, I'm not one for going abroad like (*not one for going abroad!* — that's my dad again), but there were people in all sorts of like national dress, with amazing turbans, scarves, some black lady with this massive piece of fabric tied on her head in some great big bow, real cool lookin', CA would have been well impressed. There's less of that up my way somehow, I mean, we're heavily multi-cultural, it's just that a lot of people seem to wear more of the same gear. Jeans, trainers, tracky bottoms. There's a few saris and that, long scarves and robes and stuff, but there isn't the full-on variety that's down here — It was *so* cool in fact that I felt like I practically wanted to buy a suit and bowler hat to join in (you know, in some version of me own national dress like), but then, steady on mate, maybe not, but just for a second I came over all '*Mr Benn*' — remember, that was that kid's programme from the 1970s, with those two dimensional characters that shuffled about in a roughly sketched-out world, and Mr Benn would be there in his suit and bowler hat, and he'd pop into the local costume shop where the shopkeeper would suggest some sort of fancy dress, and Mr Benn would always happily go along with him, he'd try something on, and then some magic door in the changing room would end up being a gateway to an entire world that went with his gear, and then he'd go off on these dead cool adventures — so, if he was dressed like a knight like, he'd pass through the portal and end up some place with a mighty steed, and castles, and princesses that needed rescuing, dragons that needed slayin — that's how I remember it anyhow. Amazing — and now London was populated by people all in their very own gear, just like a whole load of Mr Benns, each with their own personal little London.

One of the other top things about Mr Benn of course, was his address: 52 *Festive* Road, now you can't argue with that. I so wished Jim's family had never moved to *Burn-hope* Road, and I so wished they'd move out of it now. 'Festive Road' might well be somewhere worth considering, I figured you could do worse than Mr Benn for a neighbour. — Then it occurred to me that I hadn't actually seen anyone in a suit and bowler hat, not now, nor when I'd been down here before, in fact I think I've only ever seen men dressed like that on the telly and in films, like. So, *bingo*, that was gonna be a mission while I was down here: *find Mr Benn.* There had to be some blokes in bowler hats somewhere, had to be, at least the one.

Now it felt even more of a shame that CA wasn't around, then it could have been me and my little soulmate, the two of us, on a mission to find Mr Benn. Maybe I'd look up Nelson too, see how he was doing on that column of his, for when in London, one should probably do a few London things.

I sort of winced, shot back again to me and Jim, and dreams we'd had, of London gigs, a UK tour, songs that never happened.

## *mr ron*

## TO B&B OR NOT...

When I got off the tube I decided I'd pick up some wine at what had to have been Ron's corner shop. The folk inside were all friendly enough, Turkish, they said. I told 'em I didn't know anything about wine, the geezer behind the counter shrugged at me and smiled, he was enjoying a smoke, fair play, so I carried on looking along the rows of bottles thinking he could probably give a damn, but when I looked back I noticed that he'd taken his fag out and was resting it on the side of the counter, then he came over to the wine shelves and sort of chewed the side of his mouth a while and scanned the labels. I'd already got hold of some dusty looking bottle, a tad expensive, but I hadn't a clue. The geezer picked out another one, three quid cheaper, like a mind reader, 'Here,' he said, looking and sounding rather like Charles Bronson, 'take this, it's the same.' And then he winked at me, only nothing gay or anything, just matey. Lucky ole Ron, I thought, nice friendly local shop. I got to the counter and the geezer's fag had burned itself out, he looked disappointed but smiled anyhow. I took mine out my pocket and offered him one. Sorted.

Ron's street was a right mess; litter, black bin bags piled up and spilling their guts out, used condoms, well nasty. I stood back to check I hadn't made a wrong turn. But no, this was the right address. What a heap-of-shit kind of street was this? For the first time since I'd arrived, I had this sudden feeling that I'd made the wrong move. I felt a bit uneasy, but I shook it off, every city has a few shitty streets, and what the hell was I thinking – like I'm some toff from wherever – only that isn't it, that isn't it at all, no one, no one likes living in a dump.

I walked on and got to Ron's place; it turned out to be part of this gigantic looking Georgian building carved up into a ton of little flats. There were a load of bins outside, lids off and empty, rubbish all over the gaff. I waded through the trash, down the steps, and knocked on the door of Ron's so-called, 'Garden Flat'. While I waited for him to answer I lit up again and wondered how come he was living in a flat and not a house, the guy was loaded, that much I do remember. He was born loaded. Those were his defaults: born loaded, and being a dick; often, and this is unfortunate, but it's true to say, the two go hand-in-hand, the result being that the bastard winds up with an easy life and is termed, *scientifically*, as being: an *easylife* – and a 'Class A' tosser. I'd barely inhaled when the door shot open and Ron greeted me with this hearty hug as though in the past we'd been really close mates, and I suppose I should have felt pleased, but I hate that, when people don't act natural, when they don't have the right measure of how things are between the two of you; there's nothing good about that sort of behaviour, nothing at all, in fact, I'd go as far as saying, it stinks. I unpeeled his too matey hands from my shoulders. There *was* someone, and only one person I'd have been happy enough to have that male to male contact with, and that was a friend I'd badly let down. So the hug, it really rattled me. That and the trash could really wind me up if I let them. He stood back and did this fake cough, so I acted as though I didn't know what it meant. He pointed to my cigarette, 'What?' I asked him.

'You *smoke?*'

Sharp, Ron, very sharp, 'Nothing gets past you, eh?' I said, as I crossed the threshold, taking another drag, and yes, I was being a wanker, it was clear he wouldn't want me smoking in his gaff, but I just wanted to make him say it. Hinting, amongst other things, is, at the end of the day, totally fake. People think it's some polite way of dealing with stuff, well it isn't.

'I didn't realise you were a smoker, Mark.'

'Really? I don't see how come, I've always smoked, smoked more than I've drawn breath probably.' He did this mock laugh. That's the worst. Being humoured is totally insulting, that kinda stuff gets me really pissed off, and I was half tempted just to walk back out again – cheap B&Bs could give a damn whether you smoke or not, and ole Ron-cheeks (he had very round, very fat cheeks) was annoying the hell out of me already. But then I remembered that he was going off on his *mission* or whatever, and that soon enough he wouldn't be around. I took a moment to consider this, and then I stepped back to the door and stubbed out my fag.

'*Oh,*' he starts up again, all high pitched, 'you're not littering with fag-ends are you?' I shot him this look and said that what with all the other shite out there I figured it didn't make a deal of difference. His laugh had a hint of nervousness in it this time, asshole. I picked up the fag-butt and went inside.

When I pulled the door shut I realised just how dark it was, and as though he read my thoughts, he shouted from further on in for me to flick a few light switches.

I started to follow his voice through to the back but then I found myself stopping halfway to scan his ridiculously-huge CD collection, (now I admit that that might sound absurd, because how is it ever possible for anyone to have *too much* music? But if the collection contains as many wrong CDs as this one, then I reckon 'ridiculous' is the only word for it). I followed Ron's voice again, it seemed like a pretty big place, I said as much.

'Oh yes, the entire ground floor's mine,' he said. 'The rest of the building is cut into the tiniest little places imaginable, but I was first in, and I bought this whole entire floor up; five bedrooms.' (Now I've watched as much American TV as the next man, but I don't reckon I ever say: *whole entire*… and if memory serves me right, Ron was from somewhere like Basingstoke.)

'Five bedrooms,' I says.

'Five, yup!' He seemed pretty pleased with himself.

'But you live alone, right?'

'Yup.' Was he going to say 'yup' all the time? It made him sound like some small yappy dog (sounded like, looked like). I know, maybe he was just trying to be 'nice', it was only small talk after all… but I felt uneasy. 'But that's not the half of it,' he carried on, 'I own three other properties.'

'In London?'

'Yup!'

I bit my lip and scanned his kitchen, hoping to spot some beers or a bottle of whiskey, but it wasn't that kind of kitchen, it was one of them designed bastards, and anything that kitchen had, had it hidden.

He must have realised my dilemma with the disintegrating fag-butt stuck in my hand (sensitive soul), as he suddenly sprang open this cabinet door, doing this half dance and swinging both arms to the right, '*Ta da!*' he says, pointing to his 'hidden' bin. So there I was dusting off a half crushed fag butt into his over-designed bin, whilst he stood there in this arse of a pose – big cheesy, waxy grin there frozen onto his chops. Then he says, 'It is *so* good to see you!' all over-emphatic, and, '*Man*, do we have some shit to catch up on'; his words made me feel dead self-concious, awkward like. There was nothing for us to 'catch up on', and now this whole scene was pissing me off, and it was clear that just like his opening greeting, he was all lined up to behave like we were 'long losts'. We weren't. And for me, his insistence on behaving like we were, it just made it worse. It's weird, but it kinda hurt.

It was a bad situation all round, too matey, too fake, and I felt hastily reminded of why I'd never really wanted to know this geezer in the first place, why I'd never kept in touch, and why I'd never replied to his cheery emails in 'light blue'. He just wasn't real. I could also see that it was one of those 'particularly' bad situations where it was all gonna end up in point scoring, and I only had myself to blame for that: I'd given the bleeder the upper hand straight off by being a total arse about smoking. I was a bit pissed with myself about that. And there has to be a way not to do that, to get things on a better footing – *but it also has to be without being complicit in someone else's lies about the past, and what top mates you used to be* – yeah, there's gotta be a way to short-circuit the bullshit, anyhow, I didn't have a clue. Some blokes just never grow up. I was one of them. And some things just have to be played out the way they are, that's honest at least, only it's uneasy too; yeah, honest but uneasy.

And so, in full wind-up mode, I says, 'So, what d'you want with four gaffs in the same city?' He shot me a look as though I was stupid.

'I'm serious,' I says (what I suspected him of was plain ole greed). He paused before answering, then all superior and with a touch of spite he says, 'Investment. They're an investment.' And then changing the subject he asked me if I 'cared for some tea?', and he started filling the kettle and fussing around; he wasn't going to explain anything to me, not if I was gonna be an arsehole about things, and believe me, I was. What can I say? Sometimes that's *my* default.

Everything in his kitchen was stainless steel, grey marble or white ceramic, smart looking, and the floor had these great slate tiles. He had taste, I give him that much (though I would just say, the lights in that place, man, they were way too bright). I passed him the wine, said as maybe we could start on that, I figured I'd rather sup on that if there wasn't any beer on offer. It certainly didn't seem like a 'tea' moment, I was pretty sure that wasn't going to be strong enough to distract me from the desire to wind this little guy up; and while all that stuff feels buzzy at that time, like I said, it's a heap of shit.

'Wine it is,' he said, and he took the bottle, adding, 'rather dusty isn't it?' and sort of turning his nose up at it. I said it was probably alright on the inside. He gave another one of those lame laughs, and started wiping the bottle with a cloth and then he washed his hands, Howard Hughes style. *Dick.* He said I should have a look around while he uncorked it, but I felt a bit uncomfortable noseying round someone else's gaff. Still, it didn't seem like either of us was too natural at the art of conversation so I took the offer just to avoid stuff, at least for a while, you know, those silences... and the differences... and my addiction to winding up arseholes, but mostly the silences, the kind where everything just falls away and leaves you with the sum total of all that you have, and all me and Ron had between us was nothin'. Nothin' at all.

To be honest, the B&B idea was still looking more tempting, I really wasn't in the mood for *awkwardness.* I'd keep it in mind.

I walked from room to room with a sort of shiver, I don't know why. And I felt dead lonely. Ron hollered out that I should switch more lights on, but I could make things out well enough, and the whole super-bright bulb scenario was irritating me. I'd never thought about it before, how much artificial light bothers me, how it seems to suck more out of things than it 'illuminates', how it empties a place and stops you seeing.

After a bit, I sat down on the corner of this massive double bed, probably 'king size'. I dunno why, but I took me shoes off and I just sat there feeling the weight of my feet on these rough wooden floorboards, and then I felt this pain in my chest. I put my head in my hands. I felt very lost.

I wondered if, in time, I would understand Jim; I wondered if I could work out why he'd killed himself – but at the same time, I figured that maybe you can only truly understand it when you're just about to do the same, maybe you only know the 'why' of it yourself just before you go. And by then, maybe there is no 'why' anymore, and maybe that's what made him do it.

He'd left no note, not that anyone had found, but if I thought for long enough would I be able to imagine what he was feeling? Part of me wanted to know what was going through that head of his, and part of me, I guess the bigger part, was scared of that. Total coward at heart. — But how long had he been fighting it, how long had he wanted to do it? And the final decision, was that taken in that one last moment? And was there... one last moment... a snap of time when things could have been changed?

I curled up on the bed, deathly cold, and tried to push it all away again.

A while later, and I don't suppose it can have been that long, maybe half an hour or so, I woke up to this classical sort of music tinkling away in the background, and at first I didn't know where I was, then slowly I recognised Ron's voice on the phone in the distance. I'd fallen asleep again. But it made no sense. It seemed as though wherever I was, I just kept falling asleep. What a dick. I stood up and scratched my head, rubbed my eyes, and checked I hadn't crushed my fags: all intact (always check on life's essentials). Then Ron called out, 'You awake yet?' and then again but more drawn out, 'Are... you... awake yet?'

'Yup,' I answered, sarcastic as you like.

I pulled my shoes back on and moved back towards the kitchen like some stiff ole geezer.

'You were out cold,' he said.

'Was I?' I yawned. 'Sorry about that,' though I wasn't sorry at all. I rubbed my head again. He handed me a glass of wine and called it *vino*, and I started to wonder if he *was* gay, not that it mattered, but you just get to wondering sometimes, the way people talk, what it means. And it means nothing mostly, but you still find yourself wondering. 'Cheers,' I said and I slugged the glass.

'Steady on,' he said, and I said sorry again, but fuck knows why, I'd bought the bleeder. What was going on with me? What were all the 'sorrys' for? And the moment those thoughts shot through my head, I felt this weird pain in my chest again, my heart I guess. 'You alright?' he asked. I didn't answer, 'Here,' he said, 'sit down,' and he put his hand on my shoulder as I sat down, and just this once I didn't mind him touching me. It was alright, I felt OK again. Sort of.

Ron carried on trying to fuss a bit, but then he settled himself. I just sat there breathing heavy. He was alright really, for an easylife. He rattled on for a while now about how I ought to stop smoking, how that might be causing me problems, and then there was this speech about healthy living, regular exercise, aerobics (*give me a break*), and then he did his yappy dog laugh as he added, '...and the odd line of coke. I mean Mark, let's face it, nicotine's such an unworthy kind of drug.' I planted my fags on his kitchen table and shot him a glare. Wanker – '*and the odd line of coke*'. What is it about some blokes that makes them such *Formula One tossers*? But then I thought back to what Jules had told me about Trudy, and I reckoned she was pretty much just the female equivalent, with plenty of '*superior*' experiences that she dumps on other women – ole Trude, what with her pilates an' all. And the thing is, you have to admit it, however bad nicotine might be, smoking cigarettes looks pretty cool, whereas shoving coke up yer snout, well, that's just plain nasty.

'You're not planning on smoking in here while I'm away are you?' – you see, even his delivery was mincing. He topped up my glass, and as I 'sipped' I decided to carry on being a sarcastic sod, well, sometimes it's just gotta be done, 'So, I take it I'm '*in*' then, am I? Only I thought I had to be *interviewed*,' – dry as you like. He acted like he hadn't caught what I said, which was fair enough, and taking a deep breath he just banged on about smoke. 'Well it's just that the smell gets everywhere, it gets into everything, *totally*, and it costs a fortune to get the place industrially cleaned.' I laughed – and right from the belly, but he didn't, he just sat there with a whacking great question mark slapped over his chops, and then he went a bit pink. '*Industrially cleaned?*' I said, finishing off my *vino*.

'Yes Mark, and what's funny about that?'

'Million dollar question mate, that one.' He looked a bit 'irked', but that's how it was, I thought it was funny, he didn't. I could sense ole Franky Howard now, rum as you like, saying, '*Titter ye not*' in my ear-hole. — Why are so many of the best comedians the dead ones? I thought of asking Ron here, but then I bit my lip and thought better of it. Besides, it wasn't as if he'd know.

I decided that it wasn't fair to wind Ron up much more, it was time to take myself in hand, the thing is, a lot of easylifes can't take it too well, they've mostly never had things tough enough, they've usually never needed to find a funny side to anything, and so I assured him that I would only smoke *outside* (outside, like a dog). He looked relieved, if still a tad unnerved. Then he said he'd been planning to leave in a week but that he'd head off sooner now he'd got a *sitter*, catch up with a few people before he left for Costa Rica (...least, I think that's what he said), the place he was planning on 'teaching computer skills to a bunch of starving losers.'

*Nice, Ron. Nice.*

'Children?' I asked him.

'Yeah, some bunch of no-hope kids.'

I guess you can't blame him, easylifes don't realise it isn't like that for everyone, and I remembered now, with 'complete clarity' this time, why I never liked the guy. Ron seemed to think we were all born on a level playing field, and that what you had was a fair measure of what you were worth, as in: *really worth*. And as though he hadn't come across as a big enough arsehole already, he added, 'Of course, the trip's not all altruism.'

'Really?' I said, deadpan, and the thing is, sarcasm mostly just skates over an easylife's head, and I don't think they can help it, they just have this immunity to self-awareness. Can't really blame 'em, it's just how it is.

He topped up our wine glasses, and as he did I noticed a load of little white plates of food on the side, (he'd obviously been a right little 'busy bee' while I was sleeping). They were square, neat, sort of tasteful looking plates, like most of his things. There were things like olives and mushy looking stuff on them, stuff that would make a real great mess on a wall, (*I thought as how it might be in me genes, from me granddad like! And I pictured a 'whole entire' row of smileys!*) I laughed. Ron laughed too, though what he was laughing at is anyone's guess; this one really was in a class of his own.

'No,' he said suddenly, and I felt as though I must have missed part of what he was saying, like with the lady on the train, but I was pretty sure it wasn't going to be worth getting him to recap, so I just let him carry on, 'No, it's just as I was saying, Mark, I'd be lying if I told you this trip was only about helping others. The thing is, it's also about self discovery.' He paused and then he noticed me looking at my shoes. The sole was starting to come away a bit on the outside edge of one of them. It didn't matter, I just noticed, that was all. 'Is there something wrong Mark? Are you OK?'

'I'm fine, just fine.' He glanced at the floor and then at my shoes and then furrowed his brow all irritated like. 'Only,' and then he interrupted himself, 'am I… am I boring you?'

'No mate,' (what else could I say?), 'sorry… I'm still half asleep,' I yawned and he seemed satisfied enough. Bargain. 'Carry on,' I said. He started to move the little white plates over to the table, 'Just a few nibbles,' he said. I can't help it, the guy makes my skin crawl. He rattled on about this 'goal' to find himself, and the thing that worried me more than anything else about his trip, was exactly that, because in setting out to 'find himself', the plonker just might succeed. To be honest, I felt like I was being a bit of a bastard not warning him, but I figured that if the other 199 arseholes in his life weren't brave enough to prepare him, I didn't see why it should be down to me to tell him that some things are better left alone. For some, that self discovery lark really is best left alone, *well* alone. If only these geezers would include themselves on one of their mass egocentric emails, then they'd soon realise what wankers they really are, and there'd be no need to waste all that time taking a trip to the heart of darkness, finding a guru, or spending loads of dosh on therapy shite; and therapists ain't gonna tell it like it is, let's face it, the fuckers would be well out of a job if they did. I dipped an olive in some brown mushy stuff. Anyway, what did I know?

'Nice one,' I said, though god knows what I meant, I could be a right insincere bastard. Ron smiled. And it was like I said, the geezer was never gonna tell me anything more about his 'investments' if he thought all I was gonna do was take the mickey, and I was still curious.

'So what do you do with all these properties then?' He didn't answer me straight off. Some French bread appeared from some hidden bread bin. It was a pretty freaky kitchen all told, sanitary somehow, cold, dead like, and I'm not sure that that's really the line to go for in kitchens despite it looking cool. I asked if he'd got any butter but he said he *wasn't doing fats (what the fuck's that all about?)*, so I spread some of the mush on the bread instead, tasted alright, but the thing is, I do '*do*' fats, so it was a bit irritating, I have to admit.

After a couple of mouthfuls, he said he rented all the houses out. I asked why he didn't do the same with the other rooms in this gaff, but he said he didn't like the idea of lodgers, only he didn't call them that, he said, 'I'm not sharing my space with any rejects.'

'*Rejects?*'

'Lowlifes,' he clarified, and then in case he'd offended me, me being a lowlife and all, he added, 'no offence, but you know what I mean?' and he did one of those screwed up smiley faces of his that's frankly just plain weird (and really would look best splatted on a wall).

'Yeah, right,' I said. I needed a smoke, and my leg was twitching like a bastard by now, my fist too. 'I'll just pop outside,' I said, (now that is definitely a phrase I've never used! 'I'll just *pop* outside') 'I'll have a fag if you don't mind.' And I didn't give a crap if he minded, in fact, I half hoped he did, 'cos my fist was eager for some straightening out, some clearing up, some mashing. He went a funny shade of pink and I wondered if he could read me, 'No, no,' he said, 'that's fine, of course, please do.'

I'd stood up already and picked up my fags. 'Follow me,' he said, all eager like, and there was no way he was gay, gays have more self-respect, he was just some mincing bastard. 'Why don't I take this opportunity to show you the garden?'

'Oh yeah,' I said, remembering the name of his place, 'Garden Flat,' though what with all the overflowing bins and shite outside the front it might just as well have been called, *Garbage Flat*. Even his bleedin' home suffered delusions. Then he did that, '*Ta da!*' thing again, with his arms outstretched towards these French windows at the back. I wondered if 'Costa bleedin' Rica' had any idea what was on its way? Frantic. 'Though to be perfectly honest Mark, I really would rather you didn't smoke out here either,' (I mean, *Jesus*, thank god he hasn't got a dog, if he had he'd probably expect it to absorb its own shit). He carried on, 'and I don't want fag-ends put out on the path, or at least don't leave them near the plants,' and he started nervously, but proudly, patting and prodding various bits of 'foliage'.

I inhaled deep and handed him my spent match, watching his pupils dilate as he looked down at what I'd placed in his measly little hand. 'Tidy,' I said, and then I walked off with a nod to peruse his vast acreage, not even space enough for a ruddy picnic hardly, and you'd never get a game of cricket out there, never mind footy. Garden, my arse, I've seen bigger window boxes.

I don't know if he went back inside, I didn't turn round to see, but then I panicked a minute, wondering where my few possessions were, my bag and books, and had I lost them on the way there, at the corner shop maybe? But then I remembered dropping them in the hall on the way in, and how they clanked on Ron's wooden floor, they'd still be there, CA and the lady, and the postcards. And I don't know why, but I suddenly remembered the girl at Euston station, and the tears on her face, and how I didn't ask her what was wrong; and then I remembered being on the tube, and the black lady with the massive bow; and how I'd wanted to be Mr Benn, or at least wanted to see him. The air was cold out now, the sky was a bit grey and getting dark. My heart sank a little.

I thought about this woman on the tube, not the one I'd seen at Euston, a different one; she'd got on at King's Cross, she seemed tired, that heavy kind, as though she was weary, weary of life like, and she'd stood a while, I suppose hoping for a seat; the train was packed. She'd started to cry, and silently, just like the one in the suit. I remembered that I'd looked about but no one saw her, *no one saw her*, and so no one saw her crying. Oh everyone seemed to be looking, but somewhere else, at their books or newspapers, their shopping or shoes, or the advertising high up, or else settling their gaze in that easy middle distance that catches no one else's gaze. I'd looked at her again thinking that maybe I was mistaken, maybe I'd only imagined her tears, but I hadn't. She'd cried, and no one saw, and now I felt that knot again in my throat, and my chest was tight again, and I realised, I was just the same as the rest, and it was just as though I hadn't seen her either, because then I'd looked away. Two in one day.

'We ought to think about supper,' Ron's distant voice. I put my fag out on some fake-looking rock and picked up the butt. 'And I'd better explain how things work in this place, if you're going to stay,' he sounded a bit nervous, like he was half trying to make a joke and sound like a buddy, 'and then maybe we should think about having a night on the town, to welcome you in, so to speak, and *see me off!*' Now *that* I could drink to. I sniffed and went back inside.

Ron explained a bunch of stuff, keys and that, what needed taking care of, plants and stuff, domestic stuff, I said we should talk about money and he looked a bit perplexed, only I wanted to pay my way, pay some rent like. He laughed, he said he was planning on paying *me* for looking after the place, fair play, so we decided to call it quits and leave the cash issue out of things on account of it seeming like we were each doing the other a favour. It surprised me that he could be like that, he'd struck me as a grabber at every turn, but maybe not. And no harm being proved wrong. And if it was alright by me, he'd set off the next day, catch up with those mates of his. Sorted. And more than anything in the world, I wanted to be left alone. He suggested we go to a club later on, said he knew of one that was '*Bitchin,*' I guess he meant it was good. He said it was probably the kind of thing I'd never seen, with dancers that bent themselves all the way, as in: '*all the way*' – steady mate. 'Lots of *very, very bad girls,*' he added. Now this was tricky, I couldn't be sure if this was *Ron for real* or a version he was putting together to impress, but either way, it seemed pretty rough. He said as how some new place in Soho had some '*really* young girls, *you know… like way, way young….'* I shot him a look only he was on a roll now and was uncorking a fresh bottle, he said they were well up for some *'nasty stuff.'* I interrupted him, said I'd lost my appetite for drinking, then I asked if he knew any B&Bs. He stopped talking. 'Only I was just thinking,' I said, 'maybe this whole thing's a bad idea.' He screwed his face up again and put his head on one side, the way dogs do when they aren't sure what you mean. I was tempted to tell him what I really thought of him. And now it was me that wanted to wash my hands, Howard Hughes style, and leave.

There was this long silence and then Ron stuck some more music on, wrong stuff this time, and he started talking as though he'd completely erased what I'd said about finding a B&B. He said I could pick whichever room I liked, said I could help myself and sleep in a different room each night if I wanted. Then he thrust the bunch of keys in my hand and talked as though I was some kid he was desperately trying to placate. God, he pissed me off. I'd been to Soho loads of times in the past and managed to have a perfectly boss time, and it'd never included anything along the lines he was on about. I figured it was probably down to a different way of navigating. Just different versions of the same thing. But *'Ron's Soho'* was some place I had no interest in going.

I sat down again and thought about things. Just one night, all I had to do was put up with this geezer for one night, 'And you're off in the morning then?' I said, practically pushing the guy out of his own gaff like, but you could hardly blame me. He sort of simpered, and like I said, he made my skin crawl, now especially. He said he would definitely be off first thing now he knew he'd got things 'covered here', and he smiled that smile of his again. *Nah,* there was no way I was spending even one night under the same roof as him. But I didn't see why one night had to ruin the whole show, so I told him I had stuff to do tonight and that he'd probably be best making other 'social' arrangements (I thought about his mass email address list, and I figured that out of 199, there had to be a few other sick bastards he could hang out with). I said I'd take the keys and be back the next day to 'take over,' and I also said he needn't wait around for me to get back, he should just get himself off, *get started,* like. He didn't look too happy, but it was the best I could do, he was spoiling my mood, my whole *'Dick Whittington – Mr Benn – London'* mood, and I was having none of it.

He pointed out that we hadn't had dinner yet, and didn't I at least want to have that and maybe take a shower before I went out, 'Not that you smell or anything, Mark' (total playground stuff), and that might just about have been OK, except he followed up with another kind of laugh that ain't really a laugh, it was what you might more accurately call a 'titter'. I picked up my bag, and I could feel him watching me, I said I'd had my fill, but 'thanks.'

'You are coming back aren't you? You will stay won't you?' he was looking at my rucksack, realising that I was taking it with me. Like I said, he was sharp. I jangled the keys lightly in my hand as reassurance, 'Yup,' I said, mimicking the e-jit, though it might well have been a lie, I wasn't quite sure yet what I was gonna do, nothing felt sure. Nothing at all. And spending time around this mean moron was making me less sure by the minute. Ron pulled himself up to his full height, 'OK, so in case I'm gone when you get back, you have the keys, and I think I've pretty much shown you the ropes so... feel free to make this place your own while I'm gone, and if you get stuck the neighbours upstairs are mostly OK.' And then as an urgent afterthought, '*Oh shit*, but I ought to tell you that they're used to having a monthly meeting, a sort of get together, you know, to discuss things.'

'What things?'

'Things that concern the building... as a whole....'

'Like what?' I asked, moving towards the front door. 'Well, security issues, neighbourhood issues, like noise pollution....' I smiled and dropped my head to hide the smirk that was biking its way across my face, my mood suddenly cheering up. 'What's up Mark?'

'Nothing mate.' I'd just been wondering how it was that if they'd all sat round discussing 'noise pollution', no one had ever sorted this geezer's 'sounds' out. I mean, I rather liked the piano concerto I'd woken up to, but the other stuff, that left a lot to be desired, truck loads. My gaze settled on his distant music collection. He caught me looking and it seemed to remind him of something, he said he needed to remember to take his iPod with him, and that he just hoped the '*grubby little bastards out there*' didn't steal it. Then he said that whilst he couldn't leave his 'pod' for me to listen to, I was more than welcome to help myself to his CD collection. Now that sounded like an attractive offer though probably not in the way he intended. And so I vowed to myself, that if I did come back, I would indeed help myself to his music, I would in fact give it a thorough sorting out, an 'edit' you might even say. Tidy. Anyway, Ron said he'd 'inform' the neighbours that his old university mate was house-sitting for him, and that if I wanted to join in with the house meetings while he was away I'd probably be made very welcome. He added that they were a really 'good bunch' (but that's a description for grapes, Ron, not people), and then he also assured me that they were all majorly successful, interesting types, rather like himself. One of those pauses arrived, you know, one of those that requires a fag and a beer, and possibly a beer mat, but a light switch, flicked suddenly to *off* and a door opening back onto the outside world seemed to do just as nicely right now. I wished him well and said goodbye.

I stepped out, not entirely sure where I was aiming for; all I had in mind was maybe seeing a few sights, seeing things and places me and Jim might have wanted to see, tracking Mr Benn, and Nelson on his column – finding inspiration for our songs.

# CHAPTER SEVEN

## *up all night...*

# OUR MATE, NELSON

Outside, the air was cold, the daylight gone, but it was enough with just the moon out and strips of light from the street lamps. Sorted. There's something dead comforting about the moon, it's a reassuring sort of light.

The whole Ron scenario had really bothered me, and I really couldn't help thinking that having so much wrong music had to be some of the reason for his head being so far off it, but then again, I hadn't had a *thorough* look through his collection, and it was possible I'd missed some decent stuff, only I didn't reckon that could really be the case 'cos decent stuff has a tendency to jump out at you. Decent titles and band names tend to give a nod of recognition, like: *'Alright mate,'* as though they're as familiar with you as you are with them. *Yeah,* I know how soft-headed that sounds, but it's just how it is, and nothing, not the one disc had held out its hand. But I couldn't worry about all that too much right now, I'd only just got this Ron geezer out of my hair — no point carrying the bleeder round with me now — I'd try and sort it out later, if I got to coming back. I breathed a sigh of relief, and set off up the street.

A few metres away I could see these three lads, *youths,* as I think they get called nowadays, and that's a word that implies loads of stuff isn't it? Criminal sort of stuff mainly, seems a pretty unfair deal when you think about it. I stopped, 'paused' if you like, thinking as how me and them might have a conversation about it, and whether or not it bothered them that over time young people had gradually been sold lives with practically no intrinsic value, 'cos however much I felt I'd not been given the Highway-Code-of-living, these poor bastards were probably suckled on not much more than video games and *lifestyle* shite, the lifestyle bit being the friggin' worst of it. What an empty load of shite.

Anyways, these lads looked like they were only about ten or maybes eleven. They were picking up chunks of concrete and rooting through what looked like someone's mashed-up garden for rocks and stones like, heavy stuff. I thought it was too much to think as maybe they were *making* a garden but I gave it a shot anyhow (yes, there is a part of me that is a genuine, full-on comedian, I just mostly keeps it to meself), so I asked 'em, dry as you like, if they were collecting that stuff to make a rock garden. The fat one, who also happened to be the tallest, shot me a look, he clearly wanted to be read as hard. *Dead 'ard.* His fat cheeks bulged out of a determinedly mean expression, but somehow the lamplight softened things. I was tempted to smile, only I knew he'd take it for weakness, or weirdness or some other fuckin' wrongness, and I didn't entirely want him to think I was taking the piss, so I left the smiling out and just repeated, '*So*, are you collecting that lot up to make a rock garden?'

'No mate,' said the second one, the skinny one with sticky-out ears. The fat geezer told him to, '*Shut it*' and not to talk to me, 'cos I looked like a '*right fucker, init?*' and then he put his hand to his ears and pulled them out wide, taking the piss, '*Mickey Mouse,*' he says to him, mean like, and then he paused and drew in his gut before shooting a look at both his mates and reminding them, '*We agreed, remember? I'm the boss, we said that, I'm the boss, init!*' and then he just stood there looking mean, standing his ground, only what for? He seemed to be making way too big a deal of the whole thing. And I felt like you could fast forward ten years, and imagine him eyeballing some poor sod in a bar, and getting into a scrap over nothing, nothing at all, the way some geezers do. I took a moment and then I said I just wondered what the rocks were for, 'I mean, maybe you guys are planning on some... dry-stone-walling?'

'*Wallin'?*' the second kid piped up.

'Yeah, how they do in the countryside. They sort of cleverly wedge the right size rocks and stones to build up a wall, and without any cement or anything to hold them together, so it's a pretty like, skilled affair.'

'No cement nor nuffin?' asked Skinny, and Mr Fat attempted to eyeball him only Skinny wasn't paying attention. 'No, no cement nor nothin',' I says, 'just skill. I guess they learn from their dads... or local experts, like; pretty nifty when you think about it.'

'*Yeah...*' and it seemed that Mr Skinny was impressed.

'So,' I said, 'I take it this lot isn't for building a wall then?' Skinny laughed, 'No way mate, we ain't got no skill, man.' Mr Fat had taken to shifting some of the rock pile closer to the kerb, trying to carry a few bigger rocks in the belly of his sweater and ignoring Mr Skinny's chatter.

'As long as you're not planning on using them to break anything, eh guys?' The fat geezer's haul was starting to weigh too much, he tried to draw himself up again, hoping that I couldn't tell, knowing his strength was being sapped, fronting it out. The third guy was busy piling rocks and junk in a corner, it was the first time he'd really looked round, and it was clear that Fatty had his card marked, this little fella, the Smiler, knew his place, and his job was to take instructions, and for my money, I reckoned it had to include doing so 'without question'. Mr Skinny piped up with an explanation, 'All it is mate, *is*: you see them parking meters?' and pointing, 'Them over there...' I scanned the street, my eyes were now pretty well adjusted to the streaks of light from the street lamps and the foggy offerings from the moon, but I still didn't see the meters straight off, '...on the other side mate,' Skinny added. The fat guy told him to, 'Shut it, *init*,' but unlike the Smiler, Mr Skinny was no natural-born subordinate, so he carried on explaining, rock in hand, 'All it is, is that we use these to smash 'em, just parking meters mate, so it ain't doing no harm, init.' It's a screwy kinda logic, (but to be honest, I can't quite say as I wouldn't have done the same at his age, only we never had parking meters). Mr Skinny smiled, friendly, but I looked at my feet, smiling isn't always my thing, I lit up instead. Mr Fat shot me a look, and then he and Skinny exchanged a glance, Skinny slightly bowing his head as though in acknowledgement of Fat's 'ultimate supremacy', and Fat looked pleased though he didn't smile (after all, Skinny wasn't following orders *too* closely), but it seemed that Skinny's nod had been just enough to let Fat save face, and that was probably for the best. Smiler stood up now looking well proud of his stash of missiles; the fat geezer had his arms crossed and he leant back a bit, freshly confident of his leadership skills and whatever cocky little plans he no doubt had lined up. Noticing my cigarette, Smiler suddenly spoke up (he came across as the youngest of the three, and kind of like the runt of the litter, though I bleedin' hate that word), 'Give us a fag then.' Mr Fat looked pleased with him, despite his breaking ranks and speaking independently. I said, 'They're bad for you mate.' Mr Fat huffed, and then Mr Skinny decided to take me on, 'Yeah, but you smoking in front of us like that is harming us anyways, init? So you might as well hand 'em round, right?'

'Yeah... but you see, the thing is,' and now they were all stood in a row, Mr Fat, legs astride, hands on hips, regular cowboy; Mr Skinny, lanky as you like, hair posted out the top of his head like startled spaghetti, both of 'em eyeballing me, and Smiler there, his shoulders hunched over like he'd had a day of hard labour, mostly looking down and trying to dust himself off, sneaking the odd sly glance, and grinning like a bastard (he reminded me of some weird kid out of a Dickens' novel). I told 'em, 'The thing is, I don't totally hold with that whole 'passive' argument, on account of the amount of stress some other geezers cause me just in ordinary everyday life,' and I didn't quite realise until I'd finished, but they were all listening in and pretty intense like, 'you see, I have this theory that sometimes other folk so totally stress a person out, that *that* has to count as something, you know, as some sort of equivalent, some kind of equal though maybes unintentional passing on of stress, and I reckon that *that* contributes to all sorts of illness in other people, probably even causes some of it,' I was getting carried away now, 'and I wish I had a quid for every year some bleeder's knocked off of *my* life just by passing on his own personal stressing.' I looked up and the four of us totally flipped out laughing – I felt like me ole dad prattling on like that, (only those wouldn't be his sentiments at all, like I said, he detested smoking). 'I know where you're coming from,' said Mr Skinny followed closely by the finger-snapping Smiler, 'He's well cool man init,' only that was the wrong thing to say, about me at least, and Fat walloped him. I couldn't wade in, it was tribal stuff, and he'd only get a harder slap later if I stuck up for him now. 'The thing is mate,' says Mr Skinny starting up again, 'You owe us two quid each then init?'

'How'd you work that out?'

'A quid for killing us with passive smoking, and a quid for passing on *your own personal stressing-out,* init?' Mr Fat looked puzzled, Smiler had gone back to his pile of rocks, I sort of smiled at Skinny, 'You're a cocky git,' I said.

'I'm right though init?' said Skinny. As I started to walk on he asked me where I was going. I knocked the ash off my cigarette, 'Got an appointment,' I said feeling cocky myself now, 'with Nelson.' It seemed not that unreasonable a thing to say – (and so, it was decided, I really was gonna go to Trafalgar Square, pay our Nelson a visit, and I was also gonna look for Mr Benn, a real version, legit, a geezer in a suit and bowler hat – *you're never too old to be a bit of a kid, not really* – and like I said, no one ever gets to know what shite travels through another geezer's head and passes for amusement. Even friggin' CCTV can't get the contents of your head... yet).

'*Nelson?*' I heard Skinny pipe up dead excited. And then Smiler more distantly, 'I think he's a rapper, init?'

I crossed the street smiling, 'No mate, well, not so far as I know, least not the one I'm thinking of,' and stopping to stub out my fag, I turned around and gently reminded them, at least not to use the rocks and stuff on any windows, that type of thing.

Not too far off the corner I could still faintly make out the lads' in-fighting, Fat figured Skinny had been way too friendly and that he should have pushed harder to get some cash out of me; Smiler said he was tired and didn't want to stay out all night again, and Skinny said as how I seemed like an alright bloke and wondered if I lived round there. Then Fat added that I was a right wanker and had been cruising for a smackin' *init.* And then this bloody great smashing sound followed as a rock hit the curb, I glanced over my shoulder, it had made contact about a metre behind me. A fair shot. Fat had had to make a point, I could see that, but at least the geezer was wise enough not to lob it any closer, he'd think he was sending me a warning shot, reminding me that I was on his territory, reminding the others who ultimately was boss; but deep down he must have figured that any closer and he was seriously pushing his luck. I turned the corner.

I thought about what Smiler had said about them staying out all night, I mean, they were old enough for adventures for sure, but it bothered me. And it also bothered me that sometimes decisions get made out of macho stuff and point scoring, or else in score settling mode, and some of that stuff can easily wind up being long-term crushing, for someone, one way or another. The two of them were mostly alright, but Fats... I figured he had too much to prove; but then shite, I'm no soddin' scout leader, what was I gonna do about it?

I'd left Ron behind me, he seemed easy enough to shift out of my head, but something about those wee lads seemed to linger. Were they out all night because they were playing hooky and just up for having fun, or did they *have* to stay out all night, was there stuff wrong at home like, did they even have homes? Homes that could be called *home* in any reasonable sort of way? And for Christ's sake, it was February... it didn't make any easy sense.

I felt a bit weird, and then I tripped up on the pavement like a right freakin' idiot, but what? Like now I'm Doctor bleedin' Barnardo all of a sudden. I didn't quite get this, was I now gonna start fretting about every little toerag that crossed my path, imagining stuff about them, 'cos that's all it was, I was just imagining things, I didn't know anything about them. I didn't have anything to go on at all really, and more than likely they were just like me and Jim at that age, just larking around. No real bother. I needed to calm down. So, like a bastard, I put them out of my mind.

It was Friday night after all, the city was starting to buzz, and even this far out, this far from the centre, you could still sense the beginnings of it, or the 'outer-ripples' so to speak, and it was as though I could almost feel its pulse beneath my feet, the trains there rumbling under the ground, rattling the earth around them – Manor House Underground Station – I'd arrived. I climbed down the steps to its exotic, subterranean world of shaking trains in dilapidated, low tiled tunnels.

I seemed to stumble down the last few steps of the escalator. *Steady mate.* I stopped a second and looked down at my shoe and the sole coming away; and I didn't know what was wrong with me, but something was. I figured I should maybe just slow up a bit, but there was this mad mix of tiredness and excitement going on, adrenaline pumping. I felt a tad light-headed. Probably just needed to eat, and properly, not just a bit of bread and mush, but it wasn't really that, I hadn't ever really felt like this before, like I said, it was weird, and I can't explain it, I just hoped the feeling would shift a bit and soon.

A train pulled in and I climbed aboard the dark blue Piccadilly line, a straight, deep blue line that cuts across the city; and the tube, its network, like blood vessels, pumping people round its misshapen heart.

'1967', the train's year stamped into a floor plate at the entrance. I thought, blimey, this bleeder's older than me, and I wondered if that made it a 'classic', or just some out-of-date and possibly dangerous-as-hell piece of junk? It's hard to say. But it struck me that bits of London are decidedly crumbly. It doesn't try to hide it though, and I like it for that, I like its honesty; things flaking away, falling apart, tube walls half tiled, things half fixed; it's like it's a city that's always dying, but just as it draws its last breath it sort of bucks itself up again, starts putting itself back together.

As I sat down I found myself thinking back to the women I'd seen crying, the one at Euston and then the one on the train, and I started to wonder: *just what is that all about?* Why would a woman, just some ordinary sort of woman, at the end of some ordinary day, be so very sad? It didn't make sense. You just do get to wondering.

The train pulled in and out of stations, I stayed on, except that on the tube it isn't so much a 'pulling in and out' of stations, so much as a 'stopping and starting', a 'lurching' even; and then it suddenly occurred to me that for the first time in years, years and sodding *years*, I had no plans. None of that having to be somewhere, having to meet, having to do anything. I had no plans at all. And it felt fucking great. All I had in mind right now was easy stuff, small stuff: go look at Nelson on his column, keep an eye out for a Mr Benn, maybes read that lady's book, write some postcards, that sort of thing, but nothing much else, and frankly I couldn't handle anything else, not right now.

I decided to stay on the tube for a while, not care too much about where I got off, and it's no big deal, you can only go so far and then they run back again, maybe switch a platform, but nothing more than that. I just needed to steady myself, calm it all down. In the end I must have stayed on there for ages, just running on rails, day dreaming, listening to chatter, but not taking much of it in, and that chatter – any language you like, you could totally choose your pick, but me, I couldn't identify any at all like, bit of an ignorant prick, but still.

Some geezer was reading this book and at first I was convinced he was reading the bleeder upside down, but then I noticed the page numbers and they were the right way up, and I was glad I hadn't tried to 'alert' him and made a total prick of meself – but what the hell kinda language is that with them little triangle bits in there and weird squiggles? I was well impressed. When you think about it, we only have those twenty-six letters and most of the time we find ways not to use most of them – *init!* Though I have to admit I quite like the 'shortenings' as well, it's like each generation finding its own 'speak', and you can't hardly blame 'em, the kids, not if no bastard takes time out to teach 'em any different. I thought back to the three musketeers from earlier, smart arses, hoped they'd be alright.

There was a load of random screeches and screaming at the next station, and a crowd of girls got on. They were wearing cowboy hats, white cowboy hats, and mini skirts, a hen night, just that regular Friday night stuff, and they were followed by a larger group of Muslim girls, all in black with them scarves that frame their faces, and the whole lot of them were giggling, cowgirls and Mona Lisas, separate but the same, chattering away like, all excited by their day – I think they might actually have been laughing at my broken shoe, and my big toe peeping out like that (and my stupid green socks), but no bother, easy enough, I was sure my big toe was flattered, even.

My head felt foggy again, and suddenly everything around me seemed like I was looking on from some more distant place, it's hard to describe, but as though I wasn't really there. I wasn't feeling too good again, but I couldn't get a handle on it. And when I did finally emerge from the tube I found myself walking down street after street without even bothering to notice where it was I'd come up or where it was I was going, and after a while, each time I turned a corner I kept thinking that I saw someone, someone that I knew.

It was just a slight feeling at first, the kind you might easily enough dismiss, only no matter how slight it was at the start, it gradually started to gnaw away at me. In some ways it felt like a totally crazy feeling to have, but then why should it be? People bump into people they know or people they *used* to know, all the time. *All* the time. But maybe that was it, and maybe that was why it gnawed away, because the opposite is just as bloody true, isn't it? There's all those people, or maybe just a few, and maybe just the one, just the friggin' one that you *so* want to see again, and never do. I shivered. And then I walked. I walked some more. I walked and walked, the sole of the one shoe now slowly but surely giving way. Only I couldn't care less; and I could feel my pace picking up but like I didn't have control, and soon I could feel myself almost desperately trying to push my way through, only you can't, you can't get too far forward in a city that's clogged like that with people, all moving and heaving, weaving their selves about. London, friggin' tons of people *everywhere*, flocking to bars and restaurants, others sauntering home dog-tired, laden down with shopping bags, some of them with a right bleedin' haul – and what they buying that they ain't already got? — And then tourists and day-trippers, but whoever they were and whatever speed they were doin', it was just the sheer friggin' number of them, it just totally jammed you, hemmed you in; and in amongst them all, I was sure, I was *so* damn sure I'd caught sight of someone, that someone that I knew. And now the harder I tried to push through, the more I felt held back. It felt like everyone around me was totally aggravated, and as though they were conspiring now to keep me back. But it isn't that, you just can't get bleedin' anywhere in that great mess of people. I could feel myself sweating. Totally stressed-out by now. Bodies, tons of 'em everywhere, pouring out of doorways, pushing their way up from tube stations, and all of them getting in my fuckin' way, and it wasn't their fault, *but just move you bastards, get out of my fuckin' way!* Because I had to find him, had to catch hold of him, because he was there somewhere, in amongst them all, I knew he was, I just had to find him, catch up with him, see him close up, I had to, I just had to see his face. And it was so fucking insane, because the man I ran after was a man in a bowler, and I don't know anyone, do I? I don't know anyone who owns a bowler hat. And then just as I felt I was finally losing sight of him, I thought I caught a glimpse again, just a glimpse, sideways on, and *was it… was it him? Was it Jim?*

Maybe he was messing about, not taking the piss, more larkin' about, like maybe he was playing a role, just playing a part, having some fun. I stood a moment to catch my breath, and leant against a wall.

And he was gone.

I bent over, blood rushing to my head, my hands red with cold. I tried to think of something else, anything, just to distract my stupid, bastard head, and calm things down.

It wasn't any good.

Just breathing.

*Electric guitars*, isn't that what we dreamt of? We used to play in his dad's garage, with cricket bats as air guitars, strumming away at the silence, whole fuckin' gigs going on in our heads, tweaking the monitors, get it loud, play it loud man. *Play it loud!* And then off of some jumble sale, Jim had picked up a hat, a bowler hat, and god knows how or why, and it was way too big – he thought it might suit our image, only we didn't have an image, we were *anti*-image (you are at eleven – and I guess I still am), and it didn't matter, we'd play in our pyjamas, in our school bleedin' uniforms for Christ's sake. Didn't matter, nothing mattered much then. Bowler hats and underpants, or his dad's old suit, the one he kept for best, like for funerals and weddings (a whole stack of people seemed to die when I was little, but no one ever got wed.) — Back then we were just two little lads in a band, with cricket-bat guitars; now it sounds perverted. Well it wasn't. It so fuckin' wasn't. — I lifted my head up, and just as I did I was sure, I was absolutely sure, that I'd seen him.

Pull yourself together mate. Felt like I was totally losing it, felt like I could hardly breathe. But I'd seen him, and I kept on seeing him; running now, whenever there was room enough, making room enough, and pushing along at least, and trying my damnedest to speed it all up, turning a corner and there he was, only just as I caught sight he'd gone again, moving on, way ahead. It was as though he wasn't quite real, not *really* real, and I just can't explain, and I'd hurry on behind trying to catch him up, trying to reach him, 'cos maybe... if I could just get close enough... I could put out my hand, catch his shoulder. And then we'd go in some pub, one I've been in before, or some other further up, or some place by the Thames, and we'd talk over old times, and we'd have a laugh, and tomorrow, *tomorrow*, like a right pair of sods, we'd... we'd *do* London! Set off down that Jermyn Street, pick up some shirts, or head down Savile Row, yeah, *Savile Row*, we'd get measured up all proper, get suited-up, suited and booted, the tailored treatment, and then we'd run riot just the two of us... through Trafalgar Square, the lions and the fountains, electric guitars, Jim, blasting out his lungs as the front man, and – *excuse the language like* – but with the whole friggin' full-scale Philharmonic Orchestra blasting out all around us, and Nelson up there on his column, well, we'd have sorted out the arm thing no problem, and then, and *then* he'd play bass. Picture it, just picture it. A massive gig, under a dark starry sky, blasting, blasting.

And the next day, the next day, we'd take the whole damn bleedin' lot of 'em, Nelson too, and we'd all go fishing. Think about it, the entire Philharmonic Orchestra fishin', it makes full sense, they'd be the best, 'cos no one understands silence the way that great musicians do, and no one would better understand or appreciate the ripples on the surface. And no one more than Nelson, knows why a man needs to be by the sea ('cept for maybe that Ishmael bloke in *Moby Dick*).

Me and Jim, we might not have been any good, but we could have given it a shot, we could have given it a go, and who knows, we just might have been contenders. *Yeah, I'm a dickhead! Well spotted. But right now, it feels fucking great!*

I'd stopped running now. Tried to catch my breath. For a fragment of a moment there, I thought I saw him again... and I got this feeling, like a fist inside my chest, just punching me and punching, only I felt so empty, so mixed up. But now that I'd stopped I could see where I was, I blinked, looked up at a star-filled sky, and there he was, Nelson, way up on his column, keeping watch overhead in a sparkly night-sky.

After that I'm not sure quite what happened. I think I might have blacked out. But when I came round, the good thing was, things didn't seem quite so muddled anymore, in fact my head just felt blank. I figured my dog-meat brain must have experienced a kind of 'overload', a sort of system shutdown, easy enough I suppose. And I didn't know if I'd been anywhere or done anything, but I was pretty sure I hadn't, pretty sure I'd stayed in the one place. And I must have stayed that way all night. Some people die like that. But I wasn't cold, I just felt a sort of rush and then a shiver, but somehow, deep down, I was warm enough inside.

So there I was in Trafalgar Square, laid flat on my back, my bag for a pillow, watching Nelson way up there on his pedestal, riding the clouds in endless waves of morning blue. And it really was a *blue*, blue sky. It felt amazing. Imagine it. No one else around, just me and Nelson, him at the helm, and me below decks just waiting for the word. And indeed it came, though not from Nelson – from some copper, 'What *exactly* are you doing, sir?' – *Sir! I thought: shite, I've been promoted! – knighted!* 'You are lying down, sir, in the middle of Trafalgar Square.'

'No shit, Sherlock.' Nothing gets past these guys does it, eh? Sharp as you like. Shiny boots, metal badges, all the proper gear, he was 100% pure Mr Plod in my Mr Benn world. Nice one. But then he had a bit of a go, fair play, it's like they have to, it's part of their job description, and so: he didn't care for my language, nor my sarcasm, only what with him – at a rough guess – being a Cockney, I couldn't quite fathom that. 'So sir,' he says, and then dead sarcastic and clipped and like a total goose-stepper, 'back to my original question: *What do you think you're doing?*'

What can you say? What can a person possibly say in a situation like this that's even halfway gonna satisfy a copper? I thought that if there was any possible chance of this geezer really appreciating what I was doing, lying here, enjoying my special time here out at sea, I'd have gone as far as inviting him to have a go himself, not exactly to full-on *join me,* but yeah, at least to give it a go, 'Lie down officer,' I'd have said, 'go on, lay down, relax a bit; we are men at sea, just lie back, breathe in the air, and take in the sky,' but *no*, I was pretty sure he wasn't that kinda guy. So in the end I didn't answer him. He stood a bit and then he asked me to, '*move on,*' and not nasty like, just ordinary, but it struck me as pretty lame, and pretty fucking unnecessary (I mean right now even the friggin' pigeons were closer to being law breakers).

I looked at the sky again, and just for a moment, just for that moment, I was lost to it all again, gentle rhythms and the sound of the waves lapping gently against the side of the ship; and if you pause and look just long enough, you can see how the clouds curl up just the same as the edges of waves, only with clouds it's mostly like it's all slowed down, and then you imagine, how in great storms, the skies curl down and the seas curl up, and they clasp hold of one another, take each other's hand. And then it's calm again, and there's space again for other things, for you and me to lie down again, easy like, just watching the great morning blue – that's *so* great, just picture it, it makes you feel dead good. Easy.

But it was no good now, this geezer'd ruined it. The cop was still stood there, stock still – total plank – and if we'd been at sea I'd have thrown the fucker overboard, only this wooden bastard would probably just float away like. He'd lie there on his back, '*Move on,*' he'd call out, just staring straight up, and he'd see the sky, only he wouldn't see it would he? Not for real. He wouldn't see it at all. Like he couldn't see it now.

'Move on,' he says again, monotone, and that was best really, if he'd said anything else, anything else at all, I'd have felt compelled to have a go meself, wind him up a bit on account of him 'killing the moment', only '*Move on,*' wasn't that much to hook onto. Still, I figured that a show of obedience might just pop his bubble.

I would now have to add this to my *experiences of a lifetime* list: meeting a copper who wound me up but didn't deserve any full-on aggro, though, and it had to be said, he was definitely off me Christmas card list. And that, by the way, is also why you can't ever take a copper fishing, and why you never need feel guilty if you're ever looking for an excuse not to invite 'em: they've no right sense of timing, no feeling for fine detail, no sense of what it means to just lie the fuck down and enjoy the quiet.

As I stood up, I sort of wobbled, a bit unsteady on my feet after finding the horizontal so appealing, anyhow, the copper kept his position, his face deadpan; but it did at least give me a chance to have a sort of close-up on him. A look *down on him* as it happened, it's the height issue, it's an unfair world, but I pretty much win on that front, must be: nine times out of ten. That's one of the biggest pleasures of height as it happens, never met a copper yet that I couldn't look down on. Don't get me wrong, I dare say there's plenty that do a good job, but even me granddad used to say as how half of 'em were mostly just crims in uniform, yeah, *'Crims and fuckwits',* he called 'em, guess he had his reasons, and I don't reckon he'd be far wrong. Anyhow, Mr Plod here, being so supposedly reasonable, might well have been Mr Benn dressed up in a copper's uniform, two dimensions swollen into three, but that thought freaked me out. Anyways, my getting up off the floor, albeit a slow manoeuvre, seemed to satisfy him well enough that I was indeed gonna make my way to some place else, so without 'further ado' he grunted and then strode his self off.

I brushed myself off a bit, nothing *to* brush off really, no more than a bit of city dust. But I caught a whiff of myself and thought, no wonder the copper didn't hang around, best get myself cleaned up. I looked down, I figured my shoe had held together pretty well all things considered, though it now had that kind of flip-flop feel about it. I checked my bag lest anyone had stolen from me – but no, everything was still there: fags, postcards, CA's book, and the lady's book – I figured I best get round to reading that. Nice one.

I stood there, in Trafalgar Square, making the most of my last few private moments with Nelson – wasn't this a big year for him, 2005? Wasn't this some sort of anniversary? And then it struck me as odd in some ways, that since getting off the train at Euston I'd developed this strong interest in statues and stone, and in particular *'monuments'* – you know, Stephenson and the like – *for Christ's sake! What's that all about?* And then it made me think about Jim, and Jim's lack of monument. But that's the difference isn't it, between being someone like me or Jim, and being someone 'great'. I suppose that's what you might call, the 'why' of it all. These guys had done great things, and that's why we bother so much, *why we should bother so much! Nelson* and *Stephenson,* folk like them, made in stone, their 'likeness' captured for eternity; the place where they stand, made 'landmark' – yeah, that's right really, fair dos. Though I still couldn't help but wish that Jim's funeral hadn't at least been made more 'personal'. — And then suddenly, 'tangentially', *I'd got it!* This year, it *was* a big year, and it was an anniversary: the two-hundredth anniversary of the Battle of Trafalgar! Fuck! I wondered how come Dad never mentioned it when I was up there. But then maybe he did, and maybe I just hadn't listened, hadn't taken it in, not consciously. And anyways it wouldn't have mattered, I wouldn't have cared. Not right then. All I could remember was him rattling on about Ellen MacArthur, and her sailing round the world – come to think of it, that *well* deserves a statue.

I put my hand through my hair, or tried to, it was in as much mess by now as the frazzled contents of the dopey friggin' head it grew out of.

I could hear voices nearing, early sightseers maybe, hotel staff and the like on their way to work.

I looked up one last time, at my mate Nelson – I don't reckon he was a tall geezer, but he certainly looked like one on that friggin' column. Nice one. — And it occurred to me that I had in fact – despite not feeling much in control of my 'faculties' – had a really nice time.

Thanks Nelson.

Happy enough, I lit up and walked on.

# CHAPTER EIGHT

*'...a city which, only when it shits, is not miserly,*
*calculating, greedy.'* — Italo Calvino

# COLD

After a while, I found my way back to Ron's place. The street was quiet, no one about, the parking meters were smashed, and the cars parked there now had wheel clamps. No one likes a parking meter, but we all like wheel clamps even less. Little dickheads.

I waded through the trash, and as I stuck the key in the door, I shivered a moment, lest I hadn't left it long enough, lest the wanker was still home, curled up in his pit after a night of shagging coked up strangers. I heard a window slide open, one of the flats above, and then I heard the door just up the steps start to creak open so I shot into Ron's sharpish, I'd got no interest in his neighbours.

In the dark, I stood a moment and listened, no sound; and then I checked the place out. Empty. *Shite*, I felt relieved. There was no sign of him anywhere, the fucker had gone. Sorted. I leant back on the door and then let out this yelp of sheer fuckin' delight, the place was mine, London was mine, my own friggin' life was mine! I lit up, and inhaled deep. What can you say, the place was contaminated, it was time to de-Ron it! I know, 'chuckling' is totally uncool, but I so fucking did.

I figured I'd whack on some music, only then I remembered. Fuck. But let's not be too hasty now, like I said, I could have been wrong about his collection, I needed to make a closer examination, totally check out the man's playlist, maybe I'd missed some gems.

I walked to the back of the flat, and the super cool kitchen, drank some water, flicked some lights on, then went back to the music stash in the hallway; I figured I didn't need any full-on neon experience and 'distant lighting' was gonna be the closest I could get to 'low lighting' in this gaff. It struck me as weird that, that someone could have mega cool taste in a whole load of things and then totally fuck it up by not understanding lighting and what I have come to think of as *the weather of a place*. I chuckled again, how fucking pretentious did that sound? Ah well, that's just the way it goes.

So, back to Ron's wrong music. I lit another cigarette and braced myself, my earlier optimism waning as I was now confronted by stack after stack of total tripe. What was it with this guy? There was no Dylan, no Tom Waits, no Porter, no James Taylor, no Leonard Cohen, and no Jimmy Webb. So far, not a decent songster in sight. I walked back to the kitchen, opened a window, felt the breeze. Some mange-ridden fox limped across the garden, I figured what that little critter really needed was a proper garden and preferably *fields*, yeah, fields that led off to better places, with better tunes. I went back to the CD racks. – I was being too negative, too quick to judge. Maybe there *was* some decent stuff, I just wasn't looking hard enough; I left my fag on the shelf for a minute; let's just have a looky here... no... no... nope. Nothing, not a friggin' one worth the listen. I picked up my ciggie, and then I glanced back at the garden, ole mangy had stopped for a snoop around, he suddenly looked up like he had something to say, hungry I guess, so I went and had a shuffle through Ron's top-notch kitchen cupboards, see what I could find. There was all that friggin' trash outside, but clearly there wasn't anything decent enough to keep even this poor bleeder alive. I shuffled around a bit more. And of course, *inside* the cupboards, where you needed a bastard light, it was dark as a friggin' tomb.

They're like dogs aren't they? Foxes? Only there wasn't even any dog food in there, guess there wouldn't be, and to be honest I don't think I could feed that shite to anything. I finally found some ham in the fridge and some stuff in a carton claiming to be some kind of milk. I pulled the bottom window open and stuck it through the bars on those posh little plates – would you credit it, posh gaff like this with bars on the bleedin' windows? Mental. It's like if you have posh expensive gear you have to build a friggin' prison to protect it, rather like living in a super-posh Strangeways; *what are people like, eh?* I doubt I've got anything worth nicking, me, 'cept my music, and then if it makes some geezer happy I'd be pretty much OK with that, it's nothing you can't replace. And I'd sooner have nothin' than have to live like this for permanent. Bars on windows? Nah, can't be doing with that.

I left Foxy alone with the grub and went back to my 'editing' – 'cos the worst of Ron's stuff just had to be cut out, I'm telling you, some of his stuff was way off. I looked for the Stones, but there was none of 'em, no Roses and no Rolling; no Lennon, no Stevie Wonder. *Paul Weller?* No. *Morrissey?* No. *Ian Dury?* Nope. I tried allowing for different styles like, and taste, even tried being open minded, but I still found myself having to pull out more of his crap, and it half covered his floor by now. How about: Gibb? Carole King? Sedaka? Sting even? Springsteen? No one, not one 'saving grace', no music whatsoever to save a bleeder's sanity. No wonder the geezer's such a friggin' arsehole. And there was nothin' for it, much as it's my least favourite thing to do, I'd have to go shopping, fill in the gaps in his collection. I figured that as well as all the obvious stuff that was missing, he would well benefit from a load of Ian Brown, yeah, and maybe Mike Skinner's, *'a grand don't come for free'*, that's a goodie, and how about some Edgar Jones, Edgar *'Jones'* Jones even, and his *Soothing Music for Stray Cats.* Nice one. Jeff Buckley, a must, there's simply no living without *Hallelujah*, Leonard Cohen's top lyrics like, boss songwriter. Some Richard Ashcroft too, *defo*. *'You're a slave to the money and then you die…'*, that'd be stuck in my head all day now, boss stuff. I knew there'd be a whole stack of stuff I'd end up buying the geezer, but shit, it had to be done. Probably whack in some dead recent stuff too, there's loads of top stuff about; get a Jools Holland vibe going there too, total mellow. — The door bell went. It was this old white geezer, could have been me dad like. He was dead distressed, he had tears in his eyes and he was shaking. If I'd thought proper I suppose I should have invited the guy in, but half my head was some place else, anyways, he starts to explain that his daughter had been in this dead bad car accident and how he needs to get to the hospital. He said as how his car wouldn't start, his keys shook between his fingers. I kept watching his hands, all withered by age, shaking with fright. He was so distraught. He said he lived close by like, but had run out of cash, and could I help him out? He'd drop it round later. I put my hand in my back pocket. My watch was still there in the one, I tried the other, there was that 56p I'd found on my first day on the floor at Euston like. I shoved it back. That was my 'lucky' cash – sort of like a souvenir, I'd gotta keep that; anyways, small change wasn't what we were on about right now. 'Sure,' I said, still standing in the doorway, still not thinking to bring him inside while I found my wallet. I'm a prick to the last in these cases. I asked him how much he reckoned he needed, he said that fifteen quid would probably cover the taxi. I managed to tread on a load of Ron's CDs as I went to find my dosh, in fact I damn near skated on the bastards. If I'd have thought, I could have offered to take a look at the bloke's car, that's one of the few things that I'm good at, might have got it started, only like I said, my head was half gone. In any case, he was dead upset, I probably wouldn't have managed to do it fast enough. My wallet, found it, sorted. Fifteen smackers; I figured best make it twenty, they keep you waiting for ages in hospitals, he'd need to get a cup of tea and that. I glanced in the kitchen, and out the window. The fox was sat in the middle of the grass, right smack in the centre of the window frame, he looked at me sort of curiously, like he was trying to tell me something, least ways that's what it felt like, except he probably couldn't even see that far in, me in half light like; he hadn't touched the stuff I'd put out, fussy git. I hurried back to the front door, give the ole guy the twenty and said I hoped things would turn out alright.

When I went back to the kitchen the fox had gone. I left the food out anyway in case he was just too shy or something, or thought it was too early for his dinner, scrawny fucker though, you'd have thought he'd have eaten anything, anytime, but still.

I went back to the hallway and my current conundrum: what to do with Ron's wrong-uns? A right ole stash by now, strewn across the floor. I finally stuck 'em in one of them black bin bags, tied a knot, and shoved 'em in one of the other bedrooms. Job done – well,

91

half of it, now I just needed to shop for the decent whack and fill up his stacks. I figured I'd sort out Ron's music and if by any chance he wasn't happy with my handiwork, I might cave in and tell him where I'd put his wrong stuff – *well, maybe,* or maybe I'd sling the shite out. I'd have to wait and see.

I noticed my shoe again, ought to do something about that I suppose, trouble was I liked 'em. The one wasn't much good for running, flopping about like that, but I wasn't planning on doing any, besides, I couldn't make any big decisions right now, and I figured they were good for just a wee while longer. Maybe do something about the socks though. I hate green. It's not a good colour outside of nature. Socks are best brown, or blue. And no pattern.

The bin bag reminded me… and now seemed like a good opportunity to clear up all that shite at the front (and let's face it, no one else looked too eager to take it on); sort those bins out, put the rubbish back *in* the bleeders, assuming that's where it'd started out like, and clear all that trash up off the steps. So I took myself off outside armed with a load of bin bags, a big fancy broom and a dustpan and brush, all credit to Ron, he'd got all the gear, shame he was too stuck up to use it, but there we go.

I started sorting the place out, and I was happy enough on this chilly ole morn till this geezer came along and interrupted my mood; he was laiden down with a right ole load of shopping bags, *men's fashion* mostly by the looks of it, he said he lived upstairs, and asked what I was doing. Asked if I worked for the council, says it was about time something was done, and then adds that I should make sure to clear up the used condoms lying in the road 'while I was about it'. When I didn't answer, he repeated the last bit, I guess that was in case I was a *deaf* council worker. I paused, let the air settle, then I asked him if he'd had his lunch yet, only there was supposed to be a lot of protein in sperm, and if he carried on talking out of his arse I'd have him swallow them bastards lying in the road. A few silent moments passed, I sniggered deep inside. I realised he was looking at my shoes. I said he could lend me a pair of his if he was worried about my feet getting cold. And I looked at him now, straight on. His mouth, wide open. Not pretty. The thing is, you can't blame some easylifes, they're probably suckled on smug-juice, and swathed in ignorance from birth, so it must come as a well-big shock when, on occasion, the rest of the world doesn't wanna conform to their every fucking desire and preconception. Poor sod.

'I'm living in Ron's flat for a bit,' I said after our little pause, adding, 'That thing's gonna lock if you don't shut it,' – he glanced up at his front door, I shook my head, '...your jaw, mate.' Then this saliva slipped from the corner of his mouth, he wiped it on the back of his hand and then down the leg of his jeans, messy bleeder. 'Single too long,' me nan would have said.

He introduced himself, and not awkward like any normal geezer would be after making a complete arse of their selves, no, total confidence. He said I must be Mark. Said his name was Robin, *Rob* to his 'friends' and 'close associates', (*Yeah, right*). Then there was another pause, one in which I carried on scooping up crap from outside his flat. One in which he just stood there watching. He said he'd been meaning to put a *'major clean-up'* on the *'agenda'* for one of their house meetings, and had Ron mentioned these to me? I said I thought it looked like more of a 'hands on' situation than a 'needs to be endlessly debated' kind of thing. He sniffed. Puffed his chest out. He looked about forty, tall, snooty. He said he'd been meaning to add it to their list for a *considerable time*. 'Looks like it,' I says. He asked what I meant by that? Sure, *like he was in a position to get arsy!*

I says, 'What I mean is: it looks like it ain't been cleaned up out here in friggin' ages.'

'*Excuse me!* Are you implying then, that the residents here are unhygienic?'

'Implying nothing pal, (*arsehole*), I'm *telling you*, it's a bleedin' dump out here, and it must have been a bleedin' dump for Christ knows how long.'

'I don't think that's for you to say.' *What the fuck was this geezer on?* I says, 'I don't give a monkey's pal. But what I *do* care about is, *living in a shit hole*, 'cos where I come from, we don't.'

He took a step back, 'Well, like I said,' and he cleared his throat now, 'we are planning on addressing the situation.' (*Who sounded like a fucking council worker now?*)

'*Planning on addressing it* are you? Well, I reckon we can go one better than that, eh? How about you plonk that shopping down, roll up your sleeves and give us a hand?' (And appreciate, that whilst all this friendly banter is going on, I'm still up to my elbows in other folks' shite.)

'Well I don't think that's on,' he says, 'what we need to do is… is to get down to some serious planning…'

'Planning!'

'Organise… a rota…'

'Rota my arse mate, just give us an hand, and instead of all this chat, nice though it is to be neighbourly, we'll have it all cleaned up in no time.'

'Well, I'm afraid…'

'Afraid? What you got to be afraid of?' (*'cept a bit of hard work like.*)

'I'm afraid I have to go and make some calls… I've had my car clamped.' He looked towards the far end of the street.

I know I shouldn't but I started to laugh. Nice one, musketeers. Nice one. Then I noticed the three of them sneaking about over the road, drawing attention to their selves, little e-jits. He noticed them too, and asked if I knew them, said they were trouble (*so you could see the connection…*). He prattled on about them a while, called them hoodies, though there wasn't a hood between them, not a scarf even. And then, like he was suddenly and inexplicably aware of his imminent fucking busy-ness, he puffed out his chest again and picked up his fashion hoard.

I noticed Foxy coming out from down the side of the house, Robin had the key in his door by now, but then he noticed him, 'Such a shame they're going to ban hunting those things,' he says. And like an arse I says, 'Didn't know they did it in cities.' He looked around, snide like, and I could tell that if I carried on with such 'derisory' remarks I was definitely not going to make it into the ranks of his '*close associates*'. He said that what he meant was that foxes are a pest wherever they are. I paused a moment, leaning on my broom, then I says, 'I suppose that might be true,' (though not really knowing about these things), 'but some bastards need shooting more than others, eh?'

He went on in, letting the door slam hard behind him.

The lads had scarpered. I finished things up outside. Nice and tidy. Job done. I'd worked up a bit of a sweat but now that I stopped I felt a shiver. I moved my toes about a bit, and made like they were running over a piano keyboard, something which is in fact much easier to do in the open-toed version of my shoes; bastard green socks, the one of them was wet by now. They had *so* got to go. Should go inside. Take a bath.

I wasn't sure why, but I turned around now and looked over my shoulder, and further down the road I saw the old guy, the geezer who'd come knocking at my door earlier on. Large bottle of whiskey in hand. Twenty quids' worth at a rough guess.

I dumped the brushes and stuff inside. Slammed the door. Took a deep breath. I felt whacked. — The fox knew, didn't he? The fox knew that old geezer was gonna trick me. He knew. I'm such a dick. But I guess that's just how it goes.

Take these damn shoes off, throw these fucking socks away.

My feet felt better for being set free awhile. I got undressed, and now the thought of getting cleaned up was, for the time being, erased as I climbed inside a bed instead, one that I could think of as 'my' bed, for now anyways. Wooden floors, a small bedside table, no fuss. Good taste Ron-boy.

White cotton sheets, fresh and cool around my naked, grimy soul. I lay awhile and stared into space, and soon I was thinking back to me dad.

When I'd gone back up there, I noticed how he'd fixed the gate again. I'd said as much. He'd just looked over the top of his paper, and over his glasses at me and half raised an eyebrow, but I wasn't being sarcastic. It just sort of reminded me of when mum had walked out. I was nine when that happened. I'd run down the stairs after her and into the garden. I'd shouted 'cos she hadn't said goodbye, hadn't looked back even, and then she did, she turned right round — I remember her hair, fine and blonde catching her cheek as she turned, '*I never even wanted you!*' she shouted, and then she slammed the gate hard. That was the first time I remember it being broke. Dad fixed it, and so well that you couldn't tell it had been broke at all. I watched her walk away. It seemed to take ages. It seemed like it was happening in slow motion, or maybe that's just how I remember it. And when she was completely out of sight, I remember how final it felt. I remembered thinking that if I rubbed my eyes and looked again she'd still be there, and then I remember it making my eyeballs hurt I stared so hard.

I tried so hard to make her still be there, her hand on the gate, her face when she'd turned back, and her hair in the wind, and then just that final image in the distance, just so long as she was still there.

I didn't cry, she'd taught me not to.

I went back indoors. Dad was sitting in his armchair, sobbing. He had his head in his hands. The armchair was leather, and it was worn and shiny where his arms had rested on it over the years, his tears dripped onto it making dark little patches that grew, the edges blurred. I looked at him, and then as I walked across the room I remember looking at him dead meanly and saying to him, 'Shouldn't cry, Dad. It's not manly.' What a stupid little shit. I even thought that maybe that was why she'd left: 'cos me dad wasn't *manly* (and what the frig does that mean anyway, *now* or *then*: *'manly'?*) but that's what she'd always say to me if she thought she'd spotted a tear, and to be honest I'd felt kinda proud in being able to hold it all back because later on it felt as though she'd let me kinda 'graduate', like from being told not to be a *cry-baby*, which she did 'till I was about six, to being told it *'wasn't manly'* to cry, from then on, up until she fucked off. I think it took me a while to take it on board, but by the time she'd gone I reckon I'd perfected it. I thought as maybe Dad had just never listened to her. I was such a little shit.

I'd always preferred that gate broke, that way it couldn't make that killer slam that sounded forever after like Mum's killer slam. You'd have thought my dad might have asked me why it got bust so often.

I rubbed my feet a bit on the bottom sheet. Wondered if I'd picked the wrong bed, wondered if one of the others would be more comfortable, though I didn't manage to move myself. And then I remembered the lady's book, that *Mrs. Dalloway,* and I started to read.

I read and read, and the more I read the more I couldn't put it down, only I don't reckon it would have had that effect on me if Jim

at all. Breathe, just breathe. I turned around. It was still: Walthamstow Central. Only *it* wasn't wrong, I was. I'd fucked it up, I'd gone fuckin' wrong. Blue lines. Yeah, they were fine, and if you went down one, you got off and changed at Finsbury Park. If you went down the other, the Piccadilly, you had to stay on for Ron's gaff: Finsbury Park... next stop: *Manor House*, Manor House was the stop I wanted, I should've stayed on. Total dick. Where to go? Get back on a train, and this time, *this time*, concentrate, keep my eye on the ball; and now I'd *need* to change – and then I'd finally get my arse home. Christ. This felt so bleedin' complicated, and now I was feeling agitated again, and scared of losing the few bits of information that I had got. Just walk mate, take the train, concentrate on the stops. What a muppet.

As I finally took the 'up' escalator and then climbed the steps at Manor House station I breathed this massive, and I mean *massive,* sigh of relief. The park was on the other side of the road, that felt OK, how it should be, so I could content myself with the knowledge that I had indeed finally taken the right train, and now the right exit. There was now hope that the muppet would prevail.

And then I just walked, striding out. By now I was just desperate to get inside and lie the hell down.

I got a bit further, almost to the corner, and then lo and behold, there was the old geezer again, the one who'd done me out of twenty squid at Ron's front door on account of his tremendous fuckin' thirst, (and how's that? I could remember him alright, but me own sweet name still wouldn't come back to me! — Fuckin' brain man, mashed). Anyways, the old geezer came right up close and *wham*, he was straight into his routine, all distressed, tears in his eyes, shaking like a bastard, and he didn't seem to recognise me at all. I couldn't fucking believe it, he just soddin' stood there, and after some half-blubbed, 'Excuse me Mister', he explains how his daughter's been in this dead bad car accident and how he needs to get to the hospital *tout de suite* like. Man, he freaked me out. And then he rattled on about how his car wouldn't start, and he stands there shaking his keys in his hand just like before, dead, dead distraught. A bleeding Oscar-winning performance if ever you've seen one. You had to hand it to him. Top stuff. Stupid bastard. And he just carried on like we'd never met, like he'd never clapped eyes on me. Said he lived close by, said he'd run out of cash, could I help him out? And I'm looking at him, practically nose to nose like, just waiting for that one moment of recognition, only the bastard's too far gone. Too far fucking gone. And I don't know why I bothered, why I said a single bleedin' word to him, but I did, *'Don't you recognise me?'* I said, *'From the other day? Don't you remember pulling this on me the other day?'* Nothing, he just stood there staring, his eyes empty. *'Don't you remember mate, knocking on me door?'* His arm was still in the air, the keys jangling. But there was nothing, no recognition, not a bit.

I felt wild with rage and crazed, and full of fucking misery, *'It ain't gonna work mate, it's not gonna be enough is it?'* I remember the air felt icy, *'Don't you get it? – Well don't you? You see you're gonna need more than one fucking trick to get through this life mate, more than just the one fucking trick.'* I walked on, my chest pounding; leaving him on the street there in his pissed down kecks; and I just wondered what the hell it was had happened to this old guy; what the fuck had life done to him to make him such a mess, to make him so fucking senseless that he cons people with some sick and stupid story, and that he only has the one?

# CHAPTER TWELVE

## *back to ron's*

# TO BED

I marched away from the old guy, all the while fixed with a rage and filled with some horrible feeling of emptiness, of senselessness, and with no emotion – save for anger. And I felt really fucking angry.

The bag on my back felt too heavy, and I started to wonder just what was in it, and why the hell I was carrying it around, why I hadn't just left it at Ron's; and it wasn't exactly raining, only I so fucking wished it would.

It was already dark by now, the street lights had started up; I glanced over at the park, there were vans inside, it wasn't the police, but I couldn't quite make out what it was, something like a film crew maybe; they'd got the place floodlit. I caught sight of the musketeers cutting through the fence in the distance, crafty little bleeders.

Turned into our street (*mine* for the moment, because I was passing through, *theirs* on account of them sort of ruling the joint), and the place that counted for the moment as home. Amazing, my head had like totally shut down, but somehow... somehow, it had finally worked out where I was staying. Man, I felt well crazy.

Just a few more steps, get indoors, get a fag lit. Calm it all down. I put the key in the lock, I was in a sort of spotlight by the door, the outside lights coming on as I stepped in range. I felt sort of uncomfortable, I looked back over my shoulder, then I heard a voice from above, it was Robin, his head half out the window, 'Mark, Mark!' he shouts. What was this geezer doing? Was he watching for me coming back? That's too weird. I asked what was up. 'Thought I'd better let you know,' he said, 'what with it being by your drain, well, *Ron's* drain, but you know what I mean. Wouldn't want you all blocked up now, would we?'

It was finally starting to rain a bit, the street and house lights catching the raindrops. I really didn't have the energy for this guy's crap. Disinterestedly I says, 'What you on about?'

'It's just that I happened to notice, that your little friend is dead.'

What...? I couldn't be doing with this.

What the frig was he on about? I felt *so* damn angry. I looked down at my feet. Took my hand off the key, leaving it in the door, and now I felt kinda nervous. I heard Robin's window shut and then open again, and the end of his stupid voice trailing off as he repeated how he thought he'd just, *better let me know* 'about the thing by the drain', and then he suggested I *'stick the ruddy vermin in the bin'* (he didn't know how tempting that was, only I thought a full grown man was probably too big). His window shut again. I looked round, and there was something by the drain. In the shadows I could just make it out, the legs, a tail.... And laid that still, it was dead for sure. I stepped closer, raindrops trickling down the back of my neck. I shivered. It was Foxy.

He was just lying there, half in shadow, the light catching the edges of his mangy fur, his little feet, sodden. And then I saw his eyes. Hazel. I couldn't breathe too well. I didn't want to look at him.

Then Robin's friggin' window opened *again,* 'Thought I should also warn you,' he said, 'those young lads I was mentioning... they've been seen climbing over garden walls and so forth, only we don't want a spate of burglaries, so you might want to keep a bit of an eye out, make sure the place is secure, only if they get into Ron's place it'll give them the confidence to try us upstairs.' He made it sound like we were at war. Fuckin' drama queen, and nothing like blasting information to the entire world, and if he was right, if the little devils had been close by they'd have heard him for sure. 'House meeting tomorrow night if you're interested?' he went on, 'I'm making couscous, and we've got a little coke lined up for later.' I didn't answer, only an easylife is dick enough to shout that down the friggin' street, I was half tempted to tell him I wasn't into soft drinks; he must have waited a minute, I didn't say anything, then I heard the window slide shut.

Back inside I dropped the bag. Sat in the dark awhile. Smoked. Smoked some more. I felt cold and clammy.

The fox needed to be buried.

After a bit I opened up the back of the gaff, Ron had everything, and mostly in duplicate if not more, but for once his materialism didn't bother me, three torches, one of them decent, and rooting down the side of the house I also found this load of garden tools, all shiny and bright when I shone the light on them (I was half surprised the musketeers hadn't found 'em and run off with 'em, the stash looked worth a few quid). Found a spade.

One of them black bin bags didn't seem appropriate, in fact it made me feel like a killer, but there wasn't much else around that would do to carry Foxy through to the back, so a bin bag it was.

I lay him down on the grass at the back and started to dig. The rain carried on now, steady, but I didn't really mind. Just digging now, on autopilot.

At one point I heard Robin's voice again, only this time it was overhead at the back of the gaff; he was fast becoming my own personal CCTV, nosey fucker. I didn't bother to listen anymore, I had to cut him out, 'cos if I heard that bastard's voice again too soon, I'd have no choice but to bury the fucker alongside.

My breathing was getting tricky again, shallow, but it shouldn't take too much longer, only the ground was pretty hard. It's alright, we can't all have monuments, but we do all deserve to have what's left of us dealt with properly, and with some sort of respect. Can't just leave a creature, rotting in a drain.

As I dug, my head fixed itself on Jim again, and how I should have been there to do something; how I should have been around. Stayed in touch. Because maybe that way… I'd have seen it coming. Only, is there really, anything to *see*? Are there actual *signs*? There have to be, don't there? There have to be. Only, when someone's far from home like that, far from anyone who knows them *well enough* to see, what's a person's chances? And then I thought about Trudy, because the way things turned out, it meant that at the crucial moments, the only person seeing him, was someone who couldn't *see*, who *cannot see, and, in fact, will never see!* I kept on digging, rain spattering my face, feet slipping in grass and mud.

Kept on going.

I felt sure that Jules knew, deep down, only she'd been shuffled out of position, bullied into a more minor role; and although a part of me still wants to cling to the notion that this was Trudy's fault, it couldn't be, least not entirely, that's far too easy, far too tidy, tidy in the wrong kinda way; and Jim, he'd been let down long before, and maybe in a much bigger way, and maybe in many small ways as well, and maybe that's it, maybe it's 'cumulative'.

I wiped the rain off my forehead and sniffed, drew breath. The rain eased up a bit.

The only thing Jim ever really did that pissed me off, save for dead small stuff, like stubbing my fags out (and that was only on account of him thinking I could sing, and that it'd damage my marvellous friggin' voice, and that maybe someday I would give in and front the *bless-ed* band we dreamed of – only he was wrong, he was the one for that job, he was the front man) so really, the only thing he ever did that truly got my goat, was his moving away, that was all, and like I said, even that wasn't his fault. So how could I blame him? But I did. And not only that, I hated him for it. I totally fucking hated him. In fact, I hated the lot of 'em, his whole bleedin' family. I'd never really thought about any of this before, but Jim's moving away was also Sandra's, Ray's and little Jules' movin', and even though Jules was just a kid, and his dad never said that much, it was like I lost the four of them. Four more losses. If I'm honest, it really hurt. It felt like a stab. And though they said they'd keep in touch, said they'd 'pop over', and how *I* should 'pop over' there, they never did, and I never did, so ultimately their move was it, *the end*, 'til Jules got back in touch. How fucking insane is that, the only time my best friend and me got in touch again was when he was dead.

Their leaving, yeah, it'd hurt like hell, and saying they'd keep in touch, that had soon felt like a lie. It was different with me mum, I knew with her, I knew exactly what her leaving had meant that day; and Dad could lie to himself all he liked, but I knew, and she knew, that last look in her eyes had said it all, there was no way she was ever coming back, and though that hurt, and loads, it was clear, it was definite, and as time went on, it was true. And it didn't take that long really, before I stopped colluding in Dad's protective lies about how maybe she'd show up *this* birthday, or *this* Christmas... I just accepted it, and then of course she died. No arguing with that one.

The hole was pretty much dug, not that neat, but it was hard work in the rain, and I guessed it would just about do.

We weren't allowed, weren't 'invited' to Mum's funeral. I was surprised that Dad hadn't kicked up a fuss, *at least about that,* and put up a fight, I mean, I know that isn't his way, not normally, but over something like a funeral, *her* funeral, I thought he'd have given it all he had. Truth is, I don't think he ever came to terms with her being ill, let alone passing away, and it was easier for him to kid himself along, to keep the story at the part where she'd just walked out, the place he could still just about deal with it, because if he just replayed it up to that point, then the next part, the *how it all turns out* was still left open, and he could just sit in that chair of his, and pretend to himself, imagine her walking right back in, maybe throwing another screaming fit, even giving him a slap, but things would soon be back to normal, *our normal,* and Dad, he'd be glad. Lies. Just a rotten bunch of lies, Dad.

When I thought back to Sandra and Jim and that, moving away, I knew they hadn't really lied to me, of course they hadn't, it's just what happens, it's that 'moving away' phenomenon, which leads, naturally or not, to the 'not keeping in touch' phenomenon, of which I am possibly and probably more guilty than most. And it fucking stinks, because, for every time I've thought about Jim since his death, and since I heard how he never had a better mate than me, the truth is, I realise now, I never had a better mate than him. And I'm not just being sentimental, because think about it, it's no fuckin' coincidence that I happen to be staying with some easylife-asshole instead of a proper mate. Proper mates, they're harder to come by; assholes – they're everywhere. Yeah, so *the truth is,* we were true mates, and now that he's died, a bit of me's died too; like a bit of Sandra and Ray and Jules has died an' all; because that's what happens when someone you love passes away. While they're alive they carry part of each of you around with them, and when they pass away they take that with them, and all you're left with is a hollow, an empty bit, like someone just cut a part of you away. It's a double loss, they're gone, and some of you's gone with them.

I suppose it's pride, the reason you don't get back in touch, yeah, pride, fears, worries: *they'll have moved on, they'll be dead successful now, too busy, too much in love; too 'otherwise occupied or engaged'; too changed, too into things I'm not, too full of opinions that'll clash with mine;* and anyways, *I might hate the geezer these days, he might really piss me off!* But who am I kidding? I never had any of those thoughts really, I simply forgot, I was simply too distracted by my own petty little existence, too much of a prize bleedin' wanker to get back in touch – and it's not as though I think I could have made a difference, I'm not trying to say anything as fucking wild or lame as that – no, I just have to accept that I don't know if I could have made any difference to *his* life (though by Christ I wish I'd tried) but I know for certain that staying in touch would have made a whole lot of difference to mine.

Finished.

I stood a moment. He was buried. I looked up at the moon. I was drenched, only a few moments more and then I'd go back in, get warmed up, except I just couldn't move. I was glued to the spot, and I felt dead cold, despite having just dug like a bastard.

I carried on looking up at the night sky, stars and moon.

I missed my ole mate.

I missed him.

*So, fuck you, Jim Jakes! Fuck you!*

I dropped the spade.

Back inside, I took off my things, sat on the chair by the bed in the dark, just shadows around made by flickers of the street lights slotted through the window; I leant my arms on the table. I couldn't smoke. I had cigarettes, for sure, but I couldn't smoke. Couldn't smoke, couldn't think. I put my head in my hands. Shivery.

I guess I've never got as far down as our Jim, otherwise there's a fair chance we might both have found ourselves stood at a window on a twentieth floor. But to be honest, at times, I've got close, only now it was all far more complicated, 'cos now that I'd seen what it did to everyone, it made the window option impossible, just like it had done with the bridge, and how it probably would with a rope, a blade, or a rail track, or any other friggin' means.

*Fuck you*, Jim.

But I did still wonder, whether some days Jim and I hadn't shared the very same thoughts, perhaps even at the very same time, and maybe even on that very same day, and without realising I started to picture it, the two of us, as though side by side, preparing to jump, in separate cities, living separate lives, but the same dismal little lives, furnished with the same kind of soulless equipment: the computer screens and vending machines, the phones and the faxes, the strip lighting that throws all the wretchedness into relief; and now I could see his hand on the window frame, large and white, his knuckles bare, and then my own; and the window, murky, and the view outside, but not taking it in, not seeing a thing, and together, side by side, we moved, taking that slow but sure step forward, our hands on the window, the glass moving outwards, cold air rushing in, wind and splashes of rain on our faces, and the sheer emptiness of everything, of stomach, of heart, and mind, and nothing, nothing at all, not one single thought but that pure sensation of ice-cold rain on warm flesh cheeks, and the pain of sunlight as it cuts through your eyes that one last time, a gulp of air, my stomach leapt.

And just for a moment we were weightless, and simultaneous – we'd jumped – and just as the thought stopped, I noticed my hand raised as though still touching the glass – but there wasn't any air now, and no rain, just tears, great gigantic tears, and they came, not bit by bit, and not how I thought, but like some bloated, fast flowing stream, its banks fighting to hold. And like blood flowing from wounds cut too deep, too long, the tears pushed out, from me eyes, and me nose, me mouth, as though there was so much grief inside, it could have been saving itself up for years. And maybe it had. I was sat at that bedside table, my legs like jelly. My face, wet like putty, snot and tears dripping from my nose like a bastard; my mouth dribbling, lips quivering. My hands were shaking; my shoulders and neck locked tight, my head was pounding, and now this thick pool of tears pushed its way further to the edges of the table, and I moved my hands as though I thought I might catch them just as they fell, and what for? What would I do with them? And they dry up, it doesn't matter where they fall, they just dry up, they're gone, and no one knows, and it's only ever the inside of you that knows they were ever there at all. — I thought about Mum. It's true, practically the only thing she ever taught me, was not to cry. — And then, without knowing how I'd moved there, I found myself laid on the floor, my head in my hands, my knees bent up close to my chest, and I wept, I wept so much, and not like a baby, because babies, they don't weep, they cry, they cry and cry, they *only* cry; weeping, I discovered, that's bigger, and that comes later, that's a truck load of crying.

For Jim, staying here, staying alive any longer, had stopped being an option, and I don't know how, but for me that real day hadn't arrived, only right now I wasn't sure who was best off, and until I lost Jim, I realised I had never really cried. Never cried at all, and now I didn't know how it worked, what to do, and for the first time ever, I couldn't make it stop. I lay there, and clung to myself. Pathetic, gibbering, and so alone I thought I might die.

I stayed like that two days.

# CHAPTER THIRTEEN

## *to the rescue*

## MIKE, JOE & BONO

There was a knock at the door, then a banging. Then voices. Mike, Joe and Bono. *'Bono'*, I sort of smiled to myself – that lad's mum and dad, I guess they had some ambition for the kid.

'You in there Mister?' Top kid that Mike, made me laugh, he could sound dead polite, 'I says, *are you in there?*' – well, sometimes.

It was hard to stand up, friggin' rigor mortis, man, I hurt all over. They banged on the door hard enough now to knock the fucker in, *'Mate, are you in there?'*

'Alright, alright,' I found myself croaking like some right ole wrinkly. I realised I'd taken my gear off, and it all lay in a sort of dry muddy pile by the bed. My shoes caked in mud and grass looked like some friggin' sculpture, they might win me the Turner prize, but I'd like to meet the sod that reckoned he could get those dried-up bastards on his feet. I felt hot, central heating, I hadn't sorted the timer, and Ron was one of those energy-saving dudes, the kind that likes leaving things on and saving the energy it takes to switch some of the bastards off or put them on a timer, lazy bastard – pure polar bear fodder, our Ron. So I grabbed what can only be described as a *Guest Towel* (and get this, it actually had those very words embossed on the edge, in fancy writing too. There's no fathoming some people, not the people who dream up those daft fuckin' ideas, nor them that buys 'em). Tried to wrap it round my hips, only it was too damn small. I could hear Mike chattering to his self outside the door, the other two must have given up, and by the time I opened it Bono and Joe seemed to have scarpered. I said, 'What you gobbing on about Mike?'

'Nuffin',' he looked a bit pink. I reckoned that at times, that gob of his ran on faster even than that clever little brain of his. I scratched my head, squinting at the light, 'So, what d'you want?'

'Nuffin' really, we was just checkin'…'

'Checking what? If there was anyone in?' Suspicious to the last, and like a total ole bastard I asks, 'You guys been casing the joint?' I put my hand to my face, stubble, I scratched about, and I was so faint I didn't know if what I was saying was serious or not, I didn't really know if I cared if they were on the rob or not, and frankly after bumping into that ole whiskey sluggin' liar on the street again, it was easiest just to think the worst. Mike had a look of worry about him, 'Well, we *were* sort of watchin',' he says, stepping back, 'Bono says he saw you two nights ago, after you was talking to that bloke.'

'What bloke?'

'That old man, we seen you talking to him, only Bono reckoned you were angry, init,' he looked more nervous now, 'That bloke's a bum, init, but I don't think he means no harm, mate.'

I coughed, partly amused 'cos Mike's lines made me feel like I'd opened the door onto some friggin' BBC Dickens adaptation. My head was well bent out of shape. I meant to nod, friendly like, I don't know if I did, 'Anyway Mike, what you after?'

'Just…'

'Spit it out,' I said, surprising myself and feeling as though I was now coming over like one of them mean ole twats in *Bleak House* or that *Great Expectations*.

'Bono said you looked sick init, he thought as maybe you needed to eat or somethin'; and ain't you got more clothes?'

I shivered now what with the door open. Clothes. 'And *shoes* mate, you been walking round in well bad shoes,' and breathless he adds, 'what size is your feet?'

'…?'

'About a ten, init?'

'Eleven.'

''leven, right.' Then sort of measuring his breathing he asks me for a tenner. I was tempted to ask what he wanted it for, but since honesty didn't seem too much the local currency I figured that was probably a waste of time. 'If I give you a tenner... if you get me a jar of coffee out of it, the three of yous can split the rest, how's about that?'

'Deal.'

I wasn't at all sure I'd done the right thing, but I couldn't get my head much further right now. I went back in and fumbled through my jacket pocket, nothin', and then through me muddy kecks, me lucky 56p was still there in the one, fifteen squid and change in the other. And like a dope I didn't pause to wonder what had happened to the rest of me cash, though I should have done, I'd whacked four hundred out on that first day.

I give Mike the note and the little creep practically snatched it out of my hand, shouting, cocky as you like, '*And Bono says you wanna get a wash, man, you smell well nasty, init,*' and with that he ran. Guess he ran in case I was offended, and I guess I might have been, except that he was right, him and Bono, I truly didn't smell too good.

I looked down at my gut, scrawny as that dead fox practically, and then I sniffed again, *Jesus*, I didn't smell, I *reeked*, totally reeked. I had in fact become my own personal pollution, but the thing was, the hunger thing needed tending to first. Priorities. If I fed me brain, maybe it'd start being halfway useful again, maybe I'd stop opening the friggin' front door and giving cash away to every bleeder that knocked on it. So, 'food' it was.

I found this poncy dressing gown thing, I figured I had to borrow something, my gear was mashed, and if I was gonna cook, I sure as hell didn't wanna burn me bollocks off.

I went to see what that flash kitchen could offer up, and after a good root around I found some rice crackers, and... well, not much else frankly. And no disrespect, but you can hardly keep a man alive on bleedin' rice crackers, *or can you?* (And whose idea were they anyway? Total bleedin' cardboard, man. I mean it's alright if you're like stranded somewhere, as survival food, but shite, this was friggin' Jamie-Oliver-cookbook land, and so far, not a soddin' *ingredient* in sight.) I opened up the fridge again and tugged at the drawers inside. Nope... no. And, no. But what's in this one then? Eggs. Eggs! *Beautiful*; and so, for the time being, the *Can you keep a man alive on rice crackers?* conundrum, would just have to be put on hold (*imagine my disappointment*), only I felt an omelette coming on. Bit of salt and pepper, *lovely jubbly*, as they say down here, and we were in business.

An unfed stomach can be a stomach that aches when it finally is fed. You'd think a stomach would be more grateful than to play úp at a time like this, but anyways, it had to be done, I had to eat. *Well* bad gut ache, but one damn delicious omelette, if I do say so myself.

I started to run a bath.

I distantly remembered that I should have spare boxers with me, but on the clothes front, other than me undies, things were looking a bit tricky. I noticed that Ron-chops had one of those easylife, washer-dryers, only I didn't feel too cosy about the 'dryer' settings, don't them bastards burst into flame, like? (I'm so fuckin' paranoid about that shite, best keep things easy). I could wash my gear in it, and then I'd just have to wait for it to dry on the radiators the way normal folk do. So I whacked my muddy gear in the machine along with the sheets off my bed (man, the whole lot reeked), and *rock n' roll*, we were off. My whole wee life, spinning round and round.

Time to splat some music on. Then I remembered, Ron-boy, and his collection from the Wrong Side, which I'm fairly confident is way south of the 'Dark Side'. Can't be done. Can't listen to shite, not for love nor money. Bollocks. He had some decent classical stuff, I give him that much, but that wasn't what was called for just at the moment. — I felt suddenly inclined to have a check through my rucksack, see where I was up to, and what exactly it was I had in there. And now, now it finally occurred to me, like on a more conscious level, that on my journey down to the Big Smoke, there was no way that bag was either that full or that heavy. You wonder what goes on with a head sometimes, that low battery setting, it's like that only allows for the most minor cognitive functions, and what's scary about it is just how kinda unconscious you are, of *so very much*. A bit anxious, like, I unzipped it. CDs. *CDs!* At a rough tally, some four hundred squid's worth bar the fags, booze and other minor expenses I had otherwise incurred. Only, had I actually paid for this stash? I had no memory of going anywhere near a music gaff, or of choosing the stuff out; I flicked through 'em. It would seem that on autopilot I'd picked out a load of stuff that might just about lift Ron's music collection into the light (I know that sounds pretentious, and so what? It needed to be done). And my editing wasn't the whole picture by any means, but at least it was a start. The thing was though, I had no memory of any of this. I tried to think back and figure out just how and when I might have got hold of these CDs (and whether I'd paid for them or not). The only memory I had that might be of any use was the absolute faintest sense of the bag feeling heavier when I last got off the tube; so, was that the day I'd seen Ellen MacArthur? The day I'd been stood on the bridge? I couldn't be sure.

My other few possessions were mostly scrunched up at the bottom. I had to flatten out CA's book, yeah... *again*. Clumsy sod.

And now, since I couldn't remember being in any sort of shopping frenzy (always fuckin' hated shopping), I didn't know if I hadn't just robbed this whole lot, and for all I knew I'd given even more cash away at my front door than I thought! I shrugged. Robbing wasn't my thing – or maybe it was.

I looked through my things and found my spare boxers, and even a spare pair of socks — brown, I was more efficient than I give meself credit. Turned the bath off. It was steamin'. Nice one. I slotted the new CDs in the stacks and whacked on some sounds to accompany my *ablutions* (how the frig I know a word like that *Christ* only knows, I like the sound of it though). I pressed play. No more wrong music Ron. '*Things could only get better*' – on second thoughts, let's not use that line, the last thing I needed stuck in my head right now was any politician's so-called glory song. *New Labour* – what a load of arse! — Let's just say, that with a touch of the right sounds, things were on the up. I felt myself grinning like a bastard, and then I felt something under my foot, something stuck to it, it felt well grubby, peeled it off. A receipt, for a stonking load of CDs! What did I tell you? Oh, yes, call me smug, in fact call me *well* smug; fuck I needed a drink.

Kids hadn't got back with any coffee, guess I could kiss goodbye to that idea; no worries, Ron had some top brandy stashed, *well* old, *well* tasty, a shot of that while a man has a bath, and there's no complaining. There was plenty of whiskey too, but that'd keep for later. Nice one.

As I lay there in the water, Ron's rubber duck for company, it suddenly struck me that Ron's plans to *find himself* might not be as far off the mark as I'd first thought – *oh cynical moi* – because although I was convinced he'd return from his travels completely unchanged, in fact just as big an arsehole as when he left, *whilst he had been gone* I had somehow, inadvertently like, been turning his world back here totally upside down. So far, I had righted the wrongs of his sounds, re-landscaped the fucker's garden, cleaned up the shit-hole of a place out front; and, I was arguably working absolute fucking wonders with his neighbours! Can't change the man, *can* change his world – or so it seemed. This called for a smoke. A rubber-ducky ashtray, that's what I'd be needing from Santa next time he was doing the rounds; all *Ron's* rubber duck could do was grin. I grabbed a fag, lit up and re-submerged.

Now, this is an image an artist might find worth capturing, the look of a well contented man. Shit, I hadn't washed, nor shaved, never mind bleedin' showered or had a proper bath, not in days. It felt great. Reminded me of being a kid. We had a bath once a week back then. That was plenty. And I felt so much more clean right now for having being so friggin' dirty. It was nigh on a religious experience (if you was to go for that kinda thing). I ran my hand over a well stubbly chin, something had to be done, or did it? Maybes I'd leave it be a while, wasn't too itchy or anything. Stuck my head under the water, wow, *wow*, that was great. So nice to feel clean again – happy with the easy stuff. I thought of CA – and I almost panicked, *where had I left his book?* But then I remembered seeing it on the bed, I'd laid it by the *Dalloway*, all safe.

Must have laid in that bath upwards of an hour. The water was well grimy. I could hear the lads banging at the door. Least I thought it was them. I showered off the last of my grime dead quick now (bath *and* a shower, how friggin' indulgent can a man be?).

Guest-towelled dry, and robed in Ron-chops' dressing gown (I dare say the bleeder had a whole collection of those somewheres, you know like, *in a range of colours*). I opened the door, happily stunned that they came back at all, and not only had they come back, but the little sods were indeed bearing coffee. Wonders will never fuckin' cease, I tell you. It bent my head, only little did I know, that that was only half the surprise. The little geezers stood there grinning. Mike held onto the coffee; boss man, Bono, did the talking; and smiler Joe stood third in line behind.

'Got your coffee mate,' says Bono, poking Mike in the ribs as the signal to pass it over; Joe giggled.

'Cheers,' I says, about to add something else, but I can't think what, and before the thought had formed, Bono cut back in, 'And actually, we got something else, init.' Joe shuffled about a bit and it seemed he was holding something, using Bono's back for cover. Mike looked round at him, grinning like hell, and Joe nudged Bono like he was giving him the final edge of courage to say the rest. Bono stood to one side now and pulled Mike out the way, 'The thing is, we got you shoes, init,' Joe took a half step forward and held up a pair of slightly worn looking, smart brown shoes; he held them up as though he was holding a big royal cushion with a crown on it, dead proud; his grin, it was the widest. The three of them blushed, '*They ain't new though,*' Mike shot in, 'But they looks alright, init,' Joe piped up, shuffling about a bit. Me, I was speechless, touched like. 'They was like seven quid, at a Oxfam shop,' Mike added, 'and they's like a size bigger than you wears, but better than nothin' init?' Bono pulled himself up, he now seemed to be gathering great confidence in this whole thing, and whoever's idea it was, it seemed to be working out rather tidily. Nice one. Bono carried on, basking now in their rightful glory, 'So,' he says, 'it was me and Mike's idea, 'cos you was walking round in them others what looked well bad, init,' Joe scowled at him, I guess for not getting a name-check; Bono shot him a look, a sort of: *wait your turn,* type thing, and then he carried on, 'And they ain't new, like we says, but they're better than them others, init?' And now that Bono was sure of his self, he totally held on to the reins like, keeping full command, 'The thing is, Joe had seen you... with the fox, init; said you picked the fox up even though it was dead.' Joe nodded furiously now. Top geezer. But it was Bono who kept up the talking, 'And later on, he was watching round the back, through the fence,' Joe looked down now, a bit embarrassed, but then he butt in, all urgent, '*An' I seen you, I seen you before that, when you looked like you was talking to him out the window and you put that food out for him,'* he grabbed some breath, *'and then I seen you bury him, init. In the garden.'*

I felt a sort of knot in my throat. I felt a bit weird about the burying, a bit awkward.

I looked at the shoes, amazed. Surprises, they've never been much my thing. Not much my experience to tell the truth. But this one was a winner. Guess some kids still have 'hearts of gold' (as Nan would say), and no matter how much us big 'uns try and mess with their heads, some of them come through alright (I thought of Jim's mum, and how kind she'd always been like... and me not even realising). *Man,* I felt well sentimental. But I guess that's alright.

I remembered the cricket gear they'd nabbed, and I wanted to ask if they'd taken it back. But I guess you have to let some things go. And like I said, what was I anyway – some frigging scout leader?

# CHAPTER FOURTEEN

## *just wait awhile*

## STREETS AHEAD

I felt bad when the lads had gone, I was so friggin' touched, it totally knocked me out, and I don't remember if I even said *thanks!* And to think, they could have bought half a gram of coke with that tenner, and to tell the truth, that's exactly what had shot through my tiny little mind; it would have cost three times that when I was their age (though it wasn't in your face like it is now, so it was a tad easier to avoid). — I put me socks on and slipped me feet into me new shoes; the lads were right, just a bit on the big side, but laced up tight, they'd do well enough. Sorted. I looked at my old ones sort of mournfully, me and them had been through a lot. Couldn't readily chuck my little pals away; I settled to placing them on the window sill, because, like I said, they were practically a work of friggin' art. I thought they looked a bit like them Van Gogh painted. I'd never really understood why someone would choose to paint a picture of their shoes, but now I did. Now I totally did. I lit up and then I slept, naked but for me socks and me top new shoes.

I slept so much those few days I might as well have been doing it for England, could even have been sponsored like. The thing was, I couldn't manage too much right now. Things needed to settle themselves down a bit, sort themselves in my mind.

It was like I had to wait until the streets were ahead of me. Lately, the streets I'd walked down were all in the past and they'd been scrolling their selves either backwards or down, 'forwards' still seemed way beyond me. And there was still no figuring what I'd do long-term – my old job, my old life and that whole shebang. But it wasn't the time yet for deciding. I still needed to live plot-free for a while. I lit up, and lay back against the pillows, smoke curling itself up and round, yeah, I'd wait until the streets were ahead of me.

I looked over the postcards, some a bit bent by now. Still no idea why I'd bought such a bleedin' hoard, but there we go, and I don't even remember writing 'em, only there they were, a total stack and all in my own sweet spidery hand. I went and piled them up in the next room along with CA's book. And now, despite the fact that I really didn't wanna go outside, I also had cabin fever – *how crazy is that? Feeling simultaneously claustrophobic and agoraphobic! What was I planning on doing, spending the rest of my days in friggin' doorways?* Sort yourself out matey. Well, that's easy said, but the fact was, there was no food left at all, so at the very least I had to make it as far as the corner shop.

My gear was dry by now, so me and my new brown shoes trundled off.

As I stepped outside I came face to face with Robin bleedin' Hood again from upstairs: a man of uncompromising integrity, protector of common decency, leader of the right and fuckin' true. *First class wanker more like.* He pointed out that I'd missed the 'house meeting', I said I figured that he and his band of merry men and women probably had things covered well enough, and added, out of interest like, that democracy really wasn't much my thing (especially not when it means a bunch of geezers sat round a table *dis-cuss-in* instead of just getting up and getting the bloody job done). We did agree however, that now that the bin area had been given a 'thorough' clean (so nice to feel appreciated, *arsehole*), that it would now take roughly thirty minutes to clean it out once a week. He tells me there'd been eight of them at the meeting, and that they'd talked about 'this matter' for three hours – so between them that amounted to twenty-four hours of *chat* about cleaning up, which at thirty minutes a pop would have translated into forty-eight sessions of actual clean up, which is roughly (and mind, I ain't no *mathema-fuckin-tician),* an *entire year's worth* of clean up. And get this, the guy looked well pleased with himself, 'So, Robin,' I says, 'you managed to use up a year's worth of clean-up time in talking about it, well fuckin' done.'

He went on to explain how I didn't understand the finer details, the *granularity*, (fuck off!); he said they'd drawn up a schedule, and that this was rather complex, so that they could rotate it, and all 'take turns'. Only what the fucker didn't seem to understand is that people who won't do the right thing when it's right smack in front of them are the same people who ignore schedules. Though in all fairness how could I expect him to understand, he was after all, the worst offender. 'Great,' I said, 'so, nothing's changed.' I think he must have continued gobbing on about something or other, but I walked on, – streets enough at least to see me out of earshot, and hopefully as far as my favourite corner shop.

I could be wrong, but I felt like I was met by a smile as I entered the shop. The Turkish geezer was stood there happy enough in a cloud of his favourite smoke, the others cheery, and chatting away, and it was like stepping into another little world, a sort of capsule to somewhere else. My Turkish Tardis. Trays of sweet cakes laid out all dead pretty on the counter; Turkish delight was the only one I recognised, I'm not much for sweet stuff or I'd have tried some of the other things, but there we go.

Back on autopilot, I now found that *survival-mode-Mark* had soon picked up all the 'essentials'; man, I was well loaded down. The guy behind the counter turned to pick up 40 fags from the wall behind him – 'telepathy', love it, and I dropped my haul by the till.

I fumbled now, running my hands through my pockets, only all I had was that last fiver and a load of shrapnel, and then it dawned on me, and I could feel myself shaking a bit, I'd forgot, forgot I was totally cleaned out apart from that small stuff. And I had no cards on me either (fuck knows where I'd put them!). The geezer was bagging up my stuff; I couldn't get the words out, but it was like he must have realised, 'It's alright,' he said, totally reading me, 'you pay me next time,' and then he grinned wide, 'besides,' he chuckled, 'I know where you live,' and then he had this massive laugh, dead pleased with himself and totally at ease, like, with everything.

*I know where you live* – maybe they say that in Turkey too. Nice one. And how unusual is that? I've never had anything on tick in me life, but I'm well used to seeing signs up practically warning you not to ask for credit. Top geezer. I took the stuff, but I felt dead embarrassed about the money. I said something to him about me being 'out of sorts' but that I would get the cash to him as quick as I could; he shrugged and said he could wait a few days, and then he added, 'And no worries, I won't charge you interest,' and then he laughed again, and the sound was rich and round. And I seemed suddenly to be swimming in a thick broth of human kindness. Outside it had started to rain, fucking gorgeous! Sometimes, it really is, *rain* — it's absolutely, fuckin' gorgeous!

# CHAPTER FIFTEEN

## *rest*

## SWITCH IT ALL OFF

I got back and made some coffee. I started to think that maybe it was time to call people, let them know I was alright, like. I could ring Doris, call work, me dad maybe, only he wouldn't know that I hadn't gone back home anyways. I dare say he wasn't expecting to hear from me till Christmas, although I realised by now that he'd hope I'd come home sooner, and I didn't want it to be like that anymore. I'd get back to him before then; but the thing was, right now he wouldn't be one of the ones who'd notice that I wasn't where I should be. 'Where I should be', even those friggin' words made me shiver. And like I said, Doris wouldn't specially miss us, in fact she probably wouldn't notice my going AWOL till work rang up. I thought back to the office, the faces, the lighting. I shivered again. '*Nah*', I just can't. It's just not that simple. You see, you finally *walk*, and then you have to keep going, just walk and walk, with nothing in your head, and it just has to be like that. It has to be, or something would creep back into your head, *doubt, guilt*, some shite or other and you'd be back. Right back in it. That hollow old life with nothing but nothin' to anchor you.

I started thinking about Jim again, and then about that novel, the *Dalloway*, 'cos there was something else about that Septimus character that had really touched me. I picked the book back up again, it was something about his suffering. It's the part where this doctor geezer advises that he should take some time out... time out from his family, from his whole life really, and he says this thing about how, '*the people we care for most'* aren't really very good for us when we're ill like that. I wondered about that, and it made me think about Jules again, and how she'd felt she saw things too late, or how maybe she'd not seen things well enough, not realised, and not done anything; and then I thought about Trudy again (who I suppose also felt like she loved him), how she'd made herself *self-appointed No 1 top person for dealing with the whole fucking thing*, and how ultimately she was possibly the worst one for the job. Anyway, the doctor in the *Dalloway*, he'd suggested that what Septimus really needed in order to recover was to lie down and rest a while in a beautiful house in the country – found the page again, yeah, here we go: he said he should go to a beautiful house in the country, where he could *'rest in bed; rest in solitude'*; and where he could experience *'silence and rest; rest without friends, without books, without messages; six months' rest; until a man who went in weighing seven stone comes out weighing twelve.'* I put the book down. It felt like a bleedin' revelation, enlightenment even, only I don't hold with big ole words like that too much. But that bit in the book, it just sounded like common sense. The thing is though, you can't always know when someone needs pulling out of their life, you can't always *see*, you can't always catch it, that exact moment just before they go and take themselves out and then move themselves out of the picture for good. And there's no way of knowing – not really – if *six months rest*, proper rest, away from all the folks who care so much and mean so well… *you just can't know* if that would work, or if that would be enough. I looked over the page again and what it said about rest 'without messages' that's what it said, you needed 'rest without messages' – I checked and the book was set in 1923 – and I figured it was weird that it could somehow 'resonate' so much right now, and perhaps with even more meaning than it would have had at the time, and it reminded me of my own little habit of not texting, and keeping my mobile switched off, keeping the 'contact gadgets' at bay for a bit, frankly, they make me anxious. All that fucking bleeping. Then I wondered how they would have sent messages in the 1920s, and it occurred to me that if the messaging they had then – nothing compared to what we have now like, just letters mainly I suppose – if *that* was considered stressful, then what the hell are we all doing being permanently suckled and stifled and shafted by all this constant, endless fucking messaging shite? It could now involve a serious amount of effort to get away from all of that. All I do is go for a train ride without all that shite, my phone switched off; but imagine, imagine *six months* without it, without any of it! No email, no texts, no fucking phones, man! I went into the hallway and disconnected Ron's landline. Lovely.

For the briefest moment I thought about my mobile, and my chest got all tight, but then I breathed again. Right now I didn't even know where it was, and I couldn't give a shite. I put some sounds on, lay on the floor, wiggled my toes in my new, well top, brown leather shoes, lit up. Fuckin' bliss.

# CHAPTER SIXTEEN

*beware the front door*

## MEETING KAZU

The next morning I stepped out the front door not thinking too much, and with no real plans, just checking out the street situation but without too much commitment. I ought to find a cash machine, pay the geezer back at the corner shop, but he had said it'd wait a day or two, and I figured it was probably OK to take him at his word. In any case I couldn't really face going anywheres just yet, and not on the tube for deffo.

The air seemed vaguely fresh outside, the sky a fairly decent sort of blue. I stood and breathed it all in, easy like, then I took out my fags and leant against the wall like someone with nowhere to go, only that was my big mistake 'cos when you do that someone always gets you. And it wasn't as if I hadn't had a significant number of front door episodes already, so I should have known better; and yet despite knowing this full well, it's like with other stuff, I still have this weird tendency to do the same fucking thing over and over no matter how much shite it gets me into. Sometimes I just never fuckin' learn. Besides, wherever I am, I do just like to step outside the front door, stop, take a breath and take out me fags; you see it's a sort of ritual, a nice, ordinary, everyday type thing, taking it easy, enjoying the moment, first whiff of fresh air, first or second morning fag. — Well, OK, that last bit's a lie, it's usually the third, anyways I shouldn't do it 'cos some bleeder always stops me and shakes up my day. Anyways, I was standing there lighting up when this little geezer comes past, Oriental lookin', nothing too striking, nothing much to notice about him at all, 'cept he seemed particularly short, – but then next to me he would 'cos I'm particularly tall, six-foot-three at any rate. So there I am, lit up and for the moment content, when the little geezer does a u-turn.

'Excuse me,' he says all sort of trembly, his accent, a bit on the American side, 'I… I am a student,' and he points at this little card, holding it up as sort of proof like, it's a student ID card hanging by some grubby bit of string round his neck, 'I am at UCL.'

'Oh yeah,' I says casually, 'heard of that: University College London.' He stays in front of me, not speaking but still trembling, mostly looking down at his feet now, settling his weight first on one foot and then the other; and then, everything fell quiet, a bit too quiet, odd like, so I opened my big gob again, 'You alright?' I asked all casual. And the thing is, if you don't ask the fuckers, I'm pretty sure they wouldn't volunteer the information, so the trick would be to stay schtum, only it's rather like the standing there and the pausing that I shouldn't do either – I just never learn. So, I've asked, and now of course he answers, 'I am looking for someone,' he says – on the face of it, an innocent enough opener.

'Any particular someone?' I says, like an arsehole, when of course I should just say, 'Oh right, well, good luck, cheerio,' and walk away. Just walk away.

'I am looking for someone,' he starts again, and now it's like he's in a bit of bother like with his breathing a bit and getting his thoughts together, and not serious like, more just kinda awkward. I figure maybe he's lost, so I just wait while he gets his breath. Then after a mo I prompt him a bit, 'You says you were looking for someone…?'

'Yes,' he says, and he looks up and into the distance and then down at the pavement again, and then at some empty middle distance, like not focusing on anything, 'someone who will kill me.'

You see what happens.

Should have just walked away when I had the chance. I exhaled, chewed my lip; and then I tried to meet his eyes, as though I might be able to see what was going on with him, but he just kept staring into that empty kinda middle space, that place where your gaze doesn't fix on anything, but just sort of hangs. 'I want,' he says, and then dead quiet like and slow, 'I want to die.' He stopped trembling now

and just stood still, completely still like, not a flicker; his face, white
as hell, 'And I need,' he says, 'I need someone to help me, someone
who will kill me.'

I took a very long last drag on my ciggie. Dead awkward now, I
looked down at me shoes, wriggling my toes inside, gently tapping
the sole of the one shoe on the pavement… see what it sounded like.
I took out my ciggies, lit up again, offered him one – *well I didn't know
what the fuck to do, or even if I'd heard him right*. I even give my head a
shake, check me ears weren't playing up. (It was almost as though I
thought that if I didn't want him to be saying that kinda stuff, I could
somehow erase it. Like me dad would do.) The geezer, he didn't say
anything now, didn't take a cigarette either. I bit the inside of my
mouth.

'Non-smoker?' I says. He didn't answer. I tried a sort of smile, but
I should have left that out. He looked at me blank. Still stood stock
still like. Still dead pale. My jacket wasn't done up, I had my shirt on
underneath like, but he seemed to be looking up at my chest, staring,
as though he was looking through me or trying to read something
on it, but the shirt's blank, it's just plain, no logo even, only now he
had me worried, 'cos maybe I'd spilt food down it or something, like
some dosey arse, so I looked down to make sure. Then he asked me,
in tones too gentle, and standing there, still as a post, his head slightly
tilted, 'Do you know anyone, sir? Someone who could do it? Someone
who would kill me… someone who would help me to die?' And that
was it wasn't it? Now there was no pretending he wasn't saying what
he was saying, and it was bending my head. *Nine-thirty in the sodding
morning*, hadn't even had a coffee yet and there I was stuck with a
total doughnut who wanted me to help find someone to take him
out. Fucked. Totally fucked. I couldn't be doin' with this. I figured
I'd finish this next fag and move on. Yeah, move on. Walk away like
I should have done at the start. 'Didn't you hear me?' he carried on, *'I
said, that I need someone,'* and for the briefest moment now he held out
his hands, *'anyone*, who will….' his words trailed off, it didn't much
matter, I didn't need to hear them again, I'd got the message, loud and
clear by now. I just couldn't fucking deal with it, was all.

Then he looked up right at me, right in the eyes, and piercing like, he asks, 'Will you do it? Will you kill me?' I looked away, or tried to, and I can't remember whether it was to the left or the right, and it doesn't really matter, but I just half hoped to see someone coming down the street, because maybe they'd be able to help sort this out, settle the guy down a bit, 'cos it was pretty fuckin' clear I wasn't up to the job.

I wondered where the musketeers were, not like they'd really be able to help, but it was all just so totally weird that I felt like I actually just needed someone else, *anyone*, just to confirm how mad this really was, and prove that he really was standing there in front of me saying all this stuff. Right now I would even have settled for the company of ole Robin chops from upstairs, useless as he is. But I hoped, more than anything, that when I looked back to where this little geezer was stood, that he simply wouldn't fuckin' be there, as though all he'd have been was just some soft-headed figment of my mashed imagination.

No joy.

There was no one around.

And when I looked back, the little guy was still there. Still there, and shaking some. 'I really *really* want to die sir, and I want to die today, and as soon as… possible,' he almost gagged on the last word, saliva gathering like foam at the edges of his mouth. I said, 'Listen mate, settle down…'

'SETTLE DOWN!' he screamed; his face went beetroot. — And then, *shite* he made me jump. — '*SETTLE DOWN? You say to me: SETTLE DOWN!*'

I was fucking this up, I knew I would, but there wasn't anyone else around, and to be honest it was all a bit surreal, too fuckin' surreal, 'I mean, just steady yourself there mate… take a deep breath…'

'A *deep breath!*'

'Well… yeah,' isn't that what they tell you to do, don't they advise you to do that sort of thing on the telly, those TV psychiatrists and that lot? And talk show hosts, when someone's dead upset? I dunno. I'd stopped watching TV a while back. I didn't know how to deal with this.

I wished Jules was around.

'I am not kidding!' he said, and he forced out the 'kidding' part as though he wanted to prove to me that he knew my lingo just as well as I did; I'd never have doubted it to be honest. I'd finished my cigarette. My leg was shaking. What to do? What the hell to do?

After a few seconds he started up again, 'I said, I am not *kidding!*'

'*I know, I heard you!*' I said, but I must have come over all ratty, and scared the little bugger 'cos he suddenly got all freaked out and startled, and the next thing I knew he'd run off, and well fucking fast I'm telling you, and as he did he screamed back at me, and full of force, '*Fuck you! Fuck you, you fucking wanker! I can do it — I can do it, by myself!*'

Shit.

I ran after the fucker, down the street, 'cross the main one, dodging screeching traffic, geezers honking their stupid horns, screaming stuff at me, threatening to 'do' me, I thought '*Yeah right, do the little bastard I'm running after 'cos it seems like he'd be bleedin' grateful!*' And then I had to squeeze myself through this kid-size hole in the fence which of course speedo-man there had just zapped his self through.

So then we were into the park; and I don't care too much for parks, I have to say, it's basically just fake countryside, rats running round bins, half dead pond life, stupid bits of lawn, some of which you ain't even supposed to walk on, what's the use of that? Anyways, I find parks weird, always have done. So there I was, running like some mad fucker, after some little mad fucker, afraid he's gonna top himself, meanwhile I'm practically being chased by geezers whose motors I've just cut up with my daring swerves, and who now readily wanted to 'delete' me, now that's not very nice. And then in parts it sounded like there was a woman's voice mixed in to boot, having a go. I don't wanna complain like, but running in shoes a size too big ain't the easiest, and I hadn't run anywhere in years. Man, my heart was pounding. I thought, *crikey, this ain't right, look at the little bugger go! Slow up there matey. Steady... steady... and then miraculously... I'd got him, I'd got him! Just by the scruff of his neck, and he was a fighter, but I'd got him. YEEES!* (I suppose it was a bit like fishing - without any of the calm stuff).

Then wallop, something leapt onto my back, and it was clinging, as if the little ninja I was chasing wasn't enough to contend with.

And the one on my back was screaming, all high pitched like, and ear-scratching; I twisted about to get a better take on it, this one was blonde, fairly small, and *well irritating!* Somehow I managed to shake it off – it was a girl, and a screecher; she was calling out all sorts, and bashing away as though it was *me* that was the bleedin' nutter!

So there I was with the little guy in one hand wriggling like fuck, and the bird in the other, screaming and gnashing like some frigging *Lord of the Rings* Orc-child, and kicking the shit out of my left leg. She leapt up again and I couldn't hold her off well enough, and then it suddenly occurred to me that the best thing might be: to just let go of the pair of them. So I did.

It wasn't my intention, honest, but they couldn't have collided better or harder if I'd knocked the little fuckers' heads together, but hey, so it goes. It wasn't nice. I shouldn't have laughed. But shit happens. And I was doing my best.

After a minute or two they hushed, both a bit worn out. But then she started up again about what a fucking '*asshole*' I was, and just what kind of '*freak*' was I exactly, beating the crap out of guys half my size? Like she was so sure I *was* giving him a beating, and now there was the added insinuation that this was something I probably did on a regular basis. Charming.

'*So, have you nothing to say?*' she yelled. The little guy was on his arse by this time, shaking now as though he was suffering some kind of major physical and mental exhaustion. I wasn't far off that state myself to tell the truth. — And all of this on an empty stomach. — '*So, have you nothing to say?*' she repeats. She was dead plucky I give her that.

'Guess not,' I replied, a bit bewildered like.

'You bastard!' she says, half out of breath, unhappy I suppose at what she must have taken as 'flippancy' on my part, and maybe it was, only like I said, I was pretty much as confused as the little guy.

She came at me again, but bored of being clawed and kicked at by now, I put my hand out to her forehead and held her there at arm's length, she was one well-nasty kicker, and this way, at least for a moment or two, she wasn't able to reach. 'Let the fuck go of me!' she yelled, and then, she slipped. The little guy laughed. She got back up – *like there was nothing gonna keep her down*, and this time I managed to hold her off completely, as though *the force* was totally with me, about bleedin' time too – and I have to admit, it *was* funny. Dead funny. She went pink, then her face muscles seemed to stiffen as though she was stunned, but her arms were still flailing about and she was still capable of the odd tired but nasty kick; she must only have been about four-foot something.

I couldn't have guessed what was coming next, but suddenly the little guy let himself roll back onto the grass, and then he lay there flat out and he laughed, *man*, he laughed and he laughed and he laughed.

The girl stayed silent. She flopped down on the grass, and when I looked back at her I saw this single fat tear fall down her face. I couldn't have been more surprised at either of them. One way or another this whole thing was doing my head in. Never mind a ciggie, I needed a friggin' drink. But at least the little guy had finally figured out what was going on, and he seemed delighted by it, well amused in fact at some cute blonde trying to save him. But *she*, she didn't have a fucking clue what was going on. It was all a bit mad to be honest.

I felt a bit shivery, things still seemed to keep unravelling. And my encounters with the suicidal seemed to be mounting up. I'd been too late for Jim's, to try and steer him clear; too *crap* to achieve my own; and faced with this wee geezer, and trying to stop him, I still felt clueless. It wasn't good. And the bastard of it was, this latest run-in might still not be the last. And I know it's selfish, but I felt like I would positively murder the next bleeder that died on me, specially if it was through fuckin' suicide; and let's face it, when I ran after this guy I don't reckon I was suddenly struck by 'altruism', it was *me* I was trying to protect.

He finally sat himself up. He looked at the girl, and then he spluttered out his words through these vicious, pained tears of laughter, 'You dumb bitch,' and pointing a finger at me, '*he*... he wasn't attacking me, he fucking try to stop me... he try to stop me, and my *sui*-cide! You dumb bitch!' and with that he laughed on like a maniac, crying all the while. Weird. Parks are weird. People are weird, but there we go. The shift in his moods was making me feel dead uneasy.

And I still couldn't help feeling I was the least fit person to deal with stuff like this.

I offered the girl a hand to get up and she took it but she didn't look at me; she wiped what was now a whole trail of tears from her cheek and tried to brush the dirt off her jeans. 'Asshole,' she said under her breath, I didn't know who it was meant for, but it seemed like it could cover either of us. I took out my cigarettes and lit up and with that she got all mad again, '*Ain't you gonna offer them?!*' I shrugged and surrendered the pack and then the lighter. She took one and half pulled out another, offering it to the little guy who put up his hand like a stop sign, 'No, no, I never smoke, *ne-ver* smoke. It's very bad for health.'

I butt in then myself, 'Yeah right, mate.'

I felt like I was stranded in a really bad joke. And really bad jokes make me more miserable than anything. They unravel things, they make you self-concious, and I guess if you do stand-up (the hardest job in the world) they pretty much fucking kill you.

After a few drags I looked back at him and says, 'You gonna apologise then?'

'For wanting to die?' he says, deadpan (like I said, little tosser).

'No, for messing me the fuck about, and calling this bird names!' Only, of course, *stupid me*, she hadn't take offence at the little geezer calling her a '*dumb bitch*', what she had taken offence at was me calling her a 'bird'. The ninja couldn't get a word out now 'cos the little blonde motor-mouth was giving it large again in my direction.

When she'd wore herself out, the little guy, now somehow with a fag in his hand, points to me, raises an eyebrow, and now completely full of his self what with his insults having totally passed her by, and maybe feeling like this had given him one up on me, goes, 'Ironic isn't it, she don't like your insults, not at all, but she's pretty OK with mine!'

'Listen, Fu Manchu, you *really* are starting, in fact the pair of you, are really starting to wind me up....'

He jumped up, '*Fu Manchu, you call me! Fuck you!*' he says, his hands spread wide and flat now, one leg slightly forward, leaning back on the heel of the other, ready to pounce like some bleedin' martial arts loon. Then he points to his face, 'Where?' he says, 'Where can you see a fucking moustache? Anywhere? *Anywhere? No!* No moustache, no fucking-Fu-Manchu OK? *OK?* And for your information sir,' – what was it with that *'sir'* shite? – 'for your information, I am not *Chi*-nese, I am Jap-an-ese!'

'Oh right, yeah, bathroom-tap,' I says.

'…?' he wrinkled his brow.

'Bathroom-tap… *Jap*,' I picked my fags up from the grass and lit up again, dead slow, and exhaled big, 'it's rhyming slang: 'Jap', short for Japanese, then 'Jap' becomes: bathroom-tap.'

'You can't say that!' offered motor-mouth.

'*Oh shut up bitch!*' he says, much to my surprise, though why I should be surprised at all by this little guy anymore, god only knows. He settled himself back on the ground again, this time kneeling (it's February, it's cold, like I said the guy's a total doughnut), and then he carries on, waving the ciggie around like a conductor's baton; and for the moment it seems like he's calm again, '*This*, this is very interesting to me,' he says, 'I have read about Cock-*o*-ney rhyming slang, and it is dying out, am I right?' He looked to me for confirmation so I nodded and carried on with my smoke. 'And,' he says, 'I find that most interesting. I hear there are names for any kind of people, and any kind of 'thing', in fact, it is almost a language of its own, but in these, our "Politically Correct" times – *what a load of fucking Anglo-American bullshit that is!*' he says, interrupting his self, '*Politically Correct! Fuck it, fuck it!* – Anyway… anyway…what was I saying?' He was so damn preachy by now he could justifiably have claimed time at Hyde Park's Speakers' Corner, or else he could have replaced them Christian megaphone dudes that wanna save your soul at Oxford Circus with their '*Don't be a sinner, be a winner!*' lingo.

And the all the while he was prattling on, the girl was just stood there listening in like she was dead impressed. Bizarre if you ask me, but there we go.

'Oh yes,' he carried on, having suddenly remembered what he was on about, 'in these days of being "PC," it is often the case that people are prohibited from using many kinds of language, that's a *fucking bullshit!*' I couldn't help thinking we'd hit on his two favourite words.

And he wasn't done with them yet, not by a long shot; he stood up, 'Complete and *utter fucking bullshit* in my opinion. You think people won't find new insults if that's what they fuckin' looking for!' Then he suddenly looks up at me, 'So, Mister, tell me more. In a Cock-*o*-ney rhyming slang, what do you call a Chinaman?'

'A *Chinaman*?' I took another long drag. 'Kitchen sink.'

'It doesn't rhyme.'

'Kitchen sink – *Chink*.'

'Ahhh! And also like a *chink* in the armour! I like it, I like it.' He was very over excited now, hopping about the grass.

'Well, no,' I says, and I was about to explain, but he was away with the fairies again so I left it, and anyway the Orc-child started on at me again, 'You fuckin' racist! You can't call him a Chink!' Did this bird have selective fucking hearin' or what? I closed my eyes for a moment hoping she wouldn't be there when I opened them again; I was very much hoping I had at least only imagined *her* if not the pair of them. 'I didn't call him anything,' I says. I couldn't be doing with this, certainly not any more than I'd already 'endured' that's for sure, now there's a word! Anyhow, that drink I needed, it was turning into a large one.

To be honest, I wondered why the girl didn't just walk away. When you think about it, she'd been denied any buzz at all from 'saving the guy' since it turned out that I wasn't actually attacking the little geezer, and then of course there wasn't any thanks available for *trying* to save the little sod; and since we'd stopped running and scrapping and shite, all she'd had was this great barrage of abuse hurled at her. So why didn't she go? Pride maybe? I figured that having made the wrong assumption about 'the attack', it was as though she was determined to stay until she could regain the upper hand. But I had to say, it didn't look like she was onto a winner with either of us. Waste of time, that pride shite.

'I'd best be going,' I said, already turning away.

'Are you just gonna leave him here?' she says.

I turned back, 'What is it with you?' and then I realised I was practically brandishing my cigarette lighter at her, like it was a fucking light-sabre or something. Total dick. I looked down and tried to shove it back in my pocket and all dead casual as though I was just 'timing' my next words 'cos they were like, dead important. Like I said, *dick*. Anyway, I looked up again and ran my hand through my hair, shifted my feet around in my slightly-too-big shoes and, sort of composed, I carried on, offering a nod in the little geezer's direction at the same time, 'Listen,' I says, giving it my best shot at 'authority', '*he,* was losing it, he threw a wobbly, I ran after him to see as he was alright like, and now it seems he's fine again.' OK, I admit it, it all sounded a bit lame, and I wasn't at all sure what I meant by 'fine again', the guy seemed nuts, but to be honest that seemed like it was probably normal for him, and in any case, since it looked like he'd run it out of his system for now, laughed himself silly, calmed his self down like, I figured he was probably *as close* to his own version of normality as he ever would be. Anyhow, what was I supposed to do? Hold his bleedin' hand for the rest of his natural? Like I said, I hadn't even had a coffee, and me and ninja-man here were total strangers. Yeah, and this wee chat we'd been having didn't exactly amount to much. I figured I'd pretty much done what I could. But she knew, didn't she, she knew she'd hit a nerve, I could see it in her eye, and now she looked down and did this smile to the side, sort of cute. Flirt. I wasn't having any of that. Flirting's alright like, but it's a 'time and place' type thing. 'Anyway,' I said, 'if *you* wanna babysit him, go ahead.'

Silently, and whilst me and her had been wagging our tongues, the little guy had started to run off in the other direction like the right little sprinter-ninja that he was, and with the speed of a Benny Hill run-around. Manic. And without realising, without even thinking about it, I now ran like a bastard after him, and the very moment I caught him, that was it, wasn't it? Now I was stuck with the geezer, *proper.* I felt caught out, set up like, I'm not sure which. I let go of him and he slumped to the ground again, all out of puff. I glanced back. I suppose I'd half expected the girl to follow on. Stupid really. Distantly, she smiled, proper this time, and now, for the first time I realised what a looker she was. Boss like. It's just that when birds go off on one like that, like screeching pterodactyls, it's really hard to focus on whether they're fit or not. She was fit alright, well fit.

She waved, then she turned and walked away.

I stood a moment. I thought about Jules.

The little guy had stood up again, his battery already recharged. 'You coming or what?' he says, like all of a sudden I'm Eeyore to his Winnie-the-fucking-Pooh. 'Yeah,' I said, all automatic, it was all a bit weird to be honest.

We walked on now over a fake hill and pretty much without speaking. Just me and ninja-boy, smoking.

I felt like I needed to keep him busy, distracted, in case he ran off again and maybes even 'tried' again, but I didn't really see how I was gonna achieve that. And then my head started to wander. This was truly big, this place, a real mega-size park, and I started to think that maybe the place wasn't such a bad idea after all, even if it was only fake countryside. At least this one was on a big enough scale that you could imagine it was 'real'. I spotted a fox in the distance. It's body had almost no fur, scrawny as hell.

'I have been talking to you, but you are a fucking day dreamer,' shouts the little guy all of a sudden.

'That's me,' I said, smiling like an arse as I lit up yet again, 'a full-on, friggin' "*daydream believer*" probably.'

'What?'

'Never mind.'

After a bit I offered him another ciggie. He didn't seem to want one, but he didn't say anything, just dropped his little head down a bit and sighed. It was like the mood had changed again and the air felt strange, he looked so sort of... well... *forlorn* I guess you'd call it. Man, I was well out of my depth. 'Sure you don't want one mate?' I said, holding out my fags again. He had his hands in his pockets now, and he just carried on walking in a dead straight line, and without saying anything. Then he picked up the pace again so I hurried a bit more myself, (not a good smoking speed I have to say). I thought that maybe I should try and keep talking to him, at least that might count as something of a distraction, only that fits into the category of 'random questions and idle remarks', the things that can so easily screw things up. Still, I figured I had to give it a shot, 'I was just thinking, like,' I started off, 'just in case you was... like, feeling suicidal again... anyway... d'you fancy another ciggie?' Shit. *I know, I know!* I can't believe I just said that myself. What a prize, fucking dick. Like, go on Mark, remind the guy, make out like it's all a big ole joke, deride him even, why not? Make it sound like this would be his 'last' smoke... like a 'last' request! Fuck. Ever wished you was someone else? Someone a bit less bleedin' hopeless? And while I was hurrying along trying to keep up with his speed-walking, and simultaneously trying to regain control of my thoughts *and* keep me gob from coming out with the next totally inappropriate line, *he* comes out with this, and total melancholy, 'Sorry.'

He slowed down a bit. I tried to catch my breath, I says, 'You're sorry? Sorry? For what?'

'My imposing.'

'*Imposing?*' I didn't get this guy at all. We looked at one another, only it wasn't any good, the whole eye contact thing didn't seem to be helping. I shrugged, carried on walking, carried on smoking. After a bit he spoke up again, 'I mean: my imposing my need to take my life. You see, it is a private matter. A matter to be handled, privately.'

I scratched my head. *Imposing?*

What was I doing here? Just what the frig did I think I was doing? And why was I still walking along with him? We weren't related, I wasn't his mate. I'd done what I could, hadn't I? Only now we were like Darby and Joan (and I don't exactly know who they are, it's just something me dad says), stuck with each other. And then dead cocky again he grabbed me ciggies and helped his self. He didn't light up though, he just seemed to wanna prance around with a fag in his hand.

He might have been troubled like, but I think it's fair to say he was a bit off his tree an' all. Still, there we go. *Takes all sorts,* as me nan would say.

We'd slowed down a fair bit by now, but it still seemed like we were a way off from stopping; and then he started to march up and down this one stretch of grass as though he was sussing it out, 'back and to' he was going, back and to, like he was pacing it, measuring it up.

'Cricket!' he suddenly announces, dead bold like, 'This area is ideal for cricket, don't you think so?' but he didn't really seem to need a response, he just kept on with his pacing, deep in thought. Then he

150

says, 'It's going to be the Ashes again later in this year, you know, and it's about fucking time your country won again,' still pacing, 'don't you think so?'

I shrugged, 'I guess so,' I says, dead lame like.

'Certainly it is! You have let Australia whip your asses for the last seventeen years! Better get yourselves together this time.'

What could I say, the geezer was right, but I didn't reckon I'd have that much sway with the England team itself like. I don't suppose they liked losing like that year after year, still, be nice if we could pull it out of the bag this time. He was right about that – it had been too long.

It struck me as funny though, how much this geezer was interested in stuff like cricket and that, but it weirded me out when he hopped from one subject to another, with no real link. I guess he couldn't help it, he was hardly in the most balanced frame of mind; and I hadn't exactly been *focused* myself lately (and maybe not only lately, maybe always).

'I should introduce myself,' he says all of a sudden; he'd stopped his detailed pitch assessment and was now stood as though to attention like, 'I am,' he said, with great authority, and I spotted this cheeky little twinkle in his eye, as though he could half hear an accompanying drum roll, 'I am, Haruki... *Mura*...'

'...Murakami?'

'...' he looked surprised, but he didn't say anything else, he just left his gob hanging wide open like.

'Haruki Murakami?' I says. 'The writer? *Like shit you are.*'

He dropped his head down. 'It was just a joke,' he said, only now he sounded a bit squeaky, you know, like some rubbish cartoon mouse.

'In any case, I saw your name on your student card when you first stopped to talk, it's *Kazu*, Kazuhiro Watanabe, right? Wat-a-fuking-ejit more like.' He was a sorry bugger if ever I saw one. He looked a bit embarrassed, but then after a bit he gathered his self and asked, 'So, what is *your* name?'

'Me?' I says, suddenly feeling a bout of sarcasm about to break loose, 'Well now let's see, '*Mr Haruki Murakami*', *sometimes* it's Iain Banks, and *sometimes* it's Iain *M.* Banks with the added 'M' for fun like, and sometimes it's Ian Mc–fuckin–Ewan!'

'OK, OK, I got it. I got it! We are not famous writers. It was just my little joking. I am a little asshole... *but*,' he added, that twinkle coming back, 'if I am a *little* asshole, I guess that you are a *big one*, right?'

Ever had those times when you really can only half agree with someone? And that accompanying little laugh of his, well let's just say, it got my hand twitching. Lucky for him I was currently more interested in my cigarette.

'Anyway,' he blabs on, '*really*, what is your *real* family name, sir?'

'If you mean my surname, it's Kerr.' (That '*sir*' shite was still really irritating me, but along with his laugh, I decided to let it go for now.)

He staggered about a bit, and then he laughed some more, '*Kerr!* So... let me guess, your mother has always had a fondness for Chinese names, and so your first name must be Wan! Do you get it? *Wan-ker!*' and then he ran, *again*. He just fucking ran, chuckling along like a bastard into the bargain. There was no way I was gonna let him out of my sight now, that 'sir' shite had been bad enough, but this latest asshole remark of his had just pushed things way over the line. And I'm telling you, it didn't matter how fucking funny he *thought* he was, he was now the best living proof there ever was that you don't get comic bleedin' genius just by watching it; little fucking arsehole, 'Wan-ker', I ask you!

'*Oi, Ninja-boy, Ninja-matey! I wasn't willing before, but so help me, I'll happily kill you now you little bastard! Call me a wanker? I'll fucking have you. Don't you worry about suicide mate, I've got your demise well sorted!*'

# CHAPTER SEVENTEEN

## stuck with kazu

# MERRY POPPINS

Man, that was way too much running, we must have lapped that soddin' park a dozen times. OK, so maybe not, but it bleedin' felt like it. It felt like some major punishment for my not liking parks, it was that whole 'tempting fate' shenanigans I guess: said I didn't like parks, then found myself pretty much stuck in one of the bleeders for all eternity, and with my very own head-case thrown in for free. Nice one.

Kazu finally collapsed in a little heap, practically garrotted now by that stupid bit of string wrapped round his neck. Could have strung the bleeder up by it on this bendy lookin' tree close by but it would only have snapped. Anyhow, I wasn't about to let his 'winding me up' trick me into 'doing him'. Oh no, Sunshine! I've got your card well marked (well, sort of). But I couldn't exactly just let him run off either. Like I said, I was stuck with the wee geezer.

Knackered, I flopped down on the grass myself now. Neither of us spoke. People moved about but only distantly; I could hear cars and police sirens, but they all seemed far off too. My head felt fuzzy.

There are other types of moments, 'snippets' of time that you could almost grab on to, when it's still OK, plausible like, to eject yourself from certain situations, like when I'd been stood at the front door this morning and this wee geezer had said he was looking for someone, – that was one; or, when he'd run off, that was another 'possible ejection moment', he'd run off at one hell of a speed, and I could have just let him go, after all, me shoes weren't even fitting right, I maybes wasn't totally together myself, and he seemed like a nutter; and *since* then, I could reasonably have got myself off the hook and left the bleeder, as a reaction to all his soddin' rudeness, but each time he'd run off I'd just seemed to follow. I'd missed all the 'get outs'. But the thing was, although I'd run after him I didn't really see how I could help him, or how I might be of any use at all, like I said, I wasn't his family like, or his mate… only maybe they *really* aren't the right ones either. I felt very confused. And screw it, because I really am, at times, I am thoroughly fuckin' useless.

My mind wandered and I thought back to Septimus again in that *Mrs. Dalloway*, and how maybe some time-out, away from everyone you know, maybes in the countryside like it suggested, or anywheres really, just away from it all, how that might just help − might even have helped our Jim − surely, surely something like that must work.

And then, I remembered something in *Moby Dick* that seemed to carry the same kind of meaning, about how it might actually be nice to be cut off from things for a wee bit and step out of your life awhile, only this time it was about being out at sea, and how, when you're out there, just you and the elements, this kind of, '*sublime uneventfulness invests you,*' − that's it, and how refreshing it is to spend some time when you don't hear any news or read any papers, so that nothing unruffles your feathers. Out at sea like that, it seemed it made life simple again, like it could wash away all those 'extraneous' choices that clutter up our lives. A life kept nice and simple. — Yeah, that's what's needed sometimes, '*sublime uneventfulness*', I like the sound and feel of that, that, and being '*lost in the infinite seas, with nothing ruffled but the waves.*' Man, I love that book. I fuckin' love it.

'It's OK,' says Kazu, and I didn't know if he'd been talking for long and I'd been zoned out again, but it felt that way.

'What's OK?' I asked.

He didn't answer, and then I realised that I was knelt up dead close to him on the grass, and that my hand was resting on his shoulder, and that he was looking at it, and *man* I felt embarrassed. He seemed to sense my awkwardness and so he looked the other way, he said something about the weather. It was like he was deliberately creating that moment for me to move my hand away so as I didn't need to feel more of an arse than I already did, dead perceptive, and shit I felt weird.

I stood up and tried to brush off bits of damp grass and that.

'I like English parks,' he suddenly announced, and then sort of randomly he added, 'we had some good exercise didn't we?' and this time *he* blushed, his voice a bit unsure again. I didn't know what to say. He got up now and pulled his self as tall as he could, and I felt myself half slouching down, and it was dead strange, like we were trying to meet each other halfway. One too tall, one too short. I leant back again and stood up proper.

'This weather, and the sky,' he says, 'when the sky looks like this, it always reminds me of Merry Poppins.'

'*Mary* Poppins?'

'Yes,' and he spelled it out like, 'M, E, R, R,Y: Merry Poppins. In the movie, it's a Julie Andrews, right?'

I smiled at him, that bloody Andrews woman, she gets everywhere. She was though, pretty damn 'merry', it had to be said, too bleedin' merry for my taste, but there we go. Kazu stood there in the middle of the park, breathing it all in, staring far up into the sky, and he seemed suddenly, if only momentarily, 'serene', content in his Disney UK.

I secretly tittered to meself, imagining the Andrews woman herself, here right now, brollie in hand, about to take off.

I lit up.

*Merry* Poppins…

Kazu's re-titling seemed like a big improvement on the original; and yeah, like I've said before, some cigarettes taste particularly good. We didn't speak anymore, we just walked on, and after a bit I found myself looking up at the sky again as though I half expected to see his *Merry* Poppins flying past, I can be a dick at times.

For the moment at least, this geezer was safe again. '*For the moment…*' those words again – *and was that it? Was it that simple? That fragile?* Was this whole idea of 'moments' really the key? Because there really is a moment just before the window sucks a person out – I knew that much myself, and it is literally only a single drop of time, but if it is possible to catch it or disturb it in some way, then maybe you can move a person out of it, and away from it awhile, to somewhere they feel OK, and maybe that might be enough. The thing is, capturing those moments, *seeing* them, well maybe that's too hard, like maybe it was with our Jim, because no one saw that really – or not well enough, and that made me think that seeing that moment is much more likely to be an accidental thing. Like you could be asking some geezer for directions on the underground, not realising that the train lines were pulling him, that he was planning on a jump, but in that moment, you might just have distracted him from the job in hand, and without even knowing what you'd done, yeah, you might have caught him, it might just be as accidental as that. Only, accidental ain't too fuckin' reliable is it? It made me shiver to think just how hard it might be to see those types of moments, and it hurt to think just how many people might walk around suffering, and everyone around them blind. I mean, I'd seen Kazu's moment only because he'd thrust it, fuckin' neon lit, right into my face. Maybe next time it'd be more subtle... and next time I might not see, no one might see, and that was the worry, 'cos there may well be a next time, and a next. Catching someone, that might only be a delay, it's hard to know. And it's like I said, once you've noticed the open window, it's harder to keep passing it.

# CHAPTER EIGHTEEN

*rest*

# A PROPER KIP

We left the park and I hadn't bothered to notice where we were or where we were walking to, and by now it felt like we'd been out for hours. We'd come out of some other exit, and I hadn't a clue how it related to Ron's street. The one good thing was, I spotted a cash machine, bingo, get some dosh again at least, that way the day wasn't a total shambles after all, and I could pay back the Turkish geezer and hold my head up again at least marginally higher – get some fags too. After a bit I'd got up the courage to have another go at conversation with my young Oriental friend, I figured that maybe it might help to try and establish a bit about his background and that. He said his family lived in Tokyo. He was twenty-one, and this was only his first year at Uni, and his first year abroad. I thought that was all well brave of him, amazing like, and it seemed as though them lyrics by the Kaiser Chiefs could have been written just for him: '*Oh my god I can't believe it, I've never been this far away from home,*' except I figured those lines also covered shorter distances, like from Leeds to Sheffield, or London to Manchester, because for most of us even that's far enough. And I thought about times when people I knew had moved away, and when I'd moved away meself. Sometimes that had been dead hard to handle, and maybes it hadn't always been the right thing to do, who knows.

I told him that I thought it took a long time to make friends in a new place. He shrugged, said he'd never had many friends at home either; but then as though he was protecting himself from anything that might resemble pity on my side, he waffled on a bit, explaining away the lack of mates being down to his studying so hard, and he said that was also the reason for his English being so good. He'd gone to these special cram schools and then had private lessons on top of that, he said it'd been that way right from him being a tiny little kid. I felt as though I could imagine him with a rough book just like CA's filled with rows and rows of vocabulary, and a satchel maybes, aged about six like. — Then he made this remark about *my* English, he said it didn't sound very pure. *Pure!* What was this geezer on? But then I had to admit that what with being born up north, me nan being a Londoner, and then me moving around a fair bit, all I really had fair claim on was being something of a mongrel. (No British bulldog, me.) I figured 'pure' wasn't particularly a category that appealed to me anyhow. Mongrel suited me fine. And Kazu was now so taken by the idea of me being some kinda hound that he started in on what can perhaps best be described as a 'wolf impression', you know – howling! Howling, *and* up at the sky. Mad fucker. We were just walking down the road, out in the open like, and the geezer howls like a bleedin' wolf, then he stops and says, delightedly, that *that* was his *best* dog impression, 'You know Mr Kerr, I want to sound like a *Snoopy*.'

I told him, Snoopy never made a sound like that in his life (though to be honest, I hadn't a clue, Charlie Brown was never really my thing); and then I told him to stop calling me Mr Kerr, or *sir*, 'The name is Mark.'

'Mark.'

'That's the one.'

We were back at the dreaded front door again. Back where we'd started. He seemed a bit twitchy. I didn't know what to do. As long as we chatted, or he was distracted by something: dog impressions and the like, he seemed almost alright, but the minute the air settled, so to speak, he seemed dead nervous, unsteady, like he might just float away. I shivered.

'Best come inside and have a cuppa, mate,' I says, not really knowing what the next step would be, or if this was a good idea or not. If I'd have given it half a thought, I might have realised that this was pretty much how I ended up living with that Doris, but even *half* thoughts, *proper* half thoughts were still more than I was capable of.

'A cuppa?' he smiled, 'Your English is pretty messed up, but I very much admire your use of colloquialism.'

Suicidal or not, he was a cheeky bleeder.

I opened the door, and then, *as luck would have it*, I had an idea! I'd settle him down in one of the rooms, dead comfy like, and play him a load of top sounds, that should sort him out for the time being, a wee while anyways. So I showed him the spare rooms, let him pick the one he fancied, good host to the last like, and then I whacked on some sounds. Ron might have had shite taste in music but he did have one hell of a sound system, I had to give him that.

I felt pretty exhausted myself by now, and then I remembered that I hadn't had so much as a bacon buttie all day. I called back to the wee guy from the kitchen, 'You get yourself a lie down mate, I'll throw us some food together, alright?' There wasn't any answer, but then the volume was pretty high.

No, it was no good, I couldn't settle to cookin', best just check on him. I knocked the music down a bit and went to see how he was doing. He was sat on the edge of the bed, head in his hands. I felt clumsy. 'You OK mate?'

'I...' He didn't seem like he could get any words together, then he mumbled something in Japanese, and then he just said, 'Sorry,' and sniffed.

'No need mate. You just... just take it easy, maybes have a lie down for a bit, eh? And I'll, I'll turn this music off, let you get a proper kip like.'

'*Kip?*'

'Sleep.'

'Kip,' he repeated dead soft, 'kip,' as he laid himself properly on the bed.

I turned the sounds off and went back to the kitchen, and as I did I could just catch his voice, he was muttering away like, in his own language, but every so often I could catch him saying something in English and dead gentle like, 'kip... get a proper kip'. He sounded pretty much OK, like he was just lulling himself to sleep. But then, just as I'd got my fry-up underway: eggs, bacon, sausages, tomatoes, fried bread

159

there nicely lined up like, Kazu starts screaming, and if I thought that Snoopy howl of his was an ear-bashing, that had nothing on this; *man*; that little guy was upset. I ran in there, he was sitting up terrified. I know it's cowardly, but I just wished that Jules was there or that there was at least *someone* else about, you know, and maybe this called for a woman's touch. I don't fucking know.

'Calm it down mate, calm it down,' I says, trying to sound gentle, soothing like. He looked at me straight on, but as though he'd never set eyes on me before, and then he let rip again and screeched at the top of them sharp little lungs of his. I winced. And now the smoke alarm joined in. '*Shit!* That's me fry-up!' I says, like a wanker, shifting from one foot to the other not sure which drama to tend to first. Luckily Kazu ran out of breath, I stood a moment, waiting for him to recognise me, 'It's alright matey... just a bad dream or something. I'm Mark, remember?'

'*Of course I fuckin' remember, go turn off your cooking before you burn the fucking place down!*'

I pulled back. Crikey.

OK, I thought, and obedient to the last I legged it back to the kitchen to save me sausages. But bleedin' hell, this geezer was one complicated little chappy. I couldn't quite get my head round it, and then I got to thinking again: that just 'cos a geezer's feeling suicidal – it really don't make them a charmer. Fair enough, only it has to be said, he did my head in, big time.

When I looked round he was stood in the doorway fanning smoke away from the smoke alarm, or at least trying to, it was a bit of a tall guy job to be honest. I opened the window, and then I took the battery out of the alarm. 'It's a not safe if you do that!' he says.

'You just steady yourself,' I says, 'I'll put it back later.' He must have been the only suicide on the planet that seemed more worried about dying than anyone else. Plank.

He took a quick look over at what I was cooking, plonked himself down on a chair, 'I'll have mine sunny side up,' he pipes up.

'You'll have yours what?'

'Sunny side up!'

'...?'

'My eggs,' he says, 'that's how I like my eggs, I learned this from my American teacher.'

'Well, I'm doing the cookin' mate and you'll have 'em how they come.'

I carried on cooking, trying to rescue various bits of well done this and that, it was all the same to me, I liked stuff well done and it all goes down the same way. I'd cook his lot fresh though, him being a guest, sort of.

'That kip didn't work out too well then me ole China?'

'Old China?'

I smiled like, wondering where I'd suddenly pulled that one from.

'More rhyming slang?' he asks.

'Yeah,' I says, trying to rescue a breakfast I'd had well high hopes for, 'yeah, *me ole China;* it's from 'China plate' – rhymes with 'mate'... d'yer get it?'

'I see, China plate — *mate.* I got it!' and he chuckled. I looked over me shoulder at him, and I could see him puzzling over it, 'It must have got switched around over time, right? And so finally it became – *me ole China?*'

'Something like that. – The thing is,' I says, and now I felt a bit embarrassed, a bit fake like, bit of a phoney, 'I don't think I've ever said that in my entire life, not any of that rhyming slang in fact. I must just be trying to show off a bit.' I paused a minute. 'Weird what you know, isn't it? Like we must gather all kinds of stuff in our heads, and a ton of it without even realising, and then it just pops itself out like, on special occasions, or else when your head's wanting to make an arse of you.'

'I guess so,' he says, like he was mildly contemplating my words.

'You didn't really get much of a kip then eh?'

'No, I... I'm not very good with sleeping. Not since I came here to be honest.'

'Noisy flatmates and that?'

'No. Actually, I have a room by myself. I don't have any... flatmates.' His voice trailed off. I needed to stop mentioning mates really, of any kind.

'Nighttime is the worst,' he says, 'I can't sleep, and then I start to panic.'

161

'It's a bit early for sleep anyways,' I says, a bit awkward like, 'just thought you might be a bit worn out what with all that running and stuff.' He didn't say anything.

'So,' I says, now struggling for topics, 'how long you been interested in cricket, then? I wouldn't have thought you lot would have played it, to be honest.' He looked up, pulling back slightly from the plate of prime English breakfast now set before him, '*Us lot,*' he says, raising an eyebrow, 'well, *we...*' and then correcting himself like, 'anyway, *I,* have followed cricket for many years, and I have even studied how to play. — Do you really want me to eat this?'

'Do what you like with it mate. But if you don't want it, I'll have it.'

'It's just that I need vegetables too!'

I prodded his tomato with me fork, and raised an eyebrow meself now. Ungrateful git. Then he looked at it and said, 'It's just half a tomato...'

'...?'

'Of course, it's... it's a very nice one,' he adds, and then he settled down and noshed away.

As I polished off the last of what was, *if I do say so myself,* a total beast of a breakfast, it occurred to me that this wee chap was gonna take quite some distracting, just for a day or two at least, then hopefully he'd be over the worst of it, that most dangerous period like, and mind I am only a novice, but I figure that the twenty-four hours or so straight after feeling that way, is potentially a landscape of suicide landmines, a whole load of moments that have to be negotiated, slept through, ignored somehow, side-tracked – I guess we'd have to see, take it as it comes like, and like I say, what do I know? The thing was, cricket looked like being the obvious route to keep him distracted, only that ain't my bag to be honest, never really been more than a spectator with that one (unless you count using a cricket bat as a guitar, like); and more than that, it seemed like what he really needed was to feel like he could belong somehow, feel like he was part of things here, maybes feel like he was needed. Surely that shouldn't be too hard to suss out – *shite,* listen to me, stash of egg and bacon in me belly and suddenly I've got all the friggin' answers! *Agony aunt, psychologist, carer –* oh yes,

162

Mark! Wanker, more like.

I felt like what I needed to do was to develop a whatchamacallit? – a *strategy*, that's it. *I know, I know*, it sounds like total toss, but whatever it sounded like, what I needed was a plan.

The thing was though, before I could draw up a top plan, I needed a top kip. I wondered if Kazu 'ere would settle down and finally sleep himself like, only if I had to stay awake to watch him it's fair to say I'd be useless again by evening. I was still far from firing on all pistons. And like he was reading my mind he suddenly goes, 'You are looking pretty tired, Mister.'

I grunted and rubbed my full belly. I was well satisfied.

'If you wanna sleep, I can wash the dishes and then I will make myself scarce.'

'*Scarce?*'

'I will go back to my room... back to the halls of residence. I have imposed on your kindness too much already.'

'Firstly, making yourself scarce is exactly what we're trying to avoid, and secondly, I just don't hold with this *imposing* malarkey.'

'*Malarkey?*'

'Yeah, if I didn't want you here, I'd tell you. — It ain't my gaff actually, I'm just house-sitting for some geezer, but anyways, you're welcome to stay here for a bit.'

Kazu was still caught up on the word 'malarkey' and kept muttering it to himself. He wandered off and found this big ole dictionary and started thumbing through it. He seemed to find it quick enough, he read the definition to his self and then snapped the book shut again, and now looked perfectly content.

'So,' he says, 'this is not your place, it belongs to a *mate* of yours?'

'Not a mate exactly. Anyways, it's fine for you to hang out here a bit, stay a few days like, if that feels alright. Let's just see how it goes, eh? The only thing that I will insist on, if you don't mind like...'

'...'

'Is that you do not *make yourself scarce*, 'cos that'll do my head in.'

He chuckled sort of warmly, 'OK, so no *making myself scarce malarkey*... I got it boss.'

163

'And call me Mark. Just 'Mark' will do fine.'

'OK. So,' he says, pulling himself up tall again, 'why don't you get a kip yourself if you need it, and I will wash up these dishes.'

I give him a nod, I was ready to pass out, to be honest. 'You'll be alright, like?' I says, then I pointed to the bookshelves and the music, meaning he should help his self like, he nodded back, and it looked almost like he was doing a bow, then he mumbled something in his own language and I sloped off to slumberland. Man, like I said, these last days I'd pretty much slept for England.

# CHAPTER NINETEEN

# *doors*

# THE PLAN

I woke up to this dizzying mix of top sounds – good taste, Kazu (though to be honest, the newly edited 'tune racks' were failsafe now); and then I noticed the smell, it was that cleaning stuff, you know the sort, that disinfectant kinda bleachy smell combined with flowery, fruity shite like lavender or lemon, totally fake smelling like, but somehow suggesting something in the way of clean, too fucking clean.

It turned out that Kazu had kept himself well busy; he hadn't just washed the dishes but practically any friggin' surface he could reach. I was glad I woke up when I did to be honest or the little geezer would have scrubbed himself senseless. Looked nice though. I felt a tad embarrassed like. Probably thought I was a right grubby git, but there we go. I even had to prise the sponges and bucket from his fingers to get him to stop.

'I just wanted to say thank you,' he says, and then trying to stand taller, 'I wanted the place to be spotless when you woke up.' His lips started to quiver again.

'Steady mate,' I got him a towel to dry his hands, they looked red and raw.

'I wanted,' he carried on, out of puff though by now, 'to make the place "spring clean" for you.'

'That's lovely,' I says, 'great like. You've done a top job. But stop now, eh, stop.' He took the towel and trotted off to another room. I got myself a glass of water. 'Want some water?' I shouts. There was no answer but then I suddenly heard the front door open and then slam shut, I darted through. Kazu was stood in the hallway rubbing his hands, 'There,' he says, 'all finished now. I just put out your rubbish.'

'...?'

'Just that rubbish bag, the one in that room,' he pointed, 'I chucked it out. Now I think I finished.'

'What rubbish bag?' I says, going back for more water, and not thinking things through.

'That black one, it was full of clunky stuff...'

*Shite!* – Ron's old CDs that I was stashing till he got back. Oops.

'I think the place is looking pretty tidy now,' he says. He smiled then and coloured a bit, as though he shouldn't show he was so pleased with his self.

'Nice one. Job well done,' I says, 'but like I said before, stop now, eh, relax a bit; come and have a glass of water or something.' He smiled again and followed me back to the kitchen.

I thought about my editing out Ron's wrong music, and how I was gonna check with him before actually chucking anything; oh well, looks as though it was decided now. A done deal. I could of course go and rescue the shite from the bins... but *nah,* it seemed like it was *meant to be,* and I rather liked that. Ron would now have no choice *but* to have the *right sounds* in his life! Job done.

I found myself thinking about Mr Benn again, and how important it was each time he passed though that magic door like, and how things changed for him, at least for a while. I figured I needed a door more like his. And I thought about how things needed changing for me, and how things needed changing for Kazu here, then I thought about still waiting a while — till the streets looked like they were better ones to walk down, instead of just carrying on with the 'same old, same old', till it all gets too much. Time out. I guess that's what we all need from time to time, eh.

Kazu glugged down his water, 'I also found something while you were sleeping, seemed pretty funny too.'

'What was that then?'

'Postcards!' he announced, walking away dead pleased with himself. I followed him back to the hallway.

'What?' I asked, though I was fairly certain I'd caught what he said the first time.

'Postcards!'

I felt a knot in my throat. Shit. 'What postcards?' I asked, starting to feel a tad nervous, trying to scan my stupid head to think where I'd left my own stack, remembering vaguely having moved them about, and hoping, presuming like, that mine couldn't possibly be the only ones in this place, after all, it seemed as though Ron liked to travel well enough... and he did have them 200-odd mates... so he must get sent loads.

Kazu wasn't looking at me, he was too busy skipping around now like some demented little elf, 'A whole load of postcards! And *so* cute pictures, all different scenes of London: red telephone boxes, red post boxes, red buses! The River Thames!' He tootled off to his room still listing away and with each description my stomach lurched just a little bit more, 'So many different views, even *trains*, and the London Eye, and Big Ben! And even one of Nelson at Trafalgar Square!'

No, there was no way I was imagining this, the knot in my throat had got bigger, my stomach was now aching like a bastard, and despite having just chugged an entire pint of water, my mouth was completely dry, you know, like: desert dry. But calm it down Mark, the little geezer was only going on about the pictures on the front of the cards, there was no reason for him to have read them like, and anyway, aren't postcards sort of private? Well, I guess not really, 'cos then they'd be called letters and they'd be sent and received in sealed envelopes just the same.

I didn't realise until he came back out of his room that he'd actually gone to *fetch* the stash of cards. He waltzed back into the hallway with them fanned out in his hands looking dead pleased with himself.

'And what's so funny, and so nice about them,' he says, 'is that they are all written to the same person!' He still wasn't looking at me, well not straight on at least, he was too distracted and overexcited by his find, and cataloguing what was of course *my* postcard collection. 'How cute is that?' and he stopped now and looked right at me, holding one out, the one with the red bus on it, and he beamed like, full of warm amusement. I must have gone red, but not as red as him when he realised, and I'm not entirely sure *how much* he realised: that they were mine, or that regardless of who owned them, he just shouldn't have touched them, but he realised *something* and as he did, he dropped them, the whole stack.

The cards flew across the wooden floorboards in different directions, some face up, some down.

He froze. Then he started up, 'I'm sorry, I am *so sorry*, I didn't think... I didn't think... I shouldn't have looked... but they fell down when I was cleaning and I looked at the pictures and they seemed so fun... *oh no, oh no...*' and then he rattled on a while to himself in his own language like. I put my head down, like I always do, like a total prick, thinking, as I've probably always done, that I could hide underneath my hair. I wanted to tell him it didn't matter, that it was no big deal, and 'never mind', but I couldn't, and it would only have been a load of lies anyway; it *did* matter, it *was* a big deal, and I minded like hell. If he'd had any sense at all, now would have been the time to shut the fuck up, or else, now would have been the time for him to lie to me and say that he respected that these didn't belong to him, that they had nothing whatsoever to do with him, and that he hadn't actually read them. But he didn't. He didn't shut up. And he didn't lie. Wanker. 'I couldn't make out the signature,' he carried on, 'but it's the same on all of them, and that kind of thing is pretty tricky to figure out... I guess.'

I suppose it was out of nervousness and embarrassment like, that he simply motored on, but it would have been so much better if he'd have stopped. 'It was just like a little scribble, the signature; and at first I wasn't actually going to try and read the cards, but when I noticed that all of them were written to just one person I got curious... you know? So beautiful to write so many cards to just one person. So romantic,' and then as though realising how carried away he was getting, he pulled himself up and started apologising, but all the while completely unawares of my change of mood. 'But I shouldn't... I shouldn't have read them. I realise that. It just seemed pretty strange, strange and nice, you know?'

'...'

'So many sweet cards addressed to just one person. And almost like a story, a kind of diary. But I feel pretty bad about it now. I didn't know someone would write such private matters... on a postcard.'

'...'

Some people wonder, why other people smoke —

He bent down and started to pick them up. Then he looked up at me from the floor, and finally, *finally* he comes out with it, 'It's a... it's a – your signature isn't it?'

'...'

And the thing is, some people really don't know when to give it up, do they? Kazu was one of 'em.

'*Jules*,' he said all warm and gentle, 'she... she must be very special to you.'

My leg had been twitching. My hand twitched now. 'I'm... I'm out of fags,' I says, and this wasn't entirely true, but this wasn't a moment that called for too much honesty, 'I'm going for a walk.'

'I...'

'No mate, no, I'm fine by myself.' Of course I didn't actually know what he was going to say, fact was, I wasn't too interested right now. I grabbed my jacket and did a Mr Benn.

I felt well wound up. No matter, I just needed to get out. I could go and settle up with the guy at the corner shop or something, stock up on a few more smokes like, and walk it off.

As I turned the corner I spotted Joe and Bono perched high up on a wall further on, and then Mike halfways through a window. What the frig were they up to? '*Oi*,' I shouts but still at a distance, 'what gives?' Joe of course couldn't hear me, if they were up to no good Bono would of course *pretend* not to hear, maybe Mike would respond, only like I said, right now he was wedged half inside the building. I legged it over, but what the frig should I care?

'What are you guys on?' I says, trying not to shout. Bono turned his self half round steadying himself on his perch, but he didn't answer. 'Are you guys on the rob or what?' *Man*, I was pissed at these guys. Joe blushed, 'We're...' then he looked at Bono who passed him one of those glances of his that counts as a warning, and Joe shut up. Guess I couldn't expect answers from that one, and he probably didn't wanna spin some yarn either; I couldn't really fault him on that. Mike started to groan a bit, I think he'd got himself self stuck.

I took a breath, calmed down a bit. 'Well,' I says, not quite sure what I was gonna come out with, I was still totally narked with ole Ninja chops back home, so to be honest I felt like I couldn't be doing with sorting anything out.

'To the untrained eye,' I says, 'it could well look like you lot was on the rob.' I took another breath, 'Only… I knows as well as you lot how stupid it would be if that's what you were up to, specially in broad daylight,' (total dickheads the three of 'em, it was still pretty light). 'You never learn, do you?' (And that line was so completely and utterly me dad. Amazing how quick that happens, stuff like that just sneaks up on you and you just find these parent fragments filtering their way through.) I let myself off the hook again for the moment, carried on with the breathing lark, tried to figure out where I was gonna go with all of this. All the while it seemed like Mike was genuinely stuck halfways through a too-small window; it was one of them narrow bastards, a kinda *why bother* type feature. 'So,' I says finally, 'I figure you lot must just have been walking along and then you happened to notice that someone had left their window open like, and so you decided that it might be helpful if you tried to climb up and close it in case some other, less scrupulous,' (I heard Mike trying to pronounce 'scrupulous' from inside the building), 'yeah, in case some *less scrupulous* lads tried to take advantage of the situation and go on the rob like.' Bono started this slow clap, Joe smirked but not for long. 'So, you gonna get your mate out of that fix or what?' The two of them finally looked up at Mike's predicament.

I started to walk off, feeling my bad mood come bouncing on back like a Tigger. Shite. People, they can really piss a person off.

'Oi,' shouts Joe (under orders no doubt), 'where you going?' I looked back, but said nothing. '*Oi,*' he shouts again. I stopped, then this time I shouted, 'Did you lot ever take that cricket gear back?'
'…'

'*Well, did yer?*' Bono didn't look sure about this, and when he shouted that they *had*, I figured he must have felt put out at having to admit to doing as he'd been told for once, or else he was lying. 'So,' I shouts, moving back closer to 'em again, and dead narked like,

170

'get yourselves out of there, get your mate down, get yourselves right away from there, and if you really wanna nick something, go and get that bleedin' cricket gear back.' I started to walk off again, I heard Joe calling after me with questions, and then Bono too. Then over my shoulder I yelled, 'And if you have to stay out all night again, get yourselves round my gaff.' I paused, and then added, 'Only make sure you've got something that counts as cricket gear with you.' I sounded like a bleedin' gangster, and a crap one at that. But so it goes, eh.

I kept on walking, trying to get a more even pace going, calm down like. What the frig was going on with me? *Rob stuff...? Don't rob?* Fuck knows.

I didn't exactly know *if* or *how* I'd get those guys set up to play cricket, *and* at night like, I hadn't had time to think it all through; thing was, I had to keep Kazu busy an' all (*well, let's face it, it was either that or kill the annoying little fucker!*), and it seemed like nighttime was the worst for the lot of them. The only other thing that seemed to link all four of them (discounting their similar height, like), was in fact, cricket. So, maybes get them all together, like? Oh *shite*, I dunno; and it's like I keep saying, I'm no bleedin' scout leader.

Something else that hadn't quite escaped my notice, and which might now just prove useful, was the fact that the film crew were back over in the park; they'd been setting up their lights again, I figured there might be some mileage in that...especially if they were gonna do a load of night shoots, and if not, well, fuck knows... guess we'd just have to go and rob cars – *well... I'm fucking useless at this.*

Go and rob cars!

Maybe, just maybe, one day, I finally *would...* stop saying shite I don't mean.

# CHAPTER TWENTY

## *the thrown-away*

## SAMURAI MAN

After I'd settled up at the corner shop, I finally started to chill out a bit. I was curious about the Turkish geezer when I paid and thanked him like, 'cos he just did this shrug of his, it wasn't indifference, I mean the bloke was running a bleedin' business, it was more just this sort of casual, you might even say 'warm' kind of acknowledgment, like he knew I'd come back, knew I'd cough up. Me nan would have said something about how that sort of thing restores your faith in human kindness. Only, how did he know? How did he know I'd come back? I offered him a fag, he took one and lit it, posted it between fat happy lips in that stubbly brown face of his. Happy with the easy stuff. Maybe that was it. Sorted.

When I got back, I found that Kazu had very neatly piled up my 'correspondence' and left it on me bed. He'd found a bit of string from somewheres and tied the postcards together, but he didn't say a word about them, so neither did I. I figured we were taking it like cowboys (or fishermen), making out like everything was understood – silent like. And next to the postcards lay CA's book. We didn't mention that either.

One thing was though, I didn't like his manservant act, I was havin' none of that, so I just made it clear that if he cleaned another fuckin' thing, I'd have him. He looked perplexed like, but then he just laughed. Fair enough. Guess he wasn't sure if I was kidding. I wasn't.

I'd picked up some noodles and that at the Turkish place, thought that'd be more to his taste maybes. And I figured that if them arseholes for chefs on the TV reckon they can cook, I could probably manage a half decent stir-fry.

We ate pretty late on, and seemed to get along fine, neither of us saying too much, and no need really, top sounds filling the place, top smells from my cooking – well, OK, needless to say, that part ain't exactly true, Kazu had to take over when it got a bit complicated like. 'Arsehole chefs' – it turned out I was rather better at the first part of that than the second, but there we go. Can't be good at everything – as me granddad used to say.

Later that night after Kazu had turned in, I sat alone for a while trying to remember what it was I'd yelled at the lads, but it wasn't much cop. I just knew I'd basically fucked things up a bit. I drank some whiskey and sat in the dark.

By the end of the evening I felt like my head had been bent inside out – I wasn't at all sure I could be doing with so much heavy stuff in so few days, it'd all been a bit of a rollercoaster to be honest and I was never one for fairs. British Rail is about as adventurous as it gets for me, with a preference for straight lines, and for flat ground more than peaks and troughs – philosopher all over! Go to bed mate... go to bed.

I was just snuggling down between those cold cotton sheets again, when I thought I could hear young Kazu fidgeting about, walking to and fro in the next room, and then the faint sound of his whimper. What to do? I couldn't get myself up hardly, I was well knackered. And a bit pissed.

'Kazu, Kazu,' I shouted. No answer. 'Kazu!'

'Yes?' his voice came thin and sad like.

'Get your arse in here.'

I didn't switch on the light, I could feel my head starting to ache. The door creaked open and he stood in the dark in his underpants. He looked a right sorry arse. I could have fucking cried.

'Come 'ere mate,' I says, and shifted to the other side of this well massive bed. 'What's up pal? Eh? What's up?'

He sat on the edge of the bed and choked back his tears. I sat up, and then I got out of bed and hunted down some tissues. 'Here,' I says, grabbing one for meself like. Nose was running.

'Lot of colds around, eh?'

'Yes,' he murmured.

I got back in my side of the bed and lay back, shivered a bit. The heating was off now. I'd sorted it days back.

Kazu stayed put, he just sat there on the edge of the bed, totally still.

What to do?

He must have heard me breathe dead deep like, almost a sigh, 'cos he turned around. 'I'm sorry,' he says.

'If you say *sorry*, once more…'

And he mimicked me, 'You'll *'ave me?'*

'Too fucking right.' Maybe he was a comedian after all.

After a few moments in total silence, he says softly, 'May I?' and he settled himself down proper in me bed. Didn't seem to matter. Five beds like, but he wants to sleep in mine. Like I said, it'd been a challenging few days. It struck me how the two of us sharing like this was a bit like that part in *Moby Dick* where that Ishmael geezer and Queequeg have to share a bed; and how Queequeg's got a bagful of human heads with him, and ultimately how chilled Ishmael is about the whole thing, '*Better sleep with a sober cannibal than a drunken Christian,*' I think he says. Fair play, and at least ole Kazu here hadn't landed on me with any weird bag of tricks like – so, it could have been worse.

He was still awake. I could feel it. And I felt I couldn't very well just doze off. Only I didn't know what to do. I lay there a bit and tried to think things through; Kazu's tears making their almost silent eruptions in the dark.

'The thing is,' I says, trying to keep me tone down, keep it sympathetic, 'it's really not until you're in this situation that you get to realising how friggin' incompetent you are. What I mean is: how incompetent *I* am like… And the more I think about it, the more I feel out of my depth and that I am possibly, if not *quite probably*, the absolute worst fucker you could have picked on to help you, Kazu.' Though that wasn't exactly what I'd meant to say… 'What I mean is… *what I mean is*, that I want to help, and I'll do what I can like, but I'm just a bit afraid… I'm just a bit afraid, that I won't be any good.'

He sat up again, dangling his legs over the edge of the bed. He was quiet for ages and when he finally spoke his voice sounded surprisingly alright, 'composed'. 'It is,' he started, *'only the 'thrown-away', those who have descended to the depths, that will prove useful in the time of need.'*

'Thanks a lot.' Charmed I'm sure.

'These are not my words.'

'Oh right...' like, was that supposed to make me feel better? 'But you just picked them out special did you?'

'Yes!' he announced, dead proud. 'It is a Samurai saying.'

'Is that right?' I needed a smoke.

'It means...'

'I think I got the meaning.'

'*It means,*' he says, ignoring me, 'that only those who have also suffered, will know what to do. Only they can be useful to one who *now* suffers.'

I felt a shiver again, 'I need a smoke,' I says, and I got out of bed again, 'I'll just pop outside. Be back in a minute.'

'It's... it's OK, you smoke in here if you like, if you don't mind to be with me...'

'Sure, sure mate.' I fumbled around in the dark for me ciggies. 'You want one?' I offered the pack but he didn't seem to notice, didn't seem to hear me.

'I'm very sorry, very sorry indeed for my behaviour today...' he sniffed. I lay back down smoking in the dark, just shadows and my fag for light. I could just about make out the curve of his back. 'Very sorry,' he said again.

'There's no need mate, long as you're alright now...'

'It's shameful... to involve another person like this.' He nodded to himself like the thoughts all belonged inside, almost like he didn't realise I was there.

Then after a bit he turned and focused on my ciggie.

'D'you want one?' I asked again, and I think he half smiled, 'No, no, thank you,' he said, and then measuring out his words, 'I just was thinking about its warm light. Orange. Orange is a very attractive colour isn't it?'

I nodded, slightly touched by his appreciation. Then I took a longer drag, admiring the smoke curling up from its brightly-lit end.

'You know, in Japan,' he carried on, all gentle sounding, his back turned, 'our train lines, they are all privately run, and the different ones have different colours painted on them, you know, something like your underground trains, like the red Central Line, dark blue Piccadilly line…'

'There's no orange though, eh.' I said, flippant like.

'But we have,' he says, 'it's called the Chuo Line,' and then he paused but only for a bit, and then he says, 'when someone… when a person does suicide by train in Japan….'

I didn't know where this was going. I didn't feel too comfy so I asked him if he was up for a whiskey or a brandy like and took his silence for a 'yes'. I didn't know if it was a good or a bad thing to be talking about suicide again, guess I'd just have to play it by ear, and part of me considered that maybes talking would help get some of it out of his system.

When I came back with the booze I found him sat in exactly the same position, and it was literally like I'd pressed pause 'cos he carried on from exactly where he'd left off. — I opened up the bottle and poured — '…the family of the suicide, they can get a bill…'

'A bill?'

'For costs.'

'What costs?'

I took a swig – checking it was alright, nice like – lit another ciggie, Kazu carried on, 'A kind of clean-up bill from the train company. It's different here, right? You can't get such a bill here?'

'I'm not quite with you mate…' I topped up my glass, 'are you trying to say… that a geezer's family might get charged for cleaning up after his suicide, like if he jumps in front of a train?'

'Sure, maybe not always… sometimes the train company is kind and don't send such a bill, but in the law, they can do it, they are permitted. But not in this country, right?'

I looked long at my cigarette, 'No mate,' then I scratched my head and passed him a drink, 'not so far as I know.'

'Cheers,' he said, glugging it like one in a desert, 'I thought it was different over here,' he carried on, 'but many people choose to die by the Chuo Line in Tokyo, and people say it is because on that line the bill will be the cheapest. The other train companies would charge much more, and it can be really expensive.'

I drank down the rest of mine in one now, it seemed appropriate.

'I have thought about this,' he says, 'and I think that some people choose suicide by that Chuo Line, you know, to be cheaper for their family, but some,' his voice trailed off a bit; I poured us both another drink before he carried on, 'maybe some of the people... maybe... maybe they just like orange.'

I coughed a bit. I hadn't liked the sound of all that. And then like a prick I says, 'Well you'll be alright here matey, like I says, we haven't got an orange line,' and I knocked back the last of my drink. I was knackered.

Kazu sighed, but in my drunken haze I thought he seemed a bit better for a chat and a wee drink, and after finishing up his second glass, he snuggled his self down. And as he finally settled himself off to sleep I thought I caught him say just lightly, 'My favourite colour is blue.'

I put my fag out and lay back down again. I looked across, and Kazu, wee Samurai man that he was, yeah, he seemed alright again, for the time being anyways.

Calm now, I must have drifted off to sleep.

I think that he did too.

# CHAPTER TWENTY-ONE

## *game on*

## STUMPED FOR WORDS, LIKE

Three in the morning and someone's knocking at the door. *'Three am!' For Christ's sake!*

Kazu sat up, he says, 'Shall I get it?'

'No matey. I'll sort it.' I pulled on me kecks, and performed the traditional, *'Alright, alright... I'm coming,'* croaking all the way. The lads. I knew it was them, could hear their little voices, I opened the door.

'Joe got kicked out again,' it was Mike who spoke up, all three seemed pretty wired, wide awake, bright eyed. As they stood to explain, they shivered a bit, 'You said to come round,' says Mike, and then there was this heavy woody clanking sound – they had that cricket stash with 'em. Bono spoke up now, 'You said to nick this back, so we did. You said to come round.'

'I don't think I quite meant *three in the friggin' morning!'* I scratched my head.

'You said *at night,*' said a brave soundin' Joe. I thought a moment. Fair play, guess that's what I had said. 'If we's, *gotta be out again at night,* init.'

Bono had a ball in his hand, 'That a cricket ball?' I asks. He unclenched his fist to show it, it wasn't a proper cricket ball, but it'd do, 'Looks alright,' I says, 'should do the job. Best get yourselves indoors like, while we get sorted.'

The door banged shut. I scratched my head again.

Do you think Dick Whittington ever had this much trouble? Or

Robin Hood maybe? Mr Benn?

The world feels weird at three in the morning. Not bad like, just weird.

The lads had all piled in and settled their haul on the floor, except for Mike who kept hold of the bat. Joe rubbed his arms to warm himself and Bono made for the radiator, putting his hand to the cold metal. 'Sorry mate, it's off,' I said. He tutted at me, cheeky sod. Kazu was out of bed by now but still only in his underpants. Figured I'd best introduce everyone. 'This is my mate,' I says to the guys, taking the cricket bat off of Mike like and passing it to Kazu to give it a look over. I chuckled to myself – *cricket bats and underpants* – the best. Then I noticed the lads giving him the onceover and passing around those young lad, weirded-out sideways glances. Best he get dressed really. 'Anyhow, this is… Kazuhiro Watanabe,' and then thinking on me feet, 'the famous…' I yawned and caught Kazu looking anxious about my next remark, but I managed to shoot him a sly wink without the lads noticing, 'the famous, Japanese cricket coach!'

'Yeah but, do they do that over there?' said Mike, a bit too calm like, and his brow wrinkled.

'Course they do, init!' piped up Joe, saving me from my sudden attack of acute bullshit, or giving me breathing space at least.

I noticed that Bono still seemed suspicious, he kept looking Kazu over, like he was trying to figure him out. Kazu looked far too young. 'For the youth team,' I added quick like. And then surprisingly (if that was still possible), Kazu chirped up himself, 'Yes!' he starts, 'indeed, I am the official coach for *The National Youth Cricket Team of Japan!*' — Don't overdo it matey. But it had the effect of making Joe beam from ear to ear, like he was in the presence of friggin' royalty, or way better than that, Flintoff himself. And that, that was well worth seeing.

'So,' I says, starting to shiver a fair bit myself now, 'without further ado…'

Joe tugged at me kecks and whispered, 'You ain't told him our names, init?'

'Yes, right,' I says, still trying to shake the sleep off of me, 'So, Kazuhiro, I think we can call you Kazu?' He nodded proudly, 'This, is Joe,' who beamed again (for getting to be named first at a rough guess), and this here is Bono, and this is Mike.' Bono didn't smile, just blushed a bit which seemed about right, and then Mike did this sort of bow and says, 'Pleased to meet you,' dead formal like. Kazu returned the bow, and then it all seemed sorted.

'So, we gonna play tonight?' said Joe excitedly.

'It certainly looks that way!' offered Kazu, 'That seems to be the plan doesn't it Mark?'

'Does it?' I raised an eyebrow. If I'd been more awake I'd have felt unnerved. I sure as hell didn't recollect discussing it with him, that's for sure. But my 'not being sure' seemed to be the order of the day. My memory was mashed.

'Mark,' he carried on, wry as you like, 'you already explained it all to me...'

'I did?'

'In your sleep. *Man*, don't you know? You are one *big* sleep talker.'

And oh, how those boys laughed. I felt like I right e-jit, but I didn't mind, 'Is that right?' I says.

'Sure,' he said excitedly, and then mimicking me in part, like a right bastard, 'You explained about how '*them three lads*' needed to be kept busy, and '*kept away from more serious mischief*', and then you said, '*like*', just the way you do when you are awake!' He stopped now to have a laugh himself, though I have to say, I found myself not joining in with this particular bout of jollity.

Then he carried on, 'Anyway, I guess *them three* must be *these* three, right? And then you started to mention the *little guy*', and I guessed that this was me,' he sounded chuffed now, 'and then you talked about cricket and how the *little guy* had *sussed out some top cricket space in the park*, and so then I was totally sure that you meant me! And then you kinda muttered – is that right: *muttered?*' I half nodded now. 'Something about floodlights and playing at nighttime, and then you said something more... but... I think the other matters you talked about are... yes, they are private.'

So, there we have it.

Needless to say his last remark left me a tad uneasy, but fortunately

180

I hadn't the time or energy to think just how much Kazu now knew about me what with all the postcards *and* my friggin' slumberland banter. *Shite.* And there was that Ishmael geezer thinking he had problems sleeping with a cannibal. Word of advice: *It's better to sleep alone than with an overly attentive, note-taking Oriental insomniac.*

'Marvellous,' I said, not quite sure of what I meant, and trying hard now to remember my own half-baked plans. Though in all fairness there was probably no real need for this anymore; if I ever got stuck remembering anything from my own life, my own thoughts, feelings or history like, all I'd ever need do now was *consult Kazu!* Fuck.

'So,' I says, trying to hold onto to me dignity, 'if... if our coach 'ere wants to get his self dressed,' (or drowned!), 'how about the rest of the team go fix themselves a nice hot drink in the kitchen.' — Turning into Delia-fucking-Smith now, or one of them women in *The Waltons.* The lads all looked pleased enough with this, but then Kazu shot the lot of us this big ole frown, 'I think it is better not to take anything right now, just before training.'

Joe went pale.

'*Training?*' said Bono, and he looked well put out. Mike bit into his lip and shuffled his feet about, 'I've never actually played cricket,' he said.

'I have!' said Joe.

And maybes feeling that he'd rather forego training by a major coach in favour of a mug of hot chocolate, Bono grimly added, 'Not sure I even wanna play, init.'

Kazu looked calmly stern, if that's possible, and then he said, monotone like, 'It is said, that seven out of ten things that you do not feel like doing, will result in failure.' Joe's jaw dropped as he stood in awe. It did seem pretty impressive. All in the delivery like. Nice one, Kazu. Bono shrugged, Mike looked wide-eyed. Kazu carried on, 'So, if you do not desire to play cricket, and to learn to play well, then there will be no cricket.' — Dead matter of fact – couldn't fault the guy. Centre stage.

'*No cricket!*' bleated Joe.

'This,' said Kazu, trying to shoot me one of our secret winks, 'is: The Way of the Samurai.'

The lot of us stood a moment in a chilly silence, it was well cool, I had to admit.

But then this smirk passed over Bono's chops, 'What? The *Sam-u-rai? They* used to play cricket?' And before me or Kazu could answer the smart-arse, Mike piped up, '*Yeah*, 'course they did, 'cos like...', politely taking back the cricket bat, but then still short of an ending to his sentence, Joe stepped in, '*Yeah, and like, maybe... maybe they even invented it, init?*' and he looked up at me for confirmation. I colluded with a little nod, what the heck? Kazu had started looking down at his feet, a bit uncomfortable at the manufacture of this rather larger fib.

'So,' said Joe, making himself as tall and cricket-playing as he could, 'we *are* gonna play, and we will play... just like the Sam-rai, init!'

'Me too!' said Mike.

'Well I'm gonna be Flintoff,' said Bono, snatching the bat off of Samurai Mike, but it didn't seem to matter, 'cos now all three lads were stood there grinning proud.

What could I say?

## *game on — under the stars*

## CRICKET BATS AND FLOODLIGHTS

Kazu's line about how most things don't work too well if your heart's not in them, well, I figured it covered me pretty well, I really wasn't up for cricket. And the thing was, *they* were the ones who needed busying 'cos they were up all night, whereas *me*, I just needed a good solid kip. So, having pushed the Japanese cricket coach to get his self dressed I soon found myself at the front door waving them all off, and like some right mother hen. Picture it, 3.30 in the bleeding morning, telling them all to take care, and how if the film crew hadn't got the place lit up like, or if there wasn't a bit covered well enough by street lights and stars (*stars!* What was I on? – oh twinkle twinkle little me!), that they'd all best come back like. And to keep an eye out for security blokes, pervs, and indeed, coppers, though how playing cricket could ever be considered a crime, I don't know. 'Tell 'em you're in training for the Ashes,' I called after 'em, suddenly forgetting to be quiet, and adding, 'It's 2005! And we're gonna thrash those bleedin' Aussies!' Not bad for a non-cricket man, eh?

I shuffled around the flat a bit, fully intending to go back to bed, only I couldn't quite settle now. Couldn't settle at all. I shuffled about a bit more, picked up me fags, put 'em back down again... and the thing was, I'd already got me kecks on. And did I really want a smoke? *Nope*... and then of course there was no good reason why that bleedin' shambles should have all the fun. Besides, best I go check on them, check they're alright like.

So, after a bit I shoved the rest of my gear on and got on my way, ready to find myself pole position on the terraces. I'd have to be careful though, I didn't really want them to see me, otherwise they'd no doubt have me join in, and I'd run enough this afternoon, thank you very much. No, 'spectating' seemed to be the order of the day. And what worried me even more than being drawn into playing the actual game, was speculating what Kazu's 'training' might include, the mind boggled, and there was no way I was having any of that.

Outside now it was a tad on the chilly side but nothing too hard to handle, it just called for a bit of a brisk step.

From a distance I could see the lights hung high overhead from the film crew. Sorted. They twinkled at the edges like, a bit like low hanging stars. The sky was that dead dark kinda blue-black. Stars, street lights, distant floodlights. Nice one. I speeded up a bit to keep warm, hands in my pockets. Thought I'd keep my next ciggie till I found a good spot in the park like. A spot where I could stand and relax and appreciate it fully.

Squeezing through that fence didn't feel any easier second time around, and bits of me were aching a fair bit from my earlier Olympic bid.

It was well weird inside the park at night, but a nice sort of weird as it happens, and a whole load of tunes with stars in the lyrics just sort of cascaded through my head. A pretty boss experience for a non park person. But then I guess everything's different at night, it's slower, calmer like. I walked on, easy. I wasn't too sure where I was, or how near or far I was from the 'big game', but no worries. Guess I'd hear or see 'em soon enough.

I don't know exactly how far I walked, but after a fair while I heard some noises that seemed like they might belong to the team, so I headed that way, stumbling a bit in my too big shoes, but chuffed really when I thought about how I came to have them.

I finally found the guys in that bit of a clearing, the area Kazu had marked out when we'd had our sprints in the daytime. It looked so different in the darkness. And I'd never thought about it before, but man, I love the way grass looks in the dark. Beautiful. I stepped back a bit, careful in case my shadow gave me away like, and trying not to step on anything too crunchy sounding.

I could see them all well enough by now, and the training looked as if it was in full swing. Sweet. I was desperate to light up my celebratory ciggie, only I couldn't risk it, one of them might hear me, or that extra dot of light might be just enough to give me away. I could feel my heart going now. Pounding like. I must have been full of adrenaline. Shit. *Shit*, I didn't know what I felt. I crouched down now, a bit light-headed to be honest. What a fuckin' wimp!

After a while and doing my best not to make any sound, I stood up again to get a better view. Out there on the field, there they all were working dead hard like, totally focused, and I think it's fair to say they seemed 'impassioned'.

I must have stayed there ages watching them under that beautiful blue-black sky. I felt proud of them, though it was nowt to do with me. But I wondered if this might be what it feels like to be a dad; it was a pretty top kind of feeling, whatever it was. A while later and the preparations seemed to be over and they finally started in on the game itself. The lads, they were having a truly boss time. Nice one Kazu. Nice one. Satisfied now, and a tad too cold if I'm brutally honest, I loafed on back. I could relax and have that ciggie now, go back home and settle back into me bed.

When I woke again it was morning, and this time the full-on version: sun up, birds up, neighbours slammin' doors, but it was the cricket team that woke me. I didn't mind too much, I'd finally snatched a few hours kip and I'd catch a whole load more when the lads had gone, besides, if I'd been more organised I'd have given Kazu the keys.

As they piled themselves in, all wore out and muddy, I looked out the door and up at the sky. A clear blue now, the night had opened up again and let it through, nice like, only, after the past few nights I'd been left with these dead warm feelings about nighttime to be honest. I figure that's the world's quiet time, when a whole load of stuff gets itself sorted out, when most humans are abed, and can't fuckin' interfere!

'So lads, how was it?'

I shut the door and was immediately bombarded not by three but *four* accounts of *cricket under floodlights!* Kazu, enjoying being a boy, the

185

boys enjoying being men. And the lot of them just enjoying 'being' like. – *OK,* I'm a dick, I just don't know how else to put it.

They broke down in giggles and contented exhaustion, so that's when I took over with a piece of my very own top commentary, complete with over emphatic pausing, 'So here we are folks, straight from the match in Hackney, and what can I tell you? This has been…. *this has been,* one *hell* of a game! It was never going to have been an easy match. The condition of the pitch could well have been better, with these last damp days making it a particularly tricky wicket,' (I wasn't too sure where I was going with all of this, but I felt compelled now to see it through, 'duty bound' like, so I carried on). 'But *that said,* Bono here was seen to apply the pressure of clean bowling Joe and Mike in successive balls, and wickets fell fast and furious.' (I paused long now and my leg twitched, I needed to exit this malarkey, and soon, not my scene, only like an arse I carried on.) 'But all was not lost, Joe and Mike later managing to steady the course of their ship with some slick and tight bowling of their own.' (I was flailing.) 'It… it also proved… to be… a match… marked by what can only be described as a… *bizarre* twist of fate when… *new* North London bowler, Kazu…'

Joe tugged at me kecks, 'You don't really know too much about cricket init?'

There was a big ole silence now.

Then the five of us collapsed into this friggin' crater sized laughter. *Shite.* We laughed our friggin' guts out.

I felt well proud of them lads. And dead chuffed for Kazu. He'd done a top job. Sorted. And the lads rolled off home, content.

Later, as we settled into bed I asked Kazu if he was planning on any more cricket sessions, maybes on another day.

'Oh indeed,' he says, all excited, but then dead shy, 'we are hoping at least to do the same the next few nights… if… if you do not mind?' his voice light and clear in the shadows.

'Mind?' I said, 'why should I mind? I yawned and then added, 'I said you could stay here a while. I think that's a top idea.'

'I… I just wanted to make sure.'

'You go for it,' I said with a little chuckle to myself.

There was a brief silence, we both lay completely still, and then dead meekly, dead gently he asked, 'Mark?'

'Yeah...'

'Is this... is this... like... *mates?*'

'Yeah,' I says, all casual, 'it is,' and I realised, laid still and quiet in the dark, that in that moment, I was the calmest I had been in a very long time. 'Yeah,' I repeated, quiet like, 'it's like mates.'

I'm pretty sure Kazu went straight off to sleep after that, he certainly didn't move or make a sound anyways, and though I should definitely have been able to sleep by now, for some reason I felt wide awake. Wide, wide awake.

And I lay there, dead conscious of my breathing, conscious of how close we sometimes are to not being here at all.

Jim. Jim mate.

I put my hand up to my face and wiped this fat ole tear away.

I slept then for ten whole hours.

The next days evolved into their own sweet pattern, strange days of sleep, evenings of cricket coaching under the stars, eat and sleep and not much more except maybe a few vague wonderings on my part about the 'what and where next', but with no real shape to anything. And sometimes my days and nights of sleep were hot and pained, but I'd wake with no memory of my dreams, and maybe that was best. It was strange somehow, but sharing my bed with my own sweet stranger had become almost natural, and though days before, he'd scared the living daylights out of me, knowing he was safe just now had made me feel quite calm.

# CHAPTER TWENTY-THREE

## *step by step*

# MATES

More than a week had passed and it crossed my mind whether Kazu would want to talk about anything, maybes anything he was worried about like, so I figured I might 'broach' the subject over brekkie – *oh psychoanalyst moi* – you know, just to check like, but he just blushed a bit, exactly how you'd expect, exactly how I would have done if I'd been asked the same. There was this pause and then he shook his head. Fair enough like. I got the message and got on with making the coffee.

After a few sips he looked up and asked me the weirdest thing. He asked if I was beginning to see the streets any differently now. This time I think I blushed. Then I remembered the postcards and how he really must have read the friggin' lot, and 'closely', nosey bleeder (and then of course there's the fact that I talk in me sleep, I hate that, it's crap all round). This time it was me who didn't really answer.

'Only,' he says after a moment, 'I have been thinking, you know, that maybe... maybe you shouldn't leave it too long before you deliver those postcards...'

'Deliver them? You mean 'post' them.'

'I mean, deliver them.'

'...?'

'After the mistake you made, you know... when you told her...'

I dropped the spoon, 'By *her*, you mean Jules?' Fuck, this guy was amazing, five minutes into a conversation and he was already really starting to annoy me again. *Shite.* Made my bastard coffee too hot an' all.

'Yes, *her, Jules*... anyway,' and boldly though quiet like, he carried on, 'I mean, after you screwed up and told her not to come to the station to see you off... I mean, wow, that was a fucking big time screw up.'

My hand started twitching, why didn't he just mind his own business? I drank my hot coffee almost to spite myself, burning my lips while he gabbed on. '...and then not contacting her since you got here, *you haven't, right?*' I didn't answer. 'And then writing all those beautiful words and not sending them to her. So, I think that *now,'* and he stood up for this part, getting louder, almost stroppy like, '*now, I feel...* I feel that you are duty bound, *du-ty bound*, to get back on that train, and deliver them to her in person!'

Now there was a massive fuckin' silence. I didn't know what to say. I could have thumped him, or given him some big and well-fuckin' justified lecture on minding your own business, and *'not speaking out of turn'* as Nan would say, but I didn't. I just stood there with a mug of scolding coffee, in me undies, like a right big twat. He was right, wasn't he? I could be as embarrassed and pissed off as I liked, but he was right. I hadn't been in touch the way I'd planned to, the way I'd wanted, not with anyone. In fact, the only person I'd written to at all was Jules, and I didn't have guts enough to send her even one of them postcards. And why? Because he was also right about them being like a diary, 'cept they weren't as lofty as that, just a few soft headed lyrics, stuff about the past, stuff about Jim, and how I felt about her... Jules.

His voice was quiet again now, gentle, 'But, I understand... that you had to wait, you know, wait for some days, wait some time until your mind became clear again, yes, and sort your head out. But... danger is... *ya*, the danger is, you will write only more cards, but never send, never call, never get on that train, never do what you want.' I felt a bit paralysed; he sucked in a breath and then he just motored on, '*So*, my suggestion is, you... you don't take too long.' He paused again; I ran my tongue over my burnt lips. He carried on, and gentle sounding now like before, 'Sometimes you need a long time alone, or at least time to be away from familiar things, to sort out your mind, but sometimes, it's short, you know? Yeah, sometimes it can be just a short time. And I'm not sure about this, but maybe you worry... that you are not ready... not *quite* ready?' He half raised an eyebrow, sweet like, 'And not sure you are able to move on *just yet*. But in these last days you have been spending some time to care for some other people, you know, kind of catching them... picking them up from the ground,' he pulled himself up tall as he could now, this heavy look in his eyes, 'Mark, it means you got your strength back. Now, you will be OK. I think. You will be OK... I think you can go back.'

Embarrassed, and touched if I'm honest, I didn't quite know how to respond, so I just joked around, 'You pushing me out of me own gaff now?' He ignored me. He walked back to the bedroom and pulled on his shirt.

'I have said what I believe,' he called, earnest to the last (little arsehole), and coming back to the kitchen he says, 'I just think, you don't have to wait too long, you know? Don't,' he looked a bit forlorn, 'you know... miss the second sailing.'

I had that lump back in my throat. I couldn't look at him straight on now, so I just put my coffee down, and went and got myself dressed.

The next few days were strange. This mad rollercoaster of events that I'd collided with since I'd arrived finally seemed to be settling themselves down. And my chaotic introduction to Kazu had now panned out into this gentle kind of... 'companionship' I suppose; like I said, it was strange, but it was easy, nice, like. And it seemed weird to think about maybe moving on again, but I knew I'd have to do it some time. And maybe Kazu was right, maybe I shouldn't leave it any longer.

After their first cricket session, Kazu had quickly drawn up a 'training schedule' for the lads, and it was so thorough, so organised like, you really might have thought they were gonna play for the Ashes; and with Kazu every bit as excited and dedicated as the lads like. Lately though, he said as how he might not be able to keep on coaching them much longer because of his studies. I have to admit, I was a bit surprised at first, hearing him want to quit like, the lads would be bound to miss him, but at the same time it was good of him to have done it at all, and really, it was great to hear him talk about wanting to get on with things again, especially his studies, after all, that's why he was over here. As time went on, it seemed like it was inevitable that he'd have to get on with his own stuff, and the lads would just have to get used to him being less available. Fair dos. He said he'd draw up a new timetable, a training schedule for them to follow, and maybes make 'em a few notes, tips that might help, things to remember.

Without realising it, Kazu's lecture about me and Jules and everything, it had been a kind of turning point for me, and gradually the idea of going back up north, and somehow making a go of things, new things, well it started to seem like a plan, and a good one to boot.

I lit up.

In many ways, a whole load of things seemed vastly uncomplicated to me now, it was as though in just stopping myself from thinking things over for a while, they'd pretty much decided themselves. Don't get me wrong, I wasn't kiddin' myself, it wasn't all gonna be easy, maybe none of it would be, and maybe 'easy' isn't the point anyways, that's just not the way of things. There was an absolute shit load of stuff to sort out: the job I'd walked out of; my place, the gaff I didn't wanna live in anymore; *Doris* of course, and that was just the obvious stuff, but by now it seemed like that lot was done with for the most part, it would soon all be consigned to the past, I just needed to face the practicalities of really jacking all that shite in, and walking away from it all for good.

The next lot of streets were gonna start with a train ride back up to Jules, back up to me dad, and one way or another... *it would all come out in the wash*, and I had a warm feeling that things might just turn out to be more than that. More than just 'alright'.

Kazu had gone out, 'shopping' he said. He was a good bloke, they all were – him and the three musketeers. And for the first time it suddenly occurred to me that when I moved on, I would in fact miss them.

Without thinking too much, it seemed I'd started to pack, and bit by bit my few possessions, for what they were, all found their way back into me bag: the postcards; the books, both CA's and the lady's. Was it really *that* decided? Was I really going *now*? *Soon like?* I went and stood outside, had another smoke, tried to breathe.

191

I liked the idea that if I took them books on the train with me, retracing my tracks – so to speak, then maybe we might all cross paths again. And I could ask that woman what she thought of Calvino, I could return that rough book to its rightful owner, and tell him that if he wanted to, it was quite alright to dedicate your life to the writing of songs. OK, so I *am* a dick, a romantic dick even. That's just how it goes.

And Ron's flat? Maybe Kazu could hang out a whole while longer, take over the house-sitting. No real reason he couldn't study there. It had to be a better option than his lonesome student gaff, and he'd have hot water, top sounds to listen to, friendly corner shop – couldn't go too far wrong with that like, *and,* most importantly, he'd be onsite in case the lads needed him so I wouldn't feel like I was totally abandoning 'em. Sorted. Almost too sorted in fact, still, no point knocking things when they seemed to be on the up. I stubbed out my ciggie. Contemplated another. Admired me shoes. Content, like.

When I looked up, Kazu was coming down the road, he'd got a right ole bag-load of groceries with him, and there was something else tucked under his arm, maybes a book or a magazine like. He beamed.

'Was that your first cigarette of the morning or your fourth?' he chuckled as he came up.

'My third, you cheeky bleeder.' He stopped. 'Whatcha got there then?' I says pointing to his haul. He glanced down and carefully landed the shopping bags on the pavement, then he pulled the book from under his arm, it wasn't big enough for a proper book like, and it was a bit small for a magazine.

'I…' he looked a bit nervous now, 'I just got to thinking,' he said, 'if you are going to go, you know, and take those postcards like I told you to, then… then you might need this.' He dropped his head, hiding his face, and then he held out a small, thin, blue book, 'It's not much, just that, if you are going to start writing songs again, I think you might need a… a rough book of your own,' and then he sounded all garbled, 'you know, scribble ideas down, yeah… see what you can make.'

'Thanks mate,' I took it, and as I did I realised my hand was trembling.

'Just one thing, one condition,' he said, 'if you gonna go, *you*... you fucking keep in touch, and you get some fucking postcards from where you going to, and you write the cricket team.' I went to get another fag out, it was automatic, like. He grabbed them and crunched the soddin' pack, 'And you don't need another fucking cigarette alight!'

'I...' I didn't know what to say, so I took hold of the little bleeder and hugged him. 'Get off me!' he protested, so I just ignored him and hugged him, tight like.

Back inside the flat, I plugged Ron's phone in. I'd give Kazu a call from time to time, have a bit of a chinwag with him and the lads like; and later I'd figure a way to explain things to ole Ron chops: how Kazu was a much better bet as a house-sitter, and how it was me who'd mangled his music collection and dug up his back lawn, though arguably these things hardly needed explaining, them being marked improvements like.

I guess it was time. Guess the streets ahead were now finally finding their way under my too-big shoes.

# CHAPTER TWENTY-FOUR

## *the mass of men*

## A PRIVATE MATTER

It was time. The day of my departure had indeed arrived. I picked up my bag and stood at the door, Dick Whittington again, fresh pack of ciggies in hand. The two of us had been a bit quiet since things had been decided, as though we were just easing ourselves gently into this idea of finally going our separate ways.

It was him that spoke first, 'Just don't fucking try to hug me again.'

'You should be so lucky.' I put my rough book in my bag, zipped it up. I stood for a moment, quiet like, and then I says, 'I feel a bit nervous, to be honest.'

'That's easy,' piped up our resident Samurai, 'I have a good answer for that,' (*now there's a surprise*). 'When you feel nervous, you just need to apply spit, like this, to your earlobe,' he demonstrated this, and then clearly expected me to follow suit, 'and then, breathe in deeply through your nostrils, like this.' You can just picture it can't you? — and I figured it really was about time I was moving on or before long he'd have me doing yoga and all sorts. 'Then,' he carried on, 'if you still feel troubled, you go out, outside, and you kick at something hard, you know, a tree or something.' Very sophisticated, these Samurai. 'This is the secret,' he carried on, all calm and assured, like. 'And later, if you still feel some anxiety… if you feel kind of dizzy or something, you must apply spit to your earlobe *again* and then you will immediately come back to your senses.' He raised an eyebrow and again I had to follow suit. But I have to say, and believe me, this doesn't come easy, but putting spit on me earlobes, it really was pretty calming. In fact, it felt... rather nice.

'Feel OK?' he asked.

'Yeah, sorted,' I said, adding, 'feels pretty good.' I nodded now, half wondering whether I should bow, or shake his hand, or hug him, but finally I couldn't decide on the physical stuff so I stayed still. Then, after a second, I just repeated, 'Yeah, feels good,' and I think I was still nodding. Idiot.

He smiled, 'Maybe,' he said, 'maybe, this is a bit like,' he dropped his head down now completely, 'a bit like... when you called me...' and he all but whispered the last word, 'mate.'

People say that it's not good to see a big man or a grown man cry, but actually that's alright, they've shoulders big enough, what isn't nice to see, is a little guy cry. I grabbed the wee man by the shoulders, '*Spit on your bloody earlobes will you!*' He laughed. We spat on our earlobes and we laughed. *And man, how we friggin' laughed.*

I'd told the lads I'd send a card when I got where I was headed, and how I'd look 'em up next time I was back down here in the Big Smoke, but I'd agreed to let Kazu come and see me off at the station; after what had happened with Jules I could hardly do otherwise.

We took the Piccadilly line and then switched to the Victoria, three more stops and we'd be there. I felt quite sentimental, all told, and sat next to Kazu on the train; I could happily have stayed on there all day as the tube chugged and zoomed its way beneath the city. Funny, how things work out, how things come good again, and I could feel my heart swell deep inside. Things were alright.

As we got off at Euston I noticed how quiet our Kazu had become, not really sad like, more kind of 'serene'. Little Samurai man. We passed through the tunnels and took our places on the escalator, 'Here,' he said, all matter of fact, and he handed me a letter, the envelope sealed. 'No, don't open it now,' and he blushed as his hand grabbed mine, a hand that meant to stop me from opening it.

'I'll keep it, shall I?' I said, trying to sound kind.

'That's right. You keep it until later, after you have seen Jules, after some days. It's better.' I unzipped me bag and put it with me rough book.

We stood a while under the departure board. Things flashed through my head, memories of the day I'd first arrived: the geezer from the train who'd looked a bit like Jim – how I'd watched him walk away; the lady, her heavy bag, the book she'd given me; the woman I'd seen crying. My chest felt tight, my heart felt full. I wiped my eye, just dust and that.

'That's it,' he says, as they announced the platform, 'you better go now, hurry.' It was all decided, so matter of fact, and almost obediently I did as he said, and I walked away.

I turned back after I'd made a few bold strides, but he was gone, melted away in that light that's not light, in the crowds there swarming around. It needed more practice, there must be an art to 'goodbyes'. I walked the length of the platform, aware of my tread. Still a few minutes left, a few moments to go. I took out his letter, *'a private matter'*, the envelope read. I dropped the bag, and ran.

I could barely see now as I bolted back down the platform, across that bastard concourse, people getting in my way.

Police in the distance racing in my path.

The letter in my hand, unopened, but I knew what it said.

It's that snap of time… that's only one of many.

'It's a private matter,' he'd said, 'a matter to be handled, privately.'

I ran and ran, smashing my way down that heaving escalator, my breath all spent, and then frantic I stood there, cops and underground geezers holding me back.

A disembodied voice called out, delays occuring on the Victoria Line, severe delays, something had happened, we'd all have to wait… person under a train, they said… all around me complaining… now they're going to be late.

The train hurtled in… and Kazu jumped… in a snap of time.

A woman traumatised, thought she'd heard him call out, but it made no difference, not like a cry for help, and the words, they'd made no sense, for he had called out softly, 'My favourite colour is blue.'

# NOTES FROM
# MY ROUGH BOOK

*I hadn't noticed at the time, but Kazu had etched my initials onto the cover of this wee notebook,* **MK,** *the letters tall and thin – just like* **CA***'s on his. It's taken me ages to even look at the thing, months and friggin' months, but now somehow, there's a pen in my hand. — Pens don't feel the same as ciggies, but I figure maybe they don't damage the lungs quite as much; we'll just have to see.*

*Turned out, my little Samurai mate, he'd done some more writing of his own, left the lads a note filled with a shit load of lies about how he'd gone back home. I didn't have the heart to put them straight, though they must have wondered why I was quite that twitchy. I guess he wanted to protect them, just like he'd tried with yours truly. What a shambles.*

*—Busy sorting out my own shabby little future, I'd taken my eye off the ball. Man, I let you down. And you'd told me, given me a shed load of warning, 'hints' even – but hinting, that shite always sucks. – But whatever way I think about it, I didn't see, when it came to it, Kazu, that moment – it totally passed me by. I'd done a rubbish job. You, and Jim – Let the both of you down.*

*But before I get all maudlin again, best I remember, I was given this book for the writing of songs, best I get on with it. — And what might a man need for the writing of songs? Some cigarettes, some booze, a little clarity of mind or emotion, a pen, a notebook. And space. I guess that's it really: a pen, notebook, space. Tidy, and just enough. — And who knows what comes when the ink nudges the paper – a few lame ideas; some half-arsed lyric, lines and half lines; just a semblance of song… only I'm feeling pretty nervous now… sitting here, just me and the page.*

*'What good am I?' Bob Dylan – easy enough to learn on guitar from Bob's 6 Chord Songbook, nice one, yeah, – you can pick up a load of his top songs from that wee book, easy like – might be worth CA taking a look.*

*Just the one cigarette. And yeah, maybe that is what's called for — a soddin' shed load of songs… 'A Shed Load of Songs' – possible album title? – only now I can't find me matches. I'm gonna get all twitchy again if I don't have a smoke – found the bastards! Sorted.*

*OK, I've no idea what comes, but here goes – 'cos, man, I wish I'd found your favourite songs, I'd have bought the albums, taken you to gigs, we could have smoked our soddin' lungs out, bought the bastard t-shirts, danced like pricks…*

*Nothing comes…*
*Just wait a little while…*
*Maybes have another ciggie…*

*Jules… I only did the leaving 'cos I didn't know how to stay…*
*– and now I can't get back.*

*(And) I would have loved, for all the world, to have written some words to soothe you –*
*Can't do it, man, ain't no songs in me –*

*I still haven't seen the lady, you know, to ask her what she thought – in detail like, about the Dalloway, and my Calvino; and I haven't seen CA to give him back his book and tell him how he needs to play guitar, write more songs. But I keep the two books with me, just in case.*

# Acknowledgements

First off, a big and hearty thank you to Edgar 'Jones' Jones and his *Soothing Music for Stray Cats*, an album I like very much, and a title I liked so much it strayed onto the cover. Cheers. A special thank you to Simon Lubin of the British Transport Police Media Relations. And I am ever grateful to the following people for all their help & kindness along the way: Kanayo Anraku Sugiyama, Greta Dowling Flaherty, Adam Glass, Hiroki Godengi, RM Lamming, Gwen MacKeith, Glenda Norquay, Hiromichi Tamura, Mark Thomas, and Roger Webster. Thanks also to all at Alcemi, especially Gwen Davies; and to everyone at the Marsh Agency, in particular my agent, Paul Marsh. But the biggest thanks of all goes to my mum.... One in a million,

jayne x

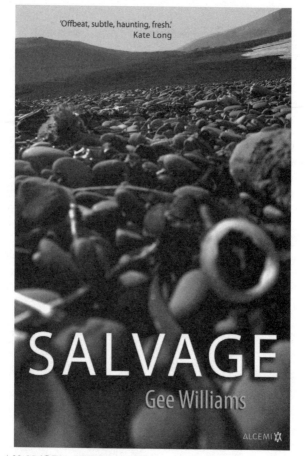

'Offbeat, subtle, haunting, fresh.'
Kate Long

# SALVAGE

## Gee Williams

ALCEMI

£9.99 ISBN: 9780955527203

## James Tait Black Memorial Prize for Fiction Nominee 2008; Winner, Pure Gold Award

*A... gifted stylist, Williams is... inspiring in her craft.* Salvage *masquerades as a murder mystery while exploring the less sunlit aspects of the Welsh shoreline. Dominant and daring, Williams relishes the act of writing.* Salvage *constantly shifts the literary goalposts from crime to romance to metafiction, while never losing immediacy of character or suspense.* **Prof Colin Nicholson, JTB Prize Judge**

*Gee Williams dextrously moulds her material, revelling in her craft... [shaping it]... to defy genre... a complex and enthralling psychological drama.* **New Welsh Review**

*Riveting... a novel that defies genre and crosses boundaries to extraordinary effect... an author utterly in control of her material... nothing superfluous... nothing merely clever.* **www.gwales.com**

# Liminal

(lĭm'ə-nəl) *adj.*

1. Of or relating to a sensory threshold.
2. A psychic transition experienced in magic, shamanism or rites of passage.

## Chris Keil

£9.99, ISBN: 9780955527210

*Evocative... Chris Keil's writing, which is limpid and often arrestingly vivid, has a charged quality that conveys the mysteries pulsing behind the everyday surfaces of things.*
**Nicolas Clee, The Guardian**

*Luminous yet unpretentious prose that leaves images lingering in the mind... an enchanting novel that continues to reveal its secrets long after you have put it down.* **New Welsh Review**

*Hypnotic.* **Jan Morris**

*Each character's individual identity and voice emerges and evolves as subtly as the narrative shifts from Welsh clifftop and museum backrooms to the harsh light of the Greek coast. Relationships, a sense of place, past and present, are subtly intertwined in this sensitive novel.*
**www.walesliterature.org**

# THE BANQUET OF
# ESTHER
# ROSENBAUM
## PENNY SIMPSON

"A born storyteller...
a richly imagined tale
written with zest."
Nicholas Murray

£9.99, ISBN: 9780955527234

*[An] extravaganza where the real and the imagined take turn
and turn about... sumptuously detailed and fantastical...
[this novel is] at once full of disturbing delicacy, and at the
same time [forceful]... [marked by its] humour, verve and
hallucinatory strangeness.* **Clare Morgan, Times Literary
Supplement**

*Magic realism at its political best, echoing the sense of
unreality that reigned as Hitler and the Nazis gradually gained
power in a country still reeling in the aftermath of the Great
War. True to the genre, Simpson uses plain language and an
understated narrative voice to speak of extraordinary things.
When I turned the last page, I found myself wanting to start the
book all over again.* **www.gwales.com**

*A feast of language... akin to those depicted in the Biblical* Book
of Esther*... served on a platter of metaphors so strong that their
aromas permeate the text.* **Jewish Book World** *(USA)*

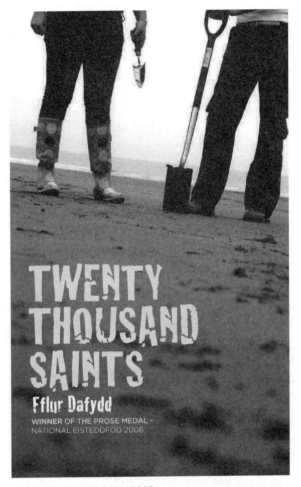

# TWENTY THOUSAND SAINTS

**Fflur Dafydd**

WINNER OF THE PROSE MEDAL -
NATIONAL EISTEDDFOD 2006

£9.99  ISBN: 9780955527227

*The most compelling novel I've read in years; a love
story, a thriller, and a profound meditation on language
and identity.*  **Peter Florence, Guardian Hay Festival
Director**

*A wild, exhilarating read.*
Catherine Taylor, **The Guardian**

**2008 Pick of the Year.** *Compelling.*
**Prospect** Magazine

*Dark, comedic thriller that explores intense bonds
between people and their loved ones... a gripping read.*
**The Spokesman** Journal

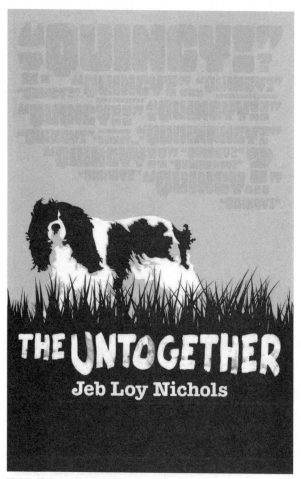

£7.99  ISBN: 9780955527241

*Demonstrates a proper allegiance to the peripheries... a supple intelligence: a sprightly, welcome voice in a time of stalled metaphors and gassy rhetoric.*
**Iain Sinclair**

*Haunting... account of lives struck by loss and threatened by love... a singular voice.*
**John Williams,** author of **The Cardiff Trilogy**

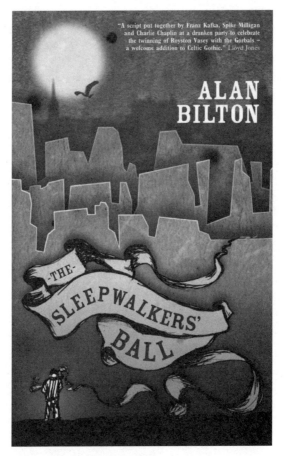

£9.99, ISBN: 9780955527265

*A script put together by Franz Kafka, Spike Milligan and Charlie Chaplin at a drunken party to celebrate the twinning of [The League of Gentlemen's] Royston Vasey with the Gorbals. A welcome addition to Celtic Gothic.*

**Lloyd Jones**

*Alan Bilton's artfully-interwoven narratives, part zany city guide, part silent film, create an imaginative whole which is poetic, inventive, surprising and pulsating with life.*

**DM Thomas, author of *The White Hotel***

**www.alcemi.eu**

TALYBONT CEREDIGION CYMRU SY24 5AP
*e-mail* gwen@ylolfa.com
*phone* (01970) 832 304
*fax* 832 782

ALCEMI Λ